THE SERIAL KILLER SUPPORT GROUP

D B STEPHENS

One More Chapter
a division of HarperCollins*Publishers* Ltd
1 London Bridge Street
London SE1 9GF
www.harpercollins.co.uk
HarperCollins*Publishers*
Macken House, 39/40 Mayor Street Upper,
Dublin 1, D01 C9W8, Ireland

This paperback edition 2025

1

First published in Great Britain in ebook format
by HarperCollins*Publishers* 2025
Copyright © D B Stephens 2025
D B Stephens asserts the moral right to be identified
as the author of this work

A catalogue record of this book is available from the British Library
ISBN: 978-0-00-869746-4

This novel is entirely a work of fiction. The names, characters and incidents portrayed in it are the work of the author's imagination. Any resemblance to actual persons, living or dead, events or localities is entirely coincidental.

Printed and bound in the UK using 100% Renewable Electricity
by CPI Group (UK) Ltd

All rights reserved. No part of this publication may be reproduced, stored in a retrieval system, or transmitted, in any form or by any means, electronic, mechanical, photocopying, recording or otherwise, without the prior permission of the publishers.

Without limiting the author's and publisher's exclusive rights, any unauthorised use of this publication to train generative artificial intelligence (AI) technologies is expressly prohibited. HarperCollins also exercise their rights under Article 4(3) of the Digital Single Market Directive 2019/790 and expressly reserve this publication from the text and data mining exception.

This is dedicated to the first person who read this book. You know who you are, and I am forever grateful.

Chapter One

JESS

31st December 2024

I promised myself, a long time ago, that I wouldn't grow up to be a woman who ever let a man lay a hand on me.

I had failed.

And maybe that was why I couldn't stop myself from crying. It wasn't because of the pain of being struck, even though it had blinded me, the blow sending a white-hot flash across my eyes, knocking me clean off my feet. It wasn't because the pain was so intense that even before I felt the blood run, I knew I was badly hurt this time. It wasn't because, for a full minute afterwards, I was sure I would be hit again. It was because I had failed. I didn't cry when he hit me, not anymore. I knew it wasn't worth it. It never helped. I doubted sobbing because of my failure would help either, but I couldn't stop myself.

'Stop crying. We cannot get help until you calm yourself down,' Lewis said beside me, and I nodded, holding the towel to my face to help stem the bleeding. My father said the same thing to my mum a long time ago, word for word, as we sat in exactly the same place as I was in now, outside A&E, and as with my mother, I wasn't allowed to get the help I needed until I had the story straight. I wasn't allowed to get help until I regained my composure. But still I cried.

My tears fell because it was a night like this one when I made my promise to not be like her. I was maybe eight, or nine, sat in the back of my father's car, helplessly watching my mum, tears streaming down her face as my father forced her to tell him again the lie he dictated, the story he had fabricated, that would ensure doctors didn't ask any questions. That night, my father told my mother to recall it, again and again, so she didn't mess it up. Just as Lewis was doing with me now.

'Tell me one more time,' Lewis said, leaning in towards me, looking over me, his wide hand taking mine, but not to offer comfort. He held it so I couldn't pull myself out of the car until he was ready for me to. I opened my mouth to speak, but my words failed, and as I fought to find them again, I noticed that the radio quietly played Taylor Swift. She was singing about being fearless, decisive, brave enough to stand on her own. I wanted to cry all over again at the irony of it all. He didn't notice.

'I fell,' I whispered, desperately trying to stop my chin wobbling.

'Don't cry.'

I nodded and sucked back my tears.

'What did you fall on?' he said, his voice quiet, threatening.

'I tripped over the laundry basket.'

'Where was it?'

'At the top of the stairs. I left it at the top of the stairs. It was my fault. I hit my face on the banister on the way down.'

'Did you?' he asked, and I was confused as to what to say. It was he who told me I had fallen over the laundry basket. An added insult to his story. The truth was, it did involve laundry, and he wanted me to be reminded of the fact that it was my fault. We were here, on New Year's Eve, because of my mistake. After he hit me, and realised the damage he had caused. That was what he said, it was my fault. It was my doing. I shouldn't have been so stupid. And he wasn't wrong. I'd washed his favourite jumper, the one he wanted to wear to the pub, on a setting too high, and shrunk it. I had done it; I had wronged him.

'Did you?' he said again, and I doubted myself.

'I ... ummm?'

'Jess, I swear to God, if you hesitate like that—' he said, raising his voice and making me flinch. I hated that he made me flinch. 'It's New Year's in a few hours. I don't wanna be stuck here seeing it in.'

'Yes. I did.'

'Did what?'

'I left the laundry at the top of the stairs, to use the bathroom, then I came out and forgot it was there and tripped over it. I caught my face on the banister on the way down.'

Lewis looked at me for a long time. 'Did you?'

'Yes, yes, of course.'

He continued to stare, and I forced myself to hold his gaze. This was a test. A doctor might stare, and I had to not back down. Eventually, he blinked.

'The going to the toilet is a nice touch. Little details help,' he said.

'Thanks.'

'You know I love you, right?' he said.

I nodded.

'That's my girl. OK. Shall we? I wanna watch Big Ben, with you, at home.'

'Don't you want to go to the pub still?'

'No,' he said, leaning back in his seat. 'You've ruined my plans. We'll make the best of it though.'

'Sorry,' I said quietly, and he smiled.

'I forgive you,' he said, leaning in to kiss me on the forehead. I flinched, and he gave me a look, telling me not to do it again. 'Come on, we can still have a few drinks and a takeaway.'

I nodded, wondering how that would end up. Over the past few years, Lewis went one of two ways. He would be drunk, that was a given, but whether he would become loving Lewis, who would talk of marriage, of kids, of 2025 being our year, or resentful Lewis, who blamed me for his lack of career, stability, future, I didn't know. Even with the beating I had received today, I still couldn't be sure he wouldn't exact his cruelty again.

Before I could respond, Lewis got out of the car and ran around to my side to open the door. He helped me out and held me in his massive frame as he and I walked across the car park towards the entrance to A&E. He looked like a man who cared, who was distraught that his partner had been hurt. One of his many faces. Lewis the Protector.

Lewis the big, strong protector.

As we entered the hospital, people looked. I had expected as much. The blood from my lip and chin had made a mess of my face and top. Lewis sat me down, then checked me in at the desk. I watched him talking, polite, concerned. He looked like the perfect partner, wanting to help his injured girlfriend. And the receptionist bought it too, hook and line. She looked my way, gave me a smile, and then spoke to Lewis once more. He nodded, thanked her and came to join me.

'Are you OK?' he asked, taking my hand in his, looking at me with tenderness that was all for show, and somehow, despite it all, still wasn't.

'Yeah, I'm OK.'

'The doctor will be with us soon. Do you need anything?'

'A bottle of water?'

'Of course.'

Lewis kissed me on the head, and then stood up.

I made sure I didn't flinch.

As he walked towards the vending machine, I looked around the waiting room. It was a Tuesday, New Year's Eve, and for most, a quiet night before the celebrations began, and the drunk and violent attended. Most people were at home, with family, resting and overeating the remaining Christmas food, or already out at a party. Many were in the clubs, drinking and laughing and dreaming of a new year, new me. Not these people, not me. There were around fifteen of us who were here, those who were injured, sick. A man in a football kit had his leg on a chair, his ankle black and swollen, his partner asleep on his shoulder. He wore an expression that told me he had been there for a while, bored out of his mind. A woman was sat further along, holding a baby who slept in her arms. An old man sat alone. There were old and young alike, all waiting to be helped, all too wrapped up in their own pain and worry to notice me watching.

All except one woman. She was sat as far away from me as possible. Beside her, a girl of maybe ten lay with her head on her mother's lap. The little girl's arm was wrapped in bandages, a burn maybe. The little girl caught my eye, and I could see she was scared. I would be too. The towel pressed to my face was bloodied, my eyes were puffy from crying, and hospitals were scary enough already. I flicked my eyebrows quickly, up and down, and her fear turned to curiosity. Then I moved the towel away from the side of my face that wasn't injured and poked out my tongue, making her giggle. Her fear faded completely for a moment, her pain too. And knowing I'd made her happier, I felt my pain vanish as well.

Upon hearing her daughter laugh, the mother looked up at me, her curiosity morphing in seconds to a look that was intense. It was like she could see straight through me and the lie that would soon come from my mouth. I tried to smile, despite the pain it caused, but she didn't smile back, her attention only shifting when Lewis walked past her. The way she looked at him, the hatred on her face, told me that somehow she knew exactly what had happened.

I needed to be careful.

'Here,' Lewis said, opening the bottle of water and handing it to me.

'Thanks,' I replied, looking once more at the woman. She gently nodded. Lewis saw me looking and turned to see what had caught my attention. Thankfully, as he did, the woman looked down at her daughter.

'Stop staring at people,' he said quietly as he sat beside me, his mass making the row of chairs shake.

'I was just trying to make that little girl laugh.'

'Why?'

'She is scared.'

'She's not your problem.'

'No, you're right. Sorry,' I said, taking a sip of water. It hurt like hell.

Lewis took my hand, smiled at me with concern. It was believable too; he was good with an audience. But then, it wasn't all a lie. Lewis did love me. Lewis did care, in his own way. I leant my head on his shoulder, knowing I needed to play to the crowd too, and closed my eyes. In the silence, I repeated the story Lewis had primed me to tell. Because the woman had unnerved me. If anyone found out, God knows what Lewis would do.

Chapter Two

For just over an hour Lewis and I sat there, quietly talking, patiently waiting, as people were called and seen by triage nurses and doctors. Some left shortly after, no doubt sent home to manage their ailment. Some, like the football player, we didn't see again.

The mum who looked through my lie and somehow knew the truth, was called with her daughter. Thirty minutes later, as they were leaving, the little girl's arm dressed properly in bandages, and were heading towards the exit, I heard my name being called.

'Jessica Pendle?'

Standing, I walked towards a nurse, an older woman who wore the expression of someone so used to exhaustion that they had a cheat code to manage it. As we made eye contact, she looked at me compassionately, and then at Lewis, who said hello. I passed the mother and her daughter, so close we could have touched. I looked at the girl and crossed my eyes, and she beamed another smile at me. I didn't want to look at her mother but I couldn't help myself. She stared at Lewis, daring him to see her. She hated him. Thankfully, Lewis didn't notice as he had dashed ahead to hold the door open for me and throw his charm at the triage nurse who had called us.

Lewis the gentleman.

Walking through with the nurse, we sat in a small room with a desk and four chairs. Beside the desk was a unit with surgical gloves, plasters, bandages and other medical paraphernalia, to help those who could be helped without the need to go further into the belly of the hospital.

'Please, take a seat,' the nurse said, and we did. 'So, Jessica? Jess?'

'Jess is fine.'

'Seems you've done a number on yourself here. Mind if I take a look?'

I nodded, and the nurse leant over and gently pulled away the towel. Some of the fibres stuck to my face, and I winced a little as it pulled free, like an old plaster.

'OK,' the nurse said, looking at my wound. 'I'm gonna clean this up a little, but I think you're gonna need a few stitches.'

'Really?' I said. 'It is that bad?'

'We could steri-strip it, but if we stitch, the scar will be smaller.'

'OK,' I said, and the nurse held my eye for a second.

'We might need to pop you through an X-ray too, just in case.'

'OK,' I mumbled again.

'What happened?'

As the nurse began to clean the wound, feel my jaw for damage and neck for mobility, I told her of my 'accident'. I could feel Lewis watching me, and I knew he would be pleased;

I was direct, precise, I didn't hesitate, didn't falter, and when I finished explaining how I had hurt my face, I could see the nurse had bought it. I looked at Lewis for reassurance that I had done well, and he sat, his eyes welling with tears.

Lewis the sensitive.

'Sounds like you were lucky you only came off with this,' the nurse said, as she applied a temporary dressing to my face.

'I was,' I lied.

'All right. So, I'm gonna send you for an X-ray quickly, make sure there's nothing damaged. Then they'll send you back here. You'll have a bed and as soon as a doctor becomes free, they will come and stitch you back up. You should be home before the new year is in.'

'Thank you,' Lewis said.

'Yes, thank you,' I echoed.

Getting up, we thanked the nurse once more, and made our way towards X-ray. Again we waited, again my name was called, and both Lewis and I stood to walk inside.

'I'm sorry. You can't come in,' the radiographer said, stopping Lewis at the door.

'Oh, of course,' Lewis replied, walking back to the seat, and just before I stepped in, I looked back at him. He smiled, telling me I would be OK, but it didn't reach his eyes. His stare said something different. It told me to keep my mouth shut. It said he would be angry if I didn't.

I took a seat where I was instructed, a huge X-ray machine beside me. The radiographer helped me position my face, my chin resting on a strap, like in an optician's, to get a clean image of my skull.

'There. Is that comfortable?' he said.

'Yes.'

'Says you fell?'

'Yes.'

'OK. I'm going to take a few shots, but I need to go behind that screen. Try not to move.'

The radiographer walked towards his computer and begun firing shots a few seconds later. I could see the images of my face on his screen.

'All right, we are just about done. I'm going to send you back towards A&E. There is a desk just before you exit into the waiting room. Go there and they will tell you where to wait for a doctor.'

'Thank you.'

'Jess, before you go. If you need to see a doctor alone, without your partner with you, all you have to do is say.'

'No, no, it's fine.'

'I'm going to ask you a direct question. I have to, as part of my duty of care.'

'All right?'

'Did your partner do this to you?'

'What? No. Of course not,' I said, unable to look at him, trying to laugh it off. 'No, I fell on the stairs.'

'Over a laundry basket, it says?'

'Yes, yes, over a laundry basket. I hit my face. Can I go now?'

'Of course, go back towards A&E, you'll be seen soon.'

'Thank you,' I said, this time able to hold his eye.

'Welcome.'

As I stood to leave and rejoin Lewis, I felt unsteady on my feet. They knew the truth, and if I failed to hide it, if I messed another thing up today, there would be hell to pay. As I reached the door, I hesitated. But, before my resolve slipped, I took a deep breath and opened it. Lewis stood and, looking past me at the radiographer, who acted as if our conversation had never happened, he smiled.

'All OK?'

'Yes, thank you.'

Chapter Three

THE CARETAKER

Seldom did people break away from their own sense of importance to know they were being judged, and on a night like New Year's Eve, in a pub as busy as the one The Caretaker found himself in, people broke away from that unjustified entitlement even less. If they had paused for a moment, lifted themselves from the intoxication of hope, alcohol, promises of change and growth, they might have noticed they were being scrutinised. The Caretaker watched, breaking everyone around him down into two categories, those who had hope, and those who didn't.

There was a young couple who couldn't keep their hands off each other, their display of affection bordering on illicit. Despite their lack of decorum – hope. Further to his right, a couple sat at a table and, though they were close, their shoulders touching, their body language was twisted: they were turned away from one another, suggesting they couldn't be further apart – no hope. Stood by the bar, a group of lads who were all dressed similarly, drinking heavily, laughing too loud at their own jokes, but harmless enough – hope. The group was diverse. The

Caretaker had hoped for a group as such; he would come back to them later. Further along the bar, up against a wall with a huge TV mounted up high, an older woman sat nursing a white wine, holding the glass as if it was not a glass at all but an extension of her right hand. As much a part of her as any other – no hope.

He wondered, if he turned a mirror on himself, what would it tell him?

As he watched, he observed that the bar, much like life, was in a constant state of chaos. But as interesting as it was to observe strangers, work out their stories, their lives, good and bad, he wasn't there for that.

Nor was he there to bring in the new year in the same way as most.

He was there for one reason only.

An eye for an eye.

The Caretaker finished his drink – a non-alcoholic pint, he needed to keep his wits – and, ordering another, he made small talk with the barmaid. Yes, I am waiting for a friend, no, he won't be long. Yes, I'm excited for the new year. She smiled, enjoying the exchange, but duty called, and she returned to serving louder and ruder customers. The Caretaker didn't mind. She had a job to do, as did he.

Then, the reason for The Caretaker being there, the job he had to do, walked in. It was a man, mid-thirties, heavier set. His name was Jamie, and in the hope-no-hope game The Caretaker knew Jamie had no hope at all. Worse, he was one who robbed others of theirs. Jamie was in The Caretaker's little blue book that lay beside him: notes on his movements, his plans, his life. The Caretaker picked it up, opened it, looked at his research.

Jamie didn't approach The Caretaker – he had no reason to, he had no idea who he was – but The Caretaker knew everything about Jamie. His age, his address, his favourite meal. He knew he was right-handed and liked to think that studying karate for a year when he was a teenager made him somehow an expert. He knew Jamie's favourite film was Cast Away, his favourite books, the Jack Reacher series. He liked to holiday in Spain but complained about there being too many Spanish people. He preferred dogs to cats, liked the colour blue, supported Queens Park Rangers. He worked as an air-conditioning contractor, drove a BMW. The Caretaker knew Jamie was a man's man, and had a temper. He knew his triggers too. Jamie was a racist, despite his ex-partner being of Jordanian descent. Jamie had hurt her too. The Caretaker knew everything there was to know about this man, and yet, for Jamie, The Caretaker was just a face in a crowd on a busy New Year's Eve celebration.

As he watched Jamie greet his friends, three men who looked like him, the muscles in The Caretaker's body began to twitch with adrenalin and excitement about what he knew was to come. But he had to wait. Jamie had the ability to control his rage when he was sober; it was when he was drunk that he got heavy-handed. The Caretaker had to wait for him to be in that state. So he returned to his alcohol-free drink, and watched.

An hour later, Jamie was four pints in, forced to catch up with his friends as he was late to the game. One more. One more should do it.

Finishing his second beer, The Caretaker gestured to the barmaid and, when she approached, smiling warmly his way, he switched from the alcohol-free pint to a double Jack Daniels and Coke. One wouldn't hurt, and he needed the courage for what came next. He drank it quickly, enjoying the heat flooding down into his stomach, and the tension loosening behind his eyes. Jamie necked a few shots of his own with his friends. He was talking louder, his words beginning to blur. Perfect.

It was time for Step One.

An eye for an eye.

Taking a deep breath, The Caretaker stood, put the blue book in his bag and began to make his way towards where Jamie and his friends were. The music pumped, shooting cortisol through his veins. His fight or flight mechanism began to heighten his senses. Everything became louder, clearer. The Caretaker apologised as he squeezed through people to get closer to his target, until he eventually passed Jamie, brushing against him as he did, and still Jamie had no idea. Standing directly behind him, so close he could reach out and punch him, The Caretaker leant on the bar that Jamie had his back to. He was right beside the younger men he had clocked earlier in the night. On the bar were several drinks belonging to those boys. The Caretaker knocked several of them over, and as pints of beer, shorts of vodka and other spirits crashed over the bar, soaking everyone around, The Caretaker jumped back, looked towards Jamie, and spoke.

'Fucking hell, mate, watch it. You just knocked over my drink.'

That was all that was needed for all those whose drinks had been carelessly knocked over to turn their eyes towards Jamie. As they did so, The Caretaker took a few steps back, so he could watch the chaos begin.

'What? I didn't touch your drink,' Jamie said indignantly.

'Mate, come on,' another man said to Jamie, trying to placate the instant aggression.

'I didn't touch your bloody drink,' Jamie spat.

'Buddy, it ain't an issue, just say sorry,' one of the other young men chipped in. The Caretaker could see they were trying to avoid conflict. He hoped they failed; he hoped Jamie was exactly the man he always was. Too stupid to argue with anything other than his fists.

'You're not listening. I didn't touch your fucking drink.'

'Wanker,' the first man said, turning away.

Perfect.

The Caretaker knew everything about Jamie, especially how he would react to being challenged by another man.

'What did you just call me?' Jamie said, grabbing the man by the shoulder and forcing him to turn. He then called the man a Paki.

'What the fuck did you just call me?' the man said, pushing Jamie off him.

Here we go, The Caretaker thought. Wishing he could film it all for posterity. Getting Jamie into a fight was the first step of the plan; the second would happen as soon as he was ejected.

Jamie shoved the man hard and sent him crashing into the bar behind, knocking more drinks over. Before the man could steady himself, one of his friends launched himself at Jamie, and his balled fist crashed into the side of his head. Jamie's racist remark ensured that though his friends tried to help, they didn't fight back. The Caretaker wondered if this was the first time they had known he was a racist, and if they were instantly trying to disassociate themselves from that. Jamie continued to spit vile words, swinging his fists, and all of the young men began to swing back.

After that, it was hard to see what was happening; fists flew, men grappled, and in the madness The Caretaker was pushed away from the action. He fought to see his target, catching glimpses of him every now and then as he either swung or was hit. He had a great view of Jamie being smashed in the head with an empty pint glass. A better one when the blood began to pour from his forehead. Bouncers waded in, splitting men apart, and most complied with what they were told, as they wanted to separate the violence rather than fuel it. Only Jamie didn't comply, and when he was grabbed by a bouncer, a man twice his size and strength, he swung, hitting him in the face.

The Caretaker understood that bouncers, like police officers, had a code. They looked after one another. As soon as Jamie struck the bouncer, The Caretaker saw the code come into play. Three huge men grabbed Jamie and, before he could swing again, he was lifted clean off his feet and carried through the pub, to the cheers of those around. The Caretaker followed as Jamie was carried out of the door and thrown into the street. He watched as Jamie tried to get up but was knocked down.

The bouncers rained a few more blows onto his body, then, knowing he had had enough, they laughed at him, and went back into the pub. Jamie pulled himself back to his feet, spat some blood onto the floor and then staggered away, wounded.

The Caretaker followed, pulling a small clear vial from his pocket. Inside was 15ml of liquid, the key ingredient for Step Two of his plan. He carefully unscrewed the top.

An eye for an eye.

Rounding a corner, Jamie paused, leant against a wall and coughed, holding his ribs. Then he became aware he wasn't alone and, turning, looked directly at The Caretaker.

'What the fuck do you want?'

The Caretaker didn't speak, didn't step any closer. Instead he threw the contents of the vial into his target's face.

For a second, nothing happened. Jamie simply stood, raising his hands to his face to rub his eyes.

Then the acid began to work and he dropped to the ground, screaming. The acid melted his flesh, giving off the smell of overcooked gammon. And despite how much he rubbed at his eyes, The Caretaker knew Jamie would never be able to stop the inevitable. He would never see daylight, never take in a sunset or watch the wind dance through the trees. He would never be able to drive a car or play football with the lads on a Saturday afternoon.

He would never be able to attack a woman again.

They say an eye for an eye, and the whole world goes blind.

Fuck what they say.

Chapter Four

JESS

I was taken into a small curtained-off room, with one bed and one chair. Lewis and I waited. I sat on the bed looking at nothing, weary and wanting to sleep. Lewis scrolled on his phone. Neither of us spoke. From all around echoed the orchestra of pain and fear. People coughed and cried; an older woman's voice moaned. The paper-thin curtains did nothing to shield anyone from the misery wrapped around us. Not being able to see but still being able to hear fuelled my imagination. Each cough became a final rattle, each cry the grief of a loved one passing. Lewis could see I was afraid and did what he could to comfort me. I hope he assumed it was the soundscape that had me rattled, and not the fact that the nurse and radiographer knew the truth, and, worse still, I wanted them to know.

Lewis wasn't always like this. In the beginning he was kind, sweet; he made me feel special. He made me feel like I was the only woman in the world. I had fought to pinpoint the exact day he changed, but no matter how hard I tried, I never could. There was no turning moment, no memory of him becoming the monster I sometimes saw. It just leaked into our little lives, an invasive knotweed that dug up from underneath, and by the time I realised it was there, it had already pushed through the foundations of my life and had wrapped its roots around me. I was choking on it, unable to stop the roots tighten.

I was more like my mother than I cared to be. Her invasive weed died when my father did, and even though she met and remarried a kind man named Steve, I know Dad had killed part of her forever. She never said it, but I knew she missed Dad when he was gone – the good things, yes, but I think his anger too. Steve didn't ever shout at her, didn't ever hit her, but I think part of her almost needed him to. After a while, all you know is all you know, and it's too late to know any other way.

Was it too late for me, though? Mum was lucky she managed to meet someone kind, but most didn't. Most went back to someone just like their ex.

All you know is all you know.

'Jess, what's on your mind?' Lewis asked, taking me away from my thoughts.

'Nothing.'

'It doesn't look like nothing,' he countered, looking at me in the way he did when I knew I had to tread carefully.

'I'm tired. I just want to go home, get some food and maybe watch the fireworks under a blanket.'

He smiled, reached over and put his hand on my leg. I looked at it. A bruise was forming on his knuckles from where he'd hit me. 'Me too.' I smiled before he returned to scrolling on his phone.

I looked at him, taking in his profile. He really had a beautiful face. His jaw was strong, his eyes sharp. But it was becoming harder and harder to see it, and I wondered, could I do it without him? Could I live without his energy in my life?

Once it was a firm no. Now, I wasn't sure. I wanted Lewis, but maybe what I wanted I couldn't have anymore. I had hoped, for so long, for a way back to what it once was. Maybe it wasn't possible. It was a new year soon, a new start, a new beginning, perhaps.

But could I leave him?

The curtain opened abruptly, making me jump, and a young doctor, younger than me, walked in pulling a small trolley. She closed the curtain behind her and looked my way. She too wore an expression of exhaustion, but she carried it in a harder way than the nurse who had helped me at triage. This doctor still hadn't grown accustomed to the long hours. But she smiled at me with kindness, and I smiled back, as painful as it was.

'Miss Pendle?'

'Yes?'

'Hi, I'm Doctor Joyce.'

'Hello.'

'So, we have had a look at your X-ray. There doesn't seem to be any damage to your jawbone.'

'I'm relieved.'

'But there is some swelling to the soft tissue around it. I'm afraid you're going to be sore for a little while. I'm going to pop a few stitches in, tidy up the wound so the scar is minimal.'

'Thank you.'

'All right. I've got to administer a local anaesthetic. It might hurt a bit.'

I nodded and she turned her attention to Lewis. 'I'm going to have to ask you to wait outside for a moment. Is that OK?'

'Oh, yes, of course,' Lewis said, getting to his feet.

'Brilliant. If you head left, towards the way you came in, there is a bank of chairs. Grab a coffee, we won't be long.'

'Are you sure I can't stay, for support?' he said.

'I'm afraid not,' she said. He nodded and turned his attention to me.

'I'll be back as soon as I'm allowed,' he said, smiling. But his eyes told me to keep quiet, to continue to do as I'd been told. To make sure the lie stuck. I heard him loud and clear.

'See you soon,' I said.

Lewis thanked the doctor and left the room, and Doctor Joyce turned her attention fully to me. When she spoke, there was a softness that hadn't been there before.

'Now, let's get you sorted, shall we?'

'Thank you.'

The doctor donned some surgical gloves and, pulling a trolley closer, prepped a needle and then administered three injections into my lower face. The first hurt, and I winced, but the painkiller took hold quickly and, besides a little pressure, I didn't feel the other two injections.

'OK, I'm gonna give this a moment before I stitch you up.'

I nodded, not trusting myself to speak. If I did, I was sure to dribble. Doctor Joyce then popped out of the curtain. She returned within a minute.

'Jess?'

I looked at her.

'If you want us to, we can help.'

I didn't react but held her eye. Not daring to blink. Not daring to move. But then, a single fat tear escaped, and rolled down my cheek.

'Is it obvious?' I eventually said, my words slurring.

'We see this kind of thing a lot, more than we should.'

'If he…'

'I cannot tell you what to do, but, if you decide to talk, we'll make sure he doesn't get to you.'

The doctor began to poke my face.

'Can you feel that?'

'No.'

'What about that?' she asked again, as she poked around my jaw. I could feel the pressure, my skin folding at her touch, but I couldn't feel the touch itself.

'No, nothing.'

'All right, I'm gonna patch you up. I need you to lie down.'

'OK.'

I did as she asked and lay on the gurney. The doctor pulled up a chair beside me. I took a deep breath, nerves getting the better of me, but I kept as still as possible whilst the doctor concentrated. She focused intently on my lip and chin. I was expecting it to take a while, but within a few minutes she was done.

'OK. Good as new. These will need to come out in about a week. Do you want to see?'

'Please.'

The doctor turned around and pulled a small mirror out of a drawer on her trolley. She held it to my face, and I could see three stitches running from my lip down the side of my chin. But I didn't look at the wound for long; instead I looked at me, deep into my own eyes. Trying to see the girl who made that promise so long ago, sat in the back of her father's car.

'I think the scar will be small, but it will look worse before it gets better,' the doctor said, putting the mirror down. She stood, pulling off her gloves, her work done, and before she could tidy away, I interrupted her. I knew if I didn't speak now, in this moment, I never would.

'Hypothetically, say if I did tell you he did this to me, say if I said to you that he hit me – what would happen?' I asked, my voice so small, so fragile it would crack at the slightest touch of compassion.

She turned and sat down opposite me. 'Well, hypothetically, I'd go to him, say I've sent you for another X-ray as I have spotted something. You would stay here, and the police would come to get him. He wouldn't come back here again. I wouldn't let him. Do you live with him?'

'Practically. I spend most of my time at his.'

'But you have your own place?'

'Yes. I do.'

'So you'd have somewhere to go?'

'Yeah, I would.'

Doctor Joyce held my eye for a moment, and then continued to tidy up. She wasn't putting the pressure on, and I respected her for that.

I took a deep breath, thought of my mum, of how her life could have been better, brighter, had she been brave enough to try. She could have met Steve before she suffered like she did.

'OK.'

She turned back to me. 'OK?'

'Yes, OK.'

'If you need help, you have to say it.'

'I need help.'

'OK,' Doctor Joyce replied. 'You've done a brave thing tonight.'

She stood, packed away and left the room, closing the curtain behind her, and I waited, barely able to breathe. I expected Lewis to burst into the room, try to kill me. I expected to hear a huge commotion from outside. But there was nothing, and despite knowing that nothing meant it was being quietly dealt with, the panic began to increase with each passing second. Eventually, maybe ten minutes later, maybe an hour, it was hard to tell, the curtain swung open, making me jump, and I prepared for whatever Lewis was going to throw my way. But it wasn't Lewis at all. It was a police officer, telling me they were going to take me home, to get a statement, and when I asked about Lewis, they said he had already left. They didn't say if it was under arrest or if he'd simply been sent home.

At the start of the day, I'd expected to see in the new year in a pub, then I thought I might spend it in hospital. Then I assumed I would go home with him. But really, I saw 2025 in, sitting in my living room, spilling my heart out to a police officer about the abuse I had sustained at the hands of my partner, stating that I wanted to press charges against him. Before they left, I was handed a leaflet about a support group that was designed to help people like me.

I thought it sounded like something I couldn't and wouldn't ever do. A support group was for people who had failed. Or so I thought.

Chapter Five

JESS

2nd January 2025

Since I spoke aloud about the abuse I had suffered, poured my heart out, left nothing unsaid, I only heard silence answer back. The police took my statement and told me they would be in touch. Lewis hadn't messaged, hadn't called, hadn't shown up. And that had left me in a liminal place, neither here nor there. My life had changed, and yet nothing seemed any different. I didn't know what I was expecting to happen after the truth came out. Maybe some sort of catharsis, a resolution perhaps? Maybe I was expecting to feel empowered, stronger. If anything, I felt more fragile than ever before. Lewis was unpredictable, volatile, but I knew those things. I knew how to manage them. This new place I was in, I didn't know how to cope with it.

I'd also expected that if I ever spoke out about what was happening, just once, I would own it, tell everyone, my friends, my family. My employer. I thought I would call my mum – she would understand what I had been through and be an ally in my healing. But every time I went to pick up the phone, I couldn't ring her. Telling strangers was one thing; telling those closest, I didn't know how.

So I tidied my flat, hung the shelf I had been meaning to for almost a year. Ordered some plants online. I watched films I had seen before and never really liked the first time, and I ate. Lewis always felt the need to inform me of the amount of sugar there was in my favourite foods, telling me the damage it would cause to my body, of how my cells wouldn't break down the glucose and instead turn it to fat. Despite how large he had let himself grow. I didn't eat a lot of chocolate. So I bought a 400g bar of Galaxy, and devoured the whole thing in one sitting. I felt sick from it, but it brought me a little joy.

Doctor Joyce was right that my face would get worse before it got better. My chin had turned a deep shade of purple that spread to just under my eye, and as the dressing had come off, to allow my stitches to dry and my cut to heal, I looked like I had been patched together by a Mary Shelley character. It also hurt every time I ate, cried and moved. However, if it wasn't for the pain, and the void I now felt in my own home, it was like New Year's Eve never happened.

As I rattled around, with nothing to do and no one to see, time began to take on a new meaning, in that it had no meaning at all. It didn't matter if it was day, or night; it didn't matter whether I was dressed or not. It just didn't matter.

Outside the weak sun dipped and the cold took hold once more, and as I looked out of my living-room window onto the street, I saw the glitter of frost forming on the cars. Up the road, a thin mist began to veil everything around. On a night like this, I wished I wasn't on the ground floor. Anything could be in the mist. Anyone could be watching. Closing my curtains, I went to my kitchen, grabbed some food and took it all back to bed. It was only just after six, but I didn't care. Turning on my TV, I went to Netflix and put on The Notebook. I knew it was going to make me feel worse, watching love as it should be, but I wanted to lean into it. I wanted to feel something.

As I ate, watched, cried, I felt my phone vibrating from somewhere in the bed, and by the time I found it buried under my pillow, whoever was ringing had stopped. There was no ID on the caller, and my first thought was that it was the police updating me. It rang again, and swallowing a mouthful of Pringles, I composed myself before answering.

'He-hello?'

The line was quiet.

'Hello?' I said again, assuming I had bad reception.

'Look out of your front window.'

Lewis's voice caught me off-guard, and I didn't reply. Instead I moved. I didn't know why; I knew what was waiting for me. As I got to my feet, I wobbled, my legs felt hollow, but still I kept moving through my flat into my living room. Pulling back my curtain, I saw Lewis standing under the streetlamp opposite, the phone pressed to his ear, staring at me.

'You broke your promise,' he said.

'Lewis, what are you doing here?' I asked, finding my voice.

'Just passing by.'

'Just...' I started, then my words trailed off into nothing. 'But I thought...'

'That I'd be in prison? Doesn't work like that, Jess.'

'Lewis, I'll...'

'You'll what?' he hissed. 'You'll what, Jess?'

I wanted to speak, to tell him I'd call the police, but the words didn't come. If he wanted to get to me, if he wanted to hurt me, there would be nothing I could do to stop him.

'I'm not staying,' he continued. 'Don't worry. But I'll see you soon, yeah?'

Lewis then turned and walked away, and I watched until he disappeared into the mist, the night swallowing him whole.

I closed the curtains, my hands shaking so hard I snagged it twice, and feeling unsafe I ran to my front door to make sure it was locked. I then checked my windows, and the back door in my kitchen.

Sitting at my kitchen table, shaking so hard I was sure I was going to be sick, I felt oppressed by the silence. I wanted to turn the radio on, or play some music from my phone to cut through it, but then, I'd not be able to hear if Lewis changed his mind and decided to come back. I felt trapped. What the fuck was he doing here anyway? Had the police done nothing? On my fridge, under the leaflet I was given about the support group, was a business card of the community support officer who had taken my statement. He said to call if I needed to. I pulled it free and dialled the number.

'Hello, PC Clement.'

'Hello, it's Jessica Pendle.'

I waited a moment. He didn't reply.

'You helped me on New Year's Eve, said I could call if I needed you.'

'Yes, of course. Are you OK, Miss Pendle?'

'My partner, Lewis, he was arrested, yes?'

'Yes.'

'He was just outside my flat.'

'Did he hurt you?'

'No.'

'Did he try to get in?'

'No, no, he just stood there. He called and just stood staring at me as he spoke.'

'Did he threaten you?'

'No – well, not really, but he said he would see me soon.'

Clement sighed. 'OK. Try not to panic, he knows he shouldn't be there. He's probably just trying to scare you.'

'He has scared me.'

'I'll get someone to have a word with him. He has conditions to his bail. He needs to behave. Do you feel safe?'

'I mean, I'm locked in my flat, so?'

'OK, stay in, call a friend or a family member. I'll have a word with him. He shouldn't be there.'

'What happened? Was he not charged?'

'No, but he was instructed that it would be best for him to leave you alone.'

'Is that it?' I said, shocked that so little had happened.

'If he comes back, ring 999. They can get someone out to you quickly.'

I hung up before he could say anymore.

Forcing myself to take measured breaths, I looked around, needing something to focus on. My fear was being replaced with rage at the injustice of it. I was the one who now had to stay in, keep my doors locked, and he was able to walk around as he pleased. Clement said to call a friend or family member, but if I did, they would have questions I wasn't ready to answer. So, instead, I pulled the leaflet for the support group off the fridge.

It didn't say much, other than the day, place and time they met. At the bottom was a number for a woman called Becky.

Before I could talk myself out if it, I dialled the number, and it rang and rang, and just as I was about to give up, she answered.

Chapter Six

3rd January 2025

I wasn't sure what I was expecting when I found the building's address that was printed on the bottom of the flyer. It wasn't a rundown old community centre, that's for sure. Maybe I expected something new, chrome and glass, a building that promoted wellbeing, Zen. But this old building, with its peeling paint, cracked glass in the doorframe and missing tiles from the roof like a retired boxer's grin, made me doubt I had found the right place. But then, I guess, the group by nature was about discretion. Being someone who had suffered domestic violence, I understood all too well that as much as there shouldn't be shame, there was, and more. My world was made up of shame and guilt and embarrassment – and fear. There was a stigma around being a victim, a sense of me being the one who had failed at life, somehow. When I looked at the building again, I realised that perhaps, after all, I should have expected it to look like this. Beaten, broken, hiding away.

Leaving my flat was a lot harder than it used to be. Once, I walked out the door without a care in the world, off to see friends and go to work. I even left after dark, when I was taking an evening course in child psychology. I went every Monday, walked to the bus stop, then took another walk to the college. I enjoyed it, before Lewis talked me out of it. He told me that it would take me a decade to get qualified and life would have passed me by. I agreed, thought he was right, but now I wasn't so sure. It didn't matter whether I wanted to try again or not. I couldn't imagine going out after dark on my own anymore. Once I didn't fear the outdoors, the unknown. Now, the door was a gateway, one that, if I was unlucky, led back to him, and knowing that he might be there, waiting, watching, meant that leaving to go to the session, even on a Friday morning, was difficult. And I was late. The session started at 10am. I checked my phone; it was twenty past. Perhaps they wouldn't let me in, perhaps they had a policy of locking the door after a certain time. I hesitated further. A man stepped out, stuffed his hands into his pockets and walked past me, giving me a mistrusting look. He walked quickly, then disappeared. It was enough to make me know I needed to get home, that I had made a mistake, and I turned to leave.

'Jess?' a voice called from behind me, and I turned to see a woman standing in the doorway to the centre. 'It's Becky. We spoke last night?'

'Hi,' I said, taking a few steps towards her. 'I'm sorry I'm so late.'

'Don't apologise, it's fine. Come in.'

I walked to her, trying to take some measured breaths. When I reached her side, she gave me a firm handshake.

'I'm glad you made it. It's tough, the first time.'

'Yeah. It is,' I said. But it wasn't just that coming to a new group was tough. It was tough because I had barely slept, wondering if Lewis was going to turn up at any moment. It was tough because, the entire journey, I was expecting him to be there, to make me pay for speaking against him. It was tough because everyone stared at me with my bruised and battered face. But more than that, it was tough because stepping into this building meant there was no going back. No undoing, no denying I was who I was. Stepping inside said, loud and clear, that I was a victim of domestic abuse. They might never make me say it, but crossing the threshold meant that there was no undoing the fact.

I followed Becky into the building, and down a narrow corridor, the walls adorned with children's paintings. As we walked, she told me about the group. I was grateful to her; I wasn't sure, if I was asked anything, I would find my voice. She also didn't comment on, or even look at, my lip and chin. It made me like her instantly.

'As you can see, this is a day centre for children. They don't open on a Friday, which is perfect for us. Do you have kids?'

'No.'

She nodded. 'So, a bit about us before we go in. We meet every Friday here, at ten.'

'I'm sorry I am so late.'

'No, honestly, it's fine. You're here. I have a session before ours, a group of men.'

'Men?' I said, my thoughts going back to the man leaving the centre, and the mistrust I could see in his eyes.

'There aren't many, but it happens. Their session is before, and some weeks, with the group's consent, they stay for a coffee after, and we have a small crossover. The last just left – the man you saw on the way in – so we haven't started our session yet.'

'Oh,' I said.

'It was actually the group who wanted it.'

'Maybe healing is healing, doesn't matter what sex you are?'

Becky nodded. 'Exactly that. I'm happy to have the crossover, and people have shared their stories. But there is no expectation to. We simply have some time together, so the women can see not all men are bad, and men can see the same too.'

'How many are in the group?'

'Usually about ten of us, give or take. And don't worry, no one is going to ask you to tell your story or anything like that.'

'Thank you.'

'It's a safe place, people only share when, or even if, they are ready. And as much as we are about helping people move forward from DV, this is just as much about people with shared experiences coming together.' As she finished, a door beside me opened and a man stepped out into the narrow space. He was big, well over six foot tall and with a jagged scar that ran from the corner of his eye across to near his ear. He smiled my way and I tried to smile back, but as he was so close to me, I felt dwarfed in his presence, like I was a child. He unnerved me.

'Hey, Geoff. You OK?' Becky said, completely relaxed in his presence.

'Yep, just sorting that leak from the tap. Think I've got it now. I'm gonna clean up and be on my way,' he replied, his voice softer than his appearance, and with a hint of an accent I knew but couldn't place.

'Thank you, love,' Becky said.

Geoff turned and smiled to me again, but unlike Becky, he did look at my face. The smile faded, and then he walked away from us into a smaller room which, when he opened the door, I could see was a store cupboard.

'That's Geoff.'

'Is he a ... ummm... Is he like me?

'No, no, he looks after this building. But he knows why we are here. He's a good man. Right, are you ready?'

I nodded.

'Don't worry, everyone you meet today was once standing where you are standing. The first step is always the hardest.'

Becky opened a door into a large room. A woman was talking, but she fell silent upon seeing me. Carpet tiles covered the floor, some of them stained with food spillages and paint. The walls were bright, rainbows and pictures of animals. A number chart hung on the wall, counting to twenty. I imagined it was a good day nursery. I didn't focus long on the wall or floor, though, for sat in the middle, in a small circle, eight women looked up at me.

'Hey, gang, this is Jess.'

I was expecting a 'Hi, Jess' in unison, but they didn't speak. They smiled, nodded my way.

'Please take a seat.'

I did as I was asked, smiling at those who looked at me. Becky then offered a hot drink, and as she went to get me a cup of tea I sat back and faked looking comfortable. The women then introduced themselves to me, and I tried to remember their names. Hannah, Madison, Kelly, Vija, Steph, Baheela, Claire, Rachel. Baheela's left cheek was horribly scarred from burns. Her left eye gone. I didn't know it then, but these women I would one day share all my secrets with.

Chapter Seven

I sat back and listened. They didn't ask me questions. Some looked at my face, but no one reacted. They just continued their conversations like I wasn't even there. I was grateful for that.

Madison picked up where she had left off before I interrupted, and began talking about her ex. I couldn't work it all out, and no one offered to fill me in, but from what I could understand, she was having issues with her child support payments.

'You should go to the police. He is breaking the law,' Steph or Vija said.

'I've been, trust me, I've been, but they don't seem to do anything.'

There was a murmur from the room. It seemed I wasn't the only one who was feeling a little let down.

'I try to be nice. I try to meet him in the middle,' Madison continued. 'But he still blames me.'

'Madison,' Kelly spoke up. 'He did it all. He was the one who hurt you. He was the one who made all of this happen.'

'Yes, but what if—'

'There is no "what if" about it. Mads, he is in the wrong, always has been. And I think I can speak for everyone when I say, you've done such an amazing job, raising your little boy with all this going on. He'll grow up never understanding how hard it's been.'

'Thanks, Kel,' Madison said, holding back a tear. 'I hate the idea of him ever knowing this.'

'He won't. I promise. His earliest memories will be of a mother who loves him, and a dad who left. Nothing more.'

Becky walked back into the room, and handing me a tea, she sat in the circle.

'What are we talking about?'

'Jake,' three of the women said in unison.

'I see. Still having issues with support?'

'You guessed it,' Madison said.

'Do you want to talk about it more?'

'No, no. I'm OK. let's get started,' Madison said.

Becky nodded and begun. 'Hello, ladies. Thanks for coming. And welcome, Jess. As I said, it takes balls to make that first step.'

I nodded.

'Today, I want to touch on the subject of triggers. As always, you share as much or as little as you want in the session. I want to know the things that trigger you, and how you can manage them. But before we get into that, I want to know the good things that are going on. Our sessions have to address the bad, and the dark – it's the only way to find ownership and healing – but it's also important to see the good things happening right now. I'll start. So, this week, I went to the cinema on my own.'

The support group all nodded and smiled. It seemed so small going to the cinema, and it told me something about

Becky: she wasn't the leader of this group to do her bit for the community. This came from a place of understanding. Becky was like me, like the rest of the women there.

'Well done, mate,' Hannah said, taking Becky's hand in hers.

'Thanks, Hannah. OK? Anyone else?'

Kelly spoke up. 'I've got a little something.' She smiled in a way that I could see, even not knowing her, suggested her little something was in fact big. 'I finally got him to agree to the divorce.'

The group clapped.

'Three fucking years and finally, it's done.'

'Kelly, that's incredible news,' Madison said.

'Yeah, it is,' Kelly agreed. Smiling broadly.

'Well done, Kelly, this has been such a battle. How do you feel about it?'

'Tired, relieved. You'd think, doing what I do, I would have found a way to speed things along, but Duncan doesn't like to let go.'

'What do you do?' I asked, shocked I had found my voice.

'Barrister,' Kelly said, and nodded, as if to say, 'Well done for asking.'

'Thanks for sharing, Kelly. Anyone else?'

'I have news. It's not good, but it made me feel good. And terrible too,' Baheela said, her voice hoarse.

'OK,' Becky said, non-judgmentally.

'Well, as you know, Jamie, my ex –' she added for my benefit – 'he always felt untouchable. Someone got to him.'

'How do you mean?' Becky asked.

'New Year's, he got really drunk; he caused a scene. He was thrown out, and then someone attacked him. Like, like he did me.'

The room fell silent, and I sat unmoving, knowing that as the new member I should not want to be a part of their conversation.

'He threw acid in my face,' she said to me. 'Seven years ago. Went to prison, was out in under four years.'

'Is that all?' I asked.

'Yep.' Baheela said.

'He had a good solicitor,' Kelly added. 'It should have carried a life sentence, a Section 18 GBH, which means he had intent to cause serious harm. It was downgraded to a Section 20, which means it was reckless infliction rather than intent.'

'What?' I said, shocked.

'The law is backwards,' Kelly replied.

'Do the police know who did it? Do they know who attacked him?' Becky asked quietly. Baheela shook her head.

'How do you feel about it?'

'Shocked,' Baheela said. 'Relieved too, and safe. It's awful. I've been told he is completely blind, and that's terrible, but now, now I know he won't come for me ever again.'

'Have the police spoken to you?' Kelly asked.

'Yes. A lot. Detectives came down from Manchester.'

'Manchester?' Kelly asked.

'It's where he moved to after he was released from prison. The way he was attacked, they want to know who knows. I told them, everyone, it was in the papers. On all the radio stations. Ladies, my question is: is it awful that I feel justice has been done properly? Does that make me as bad as him?' she asked before lowering her head and gently crying. Becky stood, approached and knelt in front of her, giving her a hug. She whispered something to her, and they both stood and left the room.

'Not many of us have our partners actually pay for what they have done to us,' Kelly said to me.

'Really?' I said, feeling hopeless. Lewis wasn't charged, and it seemed he never would be.

'Seventy-five per cent,' Hannah said.

'Sorry?'

'Seventy-five per cent of women who are brave enough to come forward are failed.'

'And even then, the justice sometimes isn't enough. Baheela has had a really tough time. He got four years, retrained inside, and then his life carried on as normal,' Steph or Vija said. I couldn't remember which was which.

'Shit,' I said, before catching myself. 'Sorry.'

'No, don't be, it is shit. It's not fair either,' Steph/Vija said. 'But that's why we have this. That's why we have each other.'

Everyone nodded, including me.

We fell into silence again, but it was short lived as Becky and Baheela came back into the room. Baheela didn't apologise for getting upset, in the usual way people did; she simply sat and smiled, and the session moved on. Everyone shared something good, and when my turn came, to my surprise I said that my good thing was picking up the phone and calling Becky. More nods, more smiles.

Becky then moved us on to talk about triggers and managing them, and I listened as women opened up, told their fears. Some were triggered by smells, by certain songs or films. By places. Hannah said hers was belts.

'It's ridiculous, I know. I wear belts. Everyone does. And if I saw yours, I'd not be triggered, so don't worry. It's if I'm in a shop or something, and see them hanging. It makes me feel tense. I wish I knew how to manage it. It's not like I can avoid clothes shops my whole life.'

'No, you can't,' Becky said. 'But I guess, now that you

understand that they trigger you, and the reasons why, in time the reaction will dilute. It will be manageable.'

'My ex had a thing for belts. He liked collecting them. He had them hanging on the back of his wardrobe door. Big metal buckles, like a fucking cowboy or something.'

Hannah took a deep breath, and she rubbed her forearm. It lifted the sleeve of her top a little, just enough for me to see a scar on her wrist. She didn't see me see, but she covered herself anyway. It seemed everyone was a little scarred, and instinctively I touched my face, knowing I was just like them. But luckier than some.

'It's OK, Hannah,' Becky said.

'At first, he liked to use them playfully, teasing me, you know, when we were intimate. I didn't mind. I thought it was a bit of fun, something to spice it up, you know? But then he got rougher, and even when I told him to stop, he wouldn't.'

Hannah looked down, and I saw a tear fall onto her jeans. 'I knew, when it wasn't about being in the bedroom, I was in trouble.'

She trailed off, and everyone sat in silence.

'So, yeah, belts.'

Becky went to open her mouth, but there was a gentle tap at the door, and she hesitated.

'That will be Geoff,' she said.

'It's OK,' Hannah replied.

'Come in.'

Geoff walked into the room and everyone said hello. He said hello back, and then apologised. I didn't know how Hannah was OK with someone walking into the room, especially a man. I knew I wouldn't be.

'Sorry, I just need to grab something, then I'll be gone. Want me to flick the kettle on before I do?'

'That would be great, thank you.'

'See you all next week,' Geoff said, looking at us all, but focusing lastly on Hannah. 'Sorry to interrupt.'

'You're OK, Geoff. It's nice knowing you're around,' Hannah said.

'I'm not going anywhere. I'll likely die keeping this building going,' Geoff said, grabbing his things and leaving the room.

Once he was gone, Becky and a few of the others were smiling. It seemed, despite his appearance, Geoff was a man they all liked. She turned her attention back to Hannah.

'Thank you for telling us that, Hannah, that was a big step.'

Hannah nodded, but didn't offer any more, so Becky announced a quick break, and everyone agreed. For Hannah's benefit, and Baheela's.

When we returned, the mood seemed lighter, and I could see Hannah felt better for saying what she'd said, and Baheela was no longer teary. I wasn't ready to open up, but I knew I would come back. In time, I might *become* ready. As the session finished, and I said my goodbyes, I actually hugged Becky.

'Sorry, I don't know what came over me,' I said, when I let her go.

'It's OK. I'm a hugger too. Will you be back next week?'

'Yes, I'd like that.'

'Me too. You have my number if you need anything before.'

'Thank you.'

As I turned to leave the room, I looked back. Most were gone, but Kelly and Madison were still seated, holding Hannah's and Baheela's hands, Kelly quietly talking to both of them. Making sure they were OK. Becky walked back and sat down with them, giving them a little extra time where it was needed.

Chapter Eight

4th January 2025

When I returned home from the support group, I was expecting to hear from Lewis, but he didn't call, didn't message, didn't show up, and when I woke, he wasn't there waiting on my doorstep. I assumed the police had acted, and he was keeping his distance. Despite my face still hurting, despite not sleeping more than a few scattered hours, I felt somehow a little better, and the only reason I could pin down was because of the support group. I hadn't shared my story, hadn't opened up. I hadn't begun my journey to acceptance, self-forgiveness and healing, but I had come away understanding I wasn't alone. Not really. What Lewis had done to me, how he'd treated me, it'd pushed me away from family, friends, it isolated me, and because of that, I'd felt like I was the only person in the world living through it. Now I knew – I had proof – that wasn't the case at all. Madison, Kelly, Hannah and the others were like me. So, although my face still looked worse for wear, and I knew I would have to lie to my employers about the reason for it, I decided to go back to work.

Life had to keep going.

I had to keep going.

When I rang my boss, Jenny, a mother to two additional-needs children whom I cared for whilst she and her husband worked, she was thrilled I was able to come back to work earlier than I'd originally said. They had had respite care-givers in to help whilst I had time off, but, like all care-givers, you build a relationship with those you care for, you understand their needs and wants without them asking. I knew that when Eva, the younger child, was upset she was usually sensory overwhelmed, and a few moments with nature helped: a walk, or even a recording of birdsong. I had noise-cancelling headphones, and sounds of nature on my phone, in case being outside wasn't an option. The gentle removal of outside noise always calmed her. I knew that when Will rocked, his legs were hurting, and a gentle massage usually helped. I knew these things because I had worked with them for almost five years. They were the reason I wanted to become a child psychologist; they were the inspiration, until Lewis took it away.

I loved Jenny's children, like I was part of the family. I almost was family, if it wasn't for the salary I received for being there. Sometimes the job was tough, when one of the children was unwell, or when Jenny or Samuel, her husband, were stuck at work, and I had to do more hours. I loved my job, and even though I knew the children might be startled at my face being so bruised and sore-looking, I couldn't wait to see them. When I called Jenny, she told me that she was taking a little overdue time off, but I was still welcome to come to work, spend the day with her and the children. I suggested we went out somewhere, and we agreed to head to the seaside for some fresh air, and fish and chips.

The drive took just under an hour, and as we travelled, we talked about New Year's Eve. I lied, saying my fall was on New Year's Day, after a wonderful evening out with Lewis. She asked how it happened, and the lie Lewis made me repeat over and over came out with ease. As guilty as it made me feel.

Spending some time out by the sea, wrapped up in layers and layers of clothes to keep the January cold out, lost in awe at the size and power of the shifting tide, made me feel even better. It worked for Jenny, Eva and Will too. There was something about the seaside that did it for everyone. It became easy, almost necessary, to reflect, to calm down, to breathe, when faced with something so much bigger than you or your problems. Jenny said it was the first time she had relaxed since before Christmas, and the children loved playing on the sand, dodging the lapping tide in their wellies and digging holes with spades we bought from one of the few open shops.

'The kids look so content,' Jenny said, as we sat on a storm surge wall, watching her children sitting twenty feet away, digging.

'Old-fashioned fun,' I said.

'Sorry?'

'That's what my mum calls it,' I said, watching the children lost in their play. 'Whenever we escaped to the seaside. Old-fashioned fun. No need for parents to play, for anything electrical. Just give a kid a spade, some space, and let nature take its course.'

'Yeah, old-fashioned fun,' Jenny said. 'This was a good idea, Jess, thank you.'

'I'm just glad to be back.'

'Me too.'

Once the children were tired, and the darkness began to draw in, we packed up, grabbed some hot fish and chips and watched the milky sun begin to wane. Then, when everyone was fed and cold, we loaded into Jenny's car and began the hour-long drive home. In the back, Will and Eva dozed, the sea air sending them off to sleep, and Jenny and I chatted quietly about what the year was going to bring for us both.

'I want to work less,' she said. 'Spend more time with the kids.'

'Do I need to worry about my job?' I asked, half joking.

'No, not at all. I want more days like today.'

'Me too.'

'What about you, Jess? What do you want for this year?'

I'd known Jenny for a long time, but she was my boss, and I didn't want to cross that line where she knew everything about me. I couldn't tell her about Lewis, about the real reason my face was battered. I couldn't tell her because I knew she would be angry with me for keeping it from her. Samuel was a solicitor, a good one too, and I knew he would want to get involved. I wasn't ready for my life to be picked apart by the people closest to me. I wanted to say I needed to be happier, to get my power back, to move on. But I didn't.

'I'm going to reconnect with old friends,' I said instead.

'I like that.' Jenny smiled.

When we got closer to home, I said I'd get an Uber, but Jenny insisted on dropping me off at my door. When we arrived, I climbed out, opened the back door of the car and gently hugged the children goodbye so I'd not wake them. I wasn't due to be back at work until Wednesday, the day after having my stitches removed, but already I couldn't wait to see them again. I thanked Jenny for a lovely day and waved her goodbye as she drove home.

With a smile on my face, I turned and walked towards my front door. Putting the key in the lock, I opened it and stepped inside.

Straightaway, I felt something was off.

'Hello?' I called out.

Closing the door behind me, I took a breath. I was being paranoid, but still, as I moved towards the kitchen, I moved with caution.

Then I saw it.

On the kitchen counter was a folded piece of paper. Picking it up, I felt my heart rate begin to increase. I knew who it was from before I opened it. I'd woken up feeling better and had a lovely day by the sea with people I loved. Life had to punish me for it.

Opening the paper, I saw my instincts were correct. It was Lewis.

Don't think that because I am keeping away, I'm not watching, I know you went to work, I know you were at the beach.

You and I, we are going to have a conversation about what you did, whether you like it or not.

Chapter Nine

I dropped the note like it was too hot to hold, and for a while I did nothing. I just stood there, dumbstruck. Lewis had been in my flat. He had let himself in and had left this note to scare me. Lewis had also followed me to the beach, and had been there watching when I played with the children and chatted with Jenny. He was there, and I didn't know. My intuition didn't warn me. My gut had failed. I felt more violated than ever, more so than from the degradation, the assaults, more so than on New Year's Eve, and when I eventually came back to my senses, I rang the police.

It took just over an hour for someone to turn up at my door. An hour of pacing, an hour or thinking that every noise within my flat was him still somewhere inside, hiding, watching me, an hour of feeling completely alone. An hour of being isolated at the will of my ex.

When the police did arrive and knocked on my door, fear flooded into my bloodstream all over again, as I wondered if it could be Lewis coming to have that talk he'd said we'd have – no, he demanded from me. I looked through the spyhole in the door, and saw it wasn't him but the police, as expected. Unlocking the door, I saw PC Clement standing there.

'Hi, Jess. Can we come in?'

I opened the door wider and let him and another officer in. The second man didn't offer his name, so Clement introduced him.

'This is DS Jones. He is dealing with your case.'

'Hello.'

Walking into the kitchen, I told them how I had been out for the day, with my employer and her children at the seaside, and came home to a note in my kitchen.

'What time was this?' DS Jones asked.

'About an hour ago.'

'And what time did you leave?'

'Just after nine this morning.'

I handed them the note, and they both read it.

'Have you found any sign of breaking and entering?' Jones asked.

'No.'

'Jess, does he have a key?' Clement asked.

I thought about it. Even though I had never given Lewis a key, as deep down perhaps I had never really trusted him, I suspected he had one. I could see him taking the spare, getting a copy cut, replacing it again so I'd never know.

'He might,' I said. 'I have never given him one, but he might.'

'OK, to be safe, I think you need to get the locks changed,' Clement said.

'Yes, of course.'

'Miss Pendle?' Jones asked, still looking at the note. 'Did you tell him you were going to the seaside?'

'No.'

'Are you sure?'

'Yes, I'm sure,' I said more defensively than I'd intended.

'This note, it says nothing about it being Lewis. I have to ask, could this note be from anyone else?'

'I–I don't understand.'

'Could someone else have written it?' he said.

'No, of course not!' I shouted.

'I'm only asking, Miss Pendle, please try and stay calm.'

'Stay calm? My ex, my abusive ex, who did this to my face' – I said, pointing at my chin – 'has been in my flat and left me a threatening note.'

'Miss Pendle, calm yourself. We'll deal with this, OK?'

'How?' I asked. 'Because when I rang the other night, saying he was outside, I was told you were going to deal with it then.'

'We'll sort it' was all DS Jones said, and as if he had heard and seen enough, he began to leave.

'Is that it?' I asked Clement.

'Jess, we can speak with him, warn him to back off. But change your locks. Most home insurance providers cover it in the policy, so check. I've no doubt DS Jones will pop and see him now.'

Clement went to leave, but I stopped him.

'PC Clement?'

'Yes?'

'I heard recently that seventy-five per cent of cases of domestic violence don't end up in a prosecution. Is that true?'

Clement didn't answer, and that said everything.

'Don't you think that's awful?'

'Honestly, Jess, it's an abomination. Now, ring a locksmith, OK?'

Clement left, and I closed the door behind him. DS Jones was already in the car, waiting to drive away. I had waited an hour for someone to come, and they were in and out within fifteen minutes.

Locking myself into the flat, I looked at my home insurance, and saw, thankfully, the cost would be mostly covered besides an excess of £150. But it was still a cost to me, a cost I had to pay because of Lewis. What else could I do?

As I waited for the locksmith to arrive – another knock at the door, another man in my home – I went to Amazon and, after a little research, bought a ring doorbell and some cheap but reliable security cameras to put outside my home, in the hope Lewis would see them and stay away from me.

Then I went on WhatsApp, to all of my archived messages from friends I'd lost touch with, and I scrolled. A few of them would probably message back, out of curiosity if nothing else. I had been a shitty friend, but some of them might forgive me. Most probably.

But still, even knowing that, I didn't message.

Chapter Ten

THE CARETAKER

7th January 2025

Wrapping up, to keep the winter wind off his face, The Caretaker was confident that the small patch of trees lining the road would keep him in the shadows. The cold was bitter, and it had moved from the frozen ground, through his boots and into the soles of his feet, creeping up his shins, into his knees and beyond. But he didn't mind; waiting was part of what he was doing. He would be warm soon enough. As each breath fogged in front of him, he watched a house across the street. A house of a person in his blue book who had singled himself out to be the next target. A house that belonged to a man named Martin. The Caretaker had watched him exclusively for the last few days, digging through notes, meticulously written in his book, of the man's movements to make sure his routine hadn't changed since he last watched him, prior to the New Year's Eve incident with Jamie.

He had committed Martin's coming and goings to memory. It was a Tuesday, and the notes said that on a Tuesday Martin left at 8am for work, was home by 6pm and then went to play darts in a local pub at 8pm. So far, two of the three timings had remained unchanged, and checking his watch, The Caretaker knew if the third was true too, the target would leave the house any moment now.

Martin didn't drive to the pub, which was just over half a mile away. He was many things, but not someone who drank and then drove. He walked, cutting through the estates before heading down a dark, narrow path that ran adjacent to the local secondary school. A wall, maybe eight feet tall, ran along one side, while on the other was a tree-lined fence that separated the path from the school grounds. In the daytime, it was full of kids vaping, or bunking lessons, but at night, apart from a rare dog walker, it was deathly quiet.

The Caretaker had a decision to make. If Martin did leave, as part of his routine, and go to the pub to have a game of darts with some friends, did he approach him before he got there? Or did he wait for him to leave after eleven? The Caretaker thought about it, and the answer became clear. He would ambush him on his way to the pub. Martin would be drunk after, and he didn't want the pain he was going to experience to be diluted in any way. All he had to do was wait.

At 8.15pm Martin's front door opened and he stepped outside.

The Caretaker took a step back, shrouding himself further in the lifeless trees, and watched as Martin, without a care in the world, zipped up his coat, put in some AirPods and headed out. The AirPods made The Caretaker smile. It was almost serendipitous: he wouldn't hear The Caretaker approaching him. It would allow him a second or two to prepare what he was going to do. And the idea of it was exciting and terrifying in equal measure. With Jamie, it was over in a flash, and as much as he enjoyed the confusion, shock and then excruciating pain, he had not been the one to cause it; the acid had done all of the work. It wasn't enough. The Caretaker needed to get involved, needed to feel the ache of a job well done. But he needed to be careful too. If he failed, Martin could and would hurt him. There was no acid this time, no instant victory.

Martin was listening to music – likely Linkin Park, as that was his favourite band – which made The Caretaker feel confident. It was as if some higher power was willing him to succeed. Martin walked quickly, and once The Caretaker was sure he wouldn't be noticed, he began to follow. At first, he kept his distance. He had never done anything like what he was about to do, and knew if he rushed in, he would fail. Martin was strong, and he was violent. Toe to toe, The Caretaker might struggle to win. He needed to ambush his prey. So, as much as adrenalin wanted him to rush in, he forced himself to slow down – so much so that a few times he lost sight of Martin. That didn't matter; he knew the route well enough. So he walked, like any other person going about their day, crunching through dead leaves frozen to the asphalt, making their way to somewhere warm. The Caretaker needed it to look that way. The police would ask for witnesses, and he needed to make sure that if anyone noticed him, he didn't look suspicious or interesting in any way. The Caretaker needed to be beige.

For several minutes, the heavily lit roads twisted and turned, with Martin taking several lefts and rights, and The Caretaker ensuring he stayed far enough away to go unnoticed. As he turned onto the final street, he saw the school, and the alley, dark and secluded, behind it. He watched as Martin stepped down it, swallowed up by the void. He hurried to catch up.

At the entrance, The Caretaker slowed again, walking

calmly, and as he walked, he pulled from his pocket a belt, a thick leather one with a brass buckle about the size of a bar of soap. He wrapped the end around his hand, gripping it tightly in his fist because he didn't want it to slip from his grasp, and once he was ready, he ran.

Even though it was nearly pitch-black, as soon as the shape of Martin came into view, it was like The Caretaker's vision became infrared. He could almost see the heat coming from his target, who, with his headphones in, didn't hear him gaining on him. Martin wasn't aware of anything at all until The Caretaker was within a few feet of him, and as he turned, his instincts making him realise someone was close, The Caretaker raised his arm and swung the buckle of the belt with all of his might. It caught Martin across the face, close to his eye, and sent him reeling. The Caretaker was shocked Martin didn't go down, but instead stumbled into the wall and hung onto it. Before Martin could correct himself, The Caretaker swung the belt again, catching him on the top of the head, opening it up, and this time Martin hit the ground.

Even in the low light, The Caretaker could see blood running down Martin's cheek and matting his hair. Martin moaned on the floor, and The Caretaker swung again, connecting with his ribs. There was a crack, a beautiful crisp crack, like a twig being stepped on. He liked the sound. He liked the sound very, very much.

Even though Martin was finished, the beating complete, The Caretaker swung again, catching Martin on the arm, the dull thud no less beautiful to the ear. And again, hip; again, leg; again, shoulder, neck and one final blow to the head.

He paused, catching his breath, and noticed that Martin didn't moan, didn't try to move. The Caretaker had knocked him out cold. He unclenched his jaw and calmed himself. He was shocked at how much he hated a man he had never properly met.

But The Caretaker didn't feel satisfied as he'd thought he would. So, discarding the belt, he began to kick his target over and over, so hard he hurt his foot and white-hot pain shot up his calf, screaming at him to stop. But still he didn't. And he heard himself speaking with each kick.

'Fuck. You. You. Fucking. Piece. Of. Shit. Fuck. You.'

Then he heard a voice shouting.

'Hey!'

He turned, saw a dog walker ahead.

'I'm calling the police!' the dog walker shouted, and The Caretaker, not wanting anyone to see his face and knowing he had done enough, began to flee. As he did, he limped, his foot angry from the repeated blows it had rained on Martin's body.

He staggered until he was close to the mouth of the alley, and turning back, he could hear the dog walker talking, mumbling that help was on the way.

The Caretaker took a deep breath, calmed the adrenalin and set off. Walking like a man without a care in the world. Which was easy. The release The Caretaker felt was euphoric, long overdue. He felt good.

He hadn't felt this good in years.

Chapter Eleven

SOPHIE SALAM

Climbing out of her car, DS Sophie Salam wrapped her coat around her tightly to shield herself from the cold wind and rang her mother, Daya. A last-minute case had come her way, and as she was scheduled to go off shift within the hour, she had the right to refuse, and have it passed on to a detective who was on the night shift. But something about it caught her interest. Something unusual. Something that made her senses tingle. She agreed to look into it. She reasoned she wouldn't be much later home than she would have been. An hour, tops. When her mum picked up the phone and said hello, Sophie could tell she was tired, and that usually only meant one thing.

'Hey, Ma.'

'Hey, love. Let me guess, you're gonna be late?'

'Yeah, sorry, but not by much, I've just gotta speak to someone. How's Lottie?' she asked, half knowing the answer because of her mum's deep yawn on the other end.

'She's OK, mild meltdown just before bed, but thankfully

not too bad. It's taken her a long time to settle, but she is calm now.'

'Is she asleep?'

'Does she ever sleep?' Daya said.

Sophie didn't reply. If she did, she knew it would come across as being defensive, and then they would likely bicker. So she changed the subject. 'Did she eat OK?'

'No more than usual. Seems to be getting harder to get food in her.'

'Sounds like it's been a tough day.'

'Nothing I can't handle. Besides, we gotta do what we gotta do, right? Would be easier, of course if Lottie's dad was—'

She cut her mum off.

'Ma, not now.'

Sophie hated that in order for her to put food on the table, she had to have her mum do so much. Her life was full of guilt. Guilt about working, guilt about not. Guilt about keeping secrets from the two people in her life she loved more than life itself. 'I've spoken with the doctor; we have an appointment next week.'

'Not sure what they can do,' her mum said.

'We are not the only ones struggling. Tens of thousands of children are born just like Lottie. And I know so many have it tough, like us. They see this sort of thing all the time. They'll have tricks we can try.'

'I hope so. Wanna message when on your way, I'll make sure the kettle is on?'

'Thanks, Ma. See you later.'

Hanging up, Sophie put her phone away and headed from the car park towards the main reception of the hospital. Sophie loved many things about her job, the variety, the problem-solving, the camaraderie with her colleagues, but the job wasn't all plain sailing. The hours were long, antisocial, and having a young daughter made it harder. It was only because she had the full support of her mum that she was able to be a detective at all. It was emotionally and physically exhausting at times, and she often joked she'd make more money stacking shelves. But she'd always loved solving puzzles – like the one she had been presented with.

When the case was handed her way, it looked like another random mugging gone wrong, and she almost passed it on. But a belt had been used. It was found near the scene of the attack. There had to be a story behind it, a reason, a hidden narrative. Sophie Salam liked a mystery.

She entered the hospital and headed towards the room where her victim lay. She didn't know much at this stage, only that there had been a serious, unprovoked attack on a man. He was in a stable but critical condition, and before she could go home to her daughter, she needed to speak to him, take a statement and feed it across the chain for whoever was working the night shift. Or, if it could wait, she would pick it up when she came back on.

As she made her way up to the fourth floor, she quickly ran over what she knew. The victim, Martin Goodfellow, had had a few run-ins with the law. Nothing major. A street fight in 2016. A charge of GBH in 2019. In 2022 he was arrested as drunk and disorderly and had had to sleep it off in a cell. There was an arrest for domestic violence a year later, but it was dropped shortly after. His rap sheet was telling. Martin Goodfellow was, on paper, anything but good. However, her job wasn't to condemn or assume. Her job was to gather the facts, investigate the crime. Take things at face value. Remain objective. Understand why a belt was used.

The Serial Killer Support Group

When she reached the fourth floor, she approached a nurse who was behind the desk, head down, scribbling on a chart.

'Hi,' she said, showing the tired and overworked staff nurse her badge. 'I'm here to talk with Martin Goodfellow. How is he?'

'Sore. He's got a few broken ribs, one broken wrist, several lacerations. His wrist needs pinning back together. Surgery will likely be tomorrow. But he'll live.'

'Thank you,' Sophie said, before heading into Martin's room. At first, she thought he was unconscious. He looked like he should be. The left side of his face was completely black from bruising, and he had several stitches under his eye. There were more stitches in the top of his head, his right arm was in a temporary plaster right up to his elbow, and she knew all too well how exhausting broken ribs felt.

'Martin?' she said quietly, and he turned towards her, opening his one good eye. 'I'm Detective Salam. I'm here to ask you a few questions about your assault. Are you up for talking?'

He nodded.

'I promise to be quick, let you get some rest. What happened?'

'I was jumped.'

'Jumped?'

'Yeah. The fucker came at me from behind. I didn't even see him until he hit me around the face.'

'Did he say anything to you before he hit you?'

'No, he just swung. If I had seen him coming, it would have ended very different.'

'OK,' Sophie said, taking a small breath. 'Start at the beginning. The more you can tell me about what happened, the more it will help us find whoever did this to you.'

Martin explained the attack, and as he did, Sophie made

notes. It was unprovoked. He didn't see the man's face. He didn't hear him speak. Not a single word was exchanged. For all intents and purposes, the man materialised from the night, attacked him and vanished just as quickly. Just like a ghost.

'Martin? Can you think of anyone who would want to do this to you?'

'No,' he said, but Sophie wasn't sure he was telling the complete truth. If he did, she might be able to help him more, but as it stood, without anything to go on, and with his injuries being bad but not life-threatening, she assumed not a lot would happen.

She thanked him for his time and said she would be in touch. As she made her way out of the hospital, she reasoned that her assumptions about the man were right, and likely the reason why he received such a beating. In his past, somewhere, Martin Goodfellow had pissed off the wrong person and they had made sure the debt was paid.

She knew that the past always catches up with you, one way or another. She knew, as much as she hated knowing.

Chapter Twelve

THE CARETAKER

The kicks The Caretaker had inflicted on the ribs of Martin Goodfellow had injured his foot. He didn't think it was broken, but suspected, when he pulled his boot off, there would be bruising, and as his boot felt tighter, swelling too. But he didn't mind. Martin had come off worse, a lot worse. The combination of his aching foot and the waning adrenalin meant that getting home was a slow process. In the distance, he heard sirens, no doubt responding to the Good Samaritan's call, but they stopped. He had got away from the scene without attracting attention. The attack, the retribution, had gone better than he could have hoped, except that he had dropped the belt. He knew they wouldn't be able to find a print or anything that linked the belt to him, so he wasn't worried. But he was disappointed. He wanted it as a trophy. To have the bloodstain become dark black in time – that would remind him of the wonderful sound it made as it gouged into flash. Thwack.

When he thought of that noise, and the moans coming from Martin's mouth, The Caretaker couldn't help but laugh. It was funny really. Absurd. How a cocky, confident man could be reduced to a guttural noise that sounded like a small animal being stood on. The big strong man had cried like a child, and The Caretaker felt no remorse for causing it. Martin Goodfellow had done so much more. He deserved the pain he felt, the fear.

This first punishment was an eye for an eye, his crimes so great they warranted nothing less. Martin Goodfellow had received his final warning. One mistake, one slip-up, and The Caretaker would finish him off.

Once inside his house, he relived the moment the buckle had met the side of Martin's face, that wonderful thwack. It made his skin tingle, and he began to giggle. He applauded himself, proud of what he had achieved, and in that state of euphoria, relief and self-adulation he waited for a knock at his door from the police that with every passing moment he knew wouldn't come.

And as night finally began to give way to a new day, without any consequence, The Caretaker knew he was ready to begin the real work, his real purpose for it all.

Jamie and Martin were the warm-up acts for a much, much bigger journey he was about to embark on.

Chapter Thirteen

JESS

8th January 2025

Since I'd found the note on my kitchen side, I didn't want to leave the house, and if it wasn't for the fact that the next day I needed to have my stitches removed, I would have locked myself away forever. I grabbed a taxi there, rather than a bus, and I didn't speak to anyone, didn't deviate. I did only what I needed to, and then, as soon as the stitches were removed, I went back home and locked my door. I never wanted to leave my flat again, but I had to; I was due back at work, and if I didn't show up, one, I would be letting Jenny down, and two, it would raise questions. Questions I didn't want to answer. Also, if I failed to go to work, Lewis would have won. There was no doubt he was winning, but I didn't want to be that woman who was entirely defeated. I didn't want to be like my own mum had been for years before her knight came and rescued her. I didn't want to rely on a man like Steve sweeping in for me. I needed to be my own knight, somehow.

So, when my alarm went off at 5:30am, I forced myself out of my warm, safe bed. I showered and dressed, and looked outside into the street whilst I drank a coffee. Apart from the faintest line in the east, darkness still had hold of the world, hanging on with its octopus grasp. Anything could be out there. Anyone.

And although I hated admitting it to myself, I didn't want to step out into that. But, again, I refused to be beaten. If I didn't walk to work, if I didn't try and carry on, I knew I would lose myself completely. The Jess I set out to be, the Jess whom I dreamed of becoming, the Jess I once was, wouldn't ever materialise. She would die.

Refocusing my gaze, I looked at my reflection in my window. The woman before me was battered, bruised. She carried her burdens. She would likely be scarred for life, both emotionally and physically. But she had to keep moving. I had to keep moving.

'Go to fucking work, Jess.'

Finishing my coffee, I put on my shoes, coat, hat and scarf and prepared to step out into the cold, ink-black early morning. Just before I left, I paused, wanting to check that he wasn't outside my door, so, logging into my ring doorbell app on my phone, I tapped the live feed and checked both the front and back of my flat. All was quiet.

Back on my security apps home screen, I saw that both cameras had recorded something in the night, and tapping on the notification, I saw that at 3.12am, a cat had walked across my back fence. Ambling along, perfectly poised without a care in the world. Lucky. I deleted it, and then looked at the front camera. I expected to see another cat, or a night-shift worker perhaps. But at 4.32am, standing in the road beyond my front path, was Lewis.

I couldn't blink as I watched him approach my front door, lower himself and peer through my letterbox. He was there for a long time, gazing into my home. And I didn't know why. I looked towards the letterbox, wondering if he had placed something inside, bridging the gap between his world of freedom and mine of confinement. Slowly I lifted the lid and peeked inside.

Nothing.

I looked back at the recorded footage. Lewis stood and then moved from the front door to my living-room window. I switched cameras and watched as he cupped his hands and tried to see inside. My curtains were closed. He didn't look for long. Then he moved again, and switching to the one camera at the back of the flat, I watched as he came into the communal garden, up to my bedroom window, and again cupped his hands. The time was 4.35am. He was standing mere feet from where I slept, and again, my intuition had failed, my gut hadn't spoken. Lewis was able to do as he pleased.

He took something from his pocket, something I couldn't see, and went back to my window before walking away.

On the main camera once more, Lewis approached my front door, stood there and then looked up directly at the camera. He knew it was there. I expected him to retreat, maybe even try and tear it off the wall, but he didn't. He smiled, waved. And then walked away.

Closing the app, I moved towards my bedroom and, opening the curtains, looked outside. On the glass, drawn in red pen, was a smiley face. He had drawn on the glass, a face that would be smiling at me as I slept. I closed the curtains quickly and left the room. I couldn't bear being in it anymore.

With shaking hands, I saved the footage and then went to ring the police. I was transferred by the 999-call operator and waited. But even as I began to tell the officer I spoke with about what happened, I knew they would do nothing about it.

Seventy-five per cent, Hannah had said, seventy-five per cent were failed, and I just knew I was part of that majority. I was completely alone in dealing with the harassment I was living through.

Alone, apart from a bunch of strangers who met once a week at the support group, whom I would see in just over forty-eight hours' time.

Chapter Fourteen

SOPHIE SALAM

Sophie's mum, Daya, usually stayed in the spare room when Sophie worked late, but decided not to today. She was fried. She didn't say it, but when Sophie returned from the hospital visit, an hour after her shift was due to end, she could see her mum had had a tough time. Her eyes were tired, her sense of humour, usually dry and quick, weakened. Lottie had been more challenging then her mum had suggested. And so, after a quick cup of tea together, Daya updated her on Lottie's day, no doubt omitting some of the challenging details, and left.

Sophie understood. Lottie was her daughter, beautiful and unique, but she was also difficult to care for properly. She wasn't like most children, and although that was a gift, it was also hard. After her mum left, Sophie went up to see her little girl. Lottie was sound asleep, angelic in her own bed, and Sophie felt awful for sometimes wanting things to be different. She climbed into her daughter's bed and lay beside her, wrapping her in her arms.

'Mumma?' Lottie stirred, her voice distant and sleepy.

'Go back to sleep, baby girl.'

Lottie closed her eyes again, and within seconds was back in her dream world. One that Sophie hoped was full of adventure, colour and sounds that made her feel safe and stimulated in just the right way. The real world was too busy, too chaotic, too disorganised for a mind like Lottie's. Dreams had to be different; at least, she hoped they were. As her daughter began to breathe deeply, Sophie's eyes filled with tears. She was remembering a really difficult time in her life, a time she couldn't tell anyone about, a time that, if the truth came out, would ruin everything she had worked so hard for. A wonderful little girl had come into her world and sometimes, especially when she was tired, she couldn't help finding it overwhelming. She pushed it down, the past, the reasons for her isolated life, the burdens she carried, the secrets she had to hold, that weren't about her daughter having complex needs. Taking in the smell of her daughter, the sweet, familiar scent that made her feel safe, she closed her eyes and drifted to sleep.

When she woke, the sun was up, a bright, crisp day, and Lottie wasn't beside her. It wasn't unusual, Lottie was always up early, so without panicking, Sophie pulled herself out of the too-small bed, stretched and, grabbing her dressing gown, went downstairs to find her.

Lottie was in the kitchen, a colouring book open on the table where she was happily scribbling away.

'Hey, baby girl, what are you drawing?'

'A seaside.'

Sophie looked at the page, thick lines in all the colours of the rainbow, and smiled.

'Oh, yes. Want to talk me through it?'

'Here is … is a beach, and there … umm … there is the sea.'

'What's that?' Sophie asked, pointing to a large pink and green scribble in the middle of the page.'

'A seahorse'

'Of course it is,' Sophie said, kissing her daughter on the head. 'Breakfast?'

'Uh-huh.'

Sophie made Lottie some breakfast and put it in front of her. Lottie didn't even acknowledge the food, but she knew not to press; if it became stressful, Lottie wouldn't eat a bite, and the pressure would likely cause a meltdown, and the quiet morning together would be ruined. So, instead, Sophie made a coffee and watched her daughter colour for another hour, then, of her own accord, Lottie ate her now mushy cereal. The small wins.

The morning continued in the same manner, quiet, calm, peaceful, and as Lottie watched TV, Sophie couldn't help but feel guilty all over again. Yesterday, Lottie was struggling, and she wondered, did her absence from her daughter cause that to happen? Her autism was so much about routine, structure, the same things at the same time. Did Sophie working shifts, having to rely on her mum, have a negative impact? But then, even if it did, could she do anything about it? Being a police officer was all she knew.

Lost in thoughts of how her life could be any different, she didn't hear her phone vibrating on the kitchen side, and by the time she realised someone was trying to get hold of her, the call had ended. The caller ID was Clarke, a colleague and her closest friend in the force. Usually, when she wasn't at work, he didn't call. He knew her life and how it was always about spinning plates, so it had to be something he would know she would want to hear. Her curiosity was piqued. She rang him back.

'Hey.'

'Hey, sorry, I know you're off today.'

'No, it's OK. What's up?' she asked, looking over to Lottie, who was lost in watching Paw Patrol.

'So, you know that assault last night?'

'The Goodfellow guy?'

'Yeah. Wanna know something interesting?'

Sophie could hear the smile in his voice, and stepping away so Lottie wouldn't hear if her attention turned, she waited for him to speak.

'Go on?'

'Guess?'

'Clarke … come on.' She smiled.

'Go on, guess.'

'All right, if I had to, I'd say it was about the belt?'

'Bingo.'

'So, go on, what about it?'

'Well, it turns out the belt actually belongs to the victim.'

'Really?'

'Yep. He didn't even know it was missing. But it is definitely his.'

'So the attack was premeditated.'

'Absolutely. And more, there was another person's blood on it.'

'No way?'

'I knew you'd like this. It's why I called.'

'Whose blood is it?'

'We don't know. Not anyone on our database. But it looks like it's not the first time someone has been assaulted with that belt.'

Sophie went quiet, trying to piece together what it all meant. She felt it was a revenge thing, but who was the one who wanted it?

'You still there?' Clarke asked.

'Do me a favour. Can you look into his past offences? See if anyone of them involved a belt as a weapon? I think it's linked to one of them. If you find anything, call me.'

'Even today? On your day off?'

'Even today. There is something not quite right about this. I just don't know what.'

Sophie hung up and, keeping the phone with her, went to join her daughter on the sofa. Lottie was so entranced by the cartoons she didn't notice her mummy was there until Sophie put her arm around her. Lottie then looked up and smiled at her. Sophie smiled back, and as the cartoon dogs raced to a scene of an accident to help save a circus, she wondered who was the first person to be assaulted by that belt. And with the offences on Martin Goodwin's record being years old, why did they wait so long to get their revenge?

Chapter Fifteen

SUPPORT GROUP CHAT

MADS 8.47PM

Hey, all, it's the mid-week check in, how are we all doing? Anything you wanna chat about before we meet Friday?

RACHEL 8.53PM

Weeks been OK. Haven't heard from my ex at all. So, feeling settled.

MADS 8.53PM

Aww, good. That's good.

CLAIRE 8.56PM

Wish I could say the same.

RACHEL 8.57PM

You all right?

CLAIRE 8.57PM

The usual shit, says he's sorry, he's changed, he'll work harder. You shouldn't have to work hard to be a decent person.

The Serial Killer Support Group

MADS 8.59PM

He's said all this shit before, so has my ex. Stay strong.

CLAIRE 9.00PM

I am, it's just so exhausting.

MADS 9.00PM

Yeah, I get that. It will get easier.

STEPH 9.03PM

Hey ladies. Sorry, kids won't settle. All OK here, see you Friday.

MADS 9.07PM

Kelly? Vija? Everything all right?

KELLY 9.23PM

Hey everyone. Catching up, have you heard?

MADS 9.23PM

What?

VIJA 9.24PM

Hey, yeah. I didn't want to say anything though. Does she know?

MADS 9.24PM

Guys, what?

KELLY 9.24PM

Yeah, she knows. Hannah's ex was attacked.

😦 3

RACHEL 9.24PM

Shit. Was he hurt badly?

KELLY 9.26PM

Yeah, bad. I've got a friend who works at the hospital. Obviously, I'm not allowed to know, however he was pretty messed up.

😦🖤 2

CLAIRE 9.26PM

Where is Hannah? Is she still in the chat?

KELLY 9.26PM

She went to her mums in Shropshire, after last week's session, she was feeling a little low.

MADS 9.26PM

Bless her.

KELLY 9.26PM

I spoke to her yesterday, told her what had happened. She's taking some time.

MADS 9.27PM

Is she OK?

KELLY 9.27PM

Shaken up. As expected. But, guys, that's not all.

STEPH 9.29PM

...

KELLY 9.29PM

He was attacked with a belt.

😦 4

VIJA 9.30PM

What????

MADS 9.30PM

Shit!

The Serial Killer Support Group

RACHEL 9.30PM

Oh fuck! Is that…

KELLY 9.30PM

Yeah, a belt.

VIJA 9.30PM

You think the police will want to talk to her?

KELLY 9.30PM

Maybe.

BAHEELA 9.31PM

Does anyone else think it's weird that on new year's, my ex was attacked with acid, and now Hannah's ex has had a beating with a belt?

KELLY 9.31PM

I thought the same. But, its likely a coincidence. Both men are gargantuan pricks. Karma always catches up.

CLAIRE 9.31PM

But, a belt? Surely that can't be a coincidence. Hannah only spoke of it last week.

KELLY 9.31PM

It is weird, I grant that. But, again, from what I know, it was a fight, I reckon it got out of hand, and the belt was the only weapon.

BAHEELA 9.31PM

It's too weird.

KELLY 9.31PM

Karma always comes back!

MADS 9.31PM

100%

KELLY 9.37PM

Can I suggest we don't talk about this on Friday, in the session? We've got that new woman with us, I don't want her to freak out. And I don't think Becky will want us to digress to it, especially if Hannah isn't back

👍 4

MADS 9.37PM

Kel, if you find out anymore, keep us posted?

KELLY 9.37PM

Of course. But I'll go to Hannah first, make sure she's OK with us talking about it. For now, let's let it lie. I just wanted you all to know.

🖤 👍 3

RACHEL 9.37PM

See you all Friday.

KELLY 9.38PM

If anyone needs a friend, we have each other in here. Keep talking ladies, we are all on the same road.

MADS 9.38PM

🖤

CLAIRE 9.41PM

🖤

VIJA 9.44PM

👍

STEPH 9.52PM

See you Friday x

BAHEELA 10.07PM

xxx

Chapter Sixteen

JESS

10th January 2025

After I discovered Lewis had been at my flat, in the middle of the night, looking through my letterbox and drawing on my bedroom window, the police were forced to take me seriously. The evidence recorded by my home security strengthened that, and I had been told that he would be brought into the station, perhaps even re-arrested, and a restraining order would be sorted by the police to make sure Lewis stayed away. My excitement waned a little when I was then advised that it could take up to two weeks for that to come through. A lot could happen in two weeks. Anything really. But I tried not to dwell on it; it was progress, maybe the final step needed to ensure Lewis left me alone, and I focused on that.

My bedroom had become another thing Lewis had taken. I could barely set foot in it; it was tainted. I'd slept on the couch since.

I didn't know if I was more confident leaving the flat afterwards, but I did so anyway. It was Friday, support group day, and although I was feeling just as nervous as the week before, in there, deep down, was a quiet excitement. These women understood; these women knew. Some might be exactly where I was, but some were out the other side. Their exes were now out of their lives and their healing had begun. And I didn't want to be late, in case someone spoke of it. I wanted to live vicariously, if that was possible. So, leaving my flat an hour before I needed to, I made my way there. The walk was slow, the footpaths still frozen from the night, and they didn't look like they would thaw. I took it steadily; the last thing I needed was to fall, hurt myself and miss the one thing that I felt might help in dealing with Lewis.

I arrived at the centre fifteen minutes before it was due to start. I hoped it would be open, so I could step inside and warm my freezing face and hands. Thankfully, when I pushed the door, it relented, and warm air from an overhead heater blasted down onto me. I closed the door behind me and called out.

'Hello?'

'Hello?' A voice called back, and from around a corner, Geoff approached. 'Oh, hello ... ummm.'

'Jess.'

'Jess, that's it. It's nice to see you again. Becky has her men's session on.'

'Oh, should I leave?'

'No, no, you're just fine. Come on, let's get a cuppa, warm you up.'

I followed Geoff down the corridor, and then into the kitchen on the other side of the main room. As he walked, I noticed he had a slight limp, and when we got to the kitchen, where the quiet voices from Becky's session were muffled, he held onto the counter and rotated his ankle.

'Are you OK?' I asked quietly.

'Oh, fine. It always plays up in the cold. I was injured, in the Falklands.'

'Oh, sorry.'

'Ah, it was a long time ago, Christ, '82, were you even born?'

I shook my head.

'Ah, I'm getting old,' he said. 'I took a bad fall, in full gear, ankle snapped like a twig.'

'Ouch.'

'Not quite the word I used, but yeah, ouch. Plays me up every now and then. Got this too in the same six months,' he said, pointing to his face.

'Sounds like a shitty six months,' I said, and Geoff laughed.

'You got that right. Most try to offer sympathy when I tell them this story. Wasn't expecting you to say that.'

'Sorry.'

'Not at all. We have to laugh about these things eventually. Or else what is the point? How'd you take your tea?'

'Just a drop of milk.'

Geoff turned, made us both a cup, and then we stood, with the tea warming our hands, chatting a little about his work for all the council-run centres in the area, as well as Becky and the groups she ran. I learned he was a dad to two girls around my age, and they lived up in Scotland, with their mother. I was surprised how easy it was to be relaxed around him. Considering my shit with Lewis, and the fact that my dad was the same kind of person, it was strange to talk with a man whom I wasn't guarded around. I'd felt intimidated when I first saw him. I'd wondered why Hannah was OK with Geoff walking into the room when she was baring her soul, but now I could see why. Geoff was a good man, no doubt a good father. I suspected he would protect his children with everything he had. Unlike my own father.

From inside the centre's main room, I heard movement as the session with the men ended. Stepping out of the kitchen, I saw Becky talking with one man, a different one from the man I saw leaving the centre the week before. He was small and wiry and looked like someone you wouldn't want to be on the wrong side of, like he might mug someone, hurt someone – and yet he was there, being consoled by Becky, just like Hannah the week before. I felt awful for judging. I'd judged Geoff too. I guess, when you are hit by a man, all men are the enemy, unless you stopped yourself going there. As soon as I entered the room, she saw me and smiled, before giving the man a final hug. ''Bye, Tim, have a good week.'

'Thanks, Becky. You too.'

'Sorry., I said as the man passed, but he didn't reply. As he reached the door, he looked back, holding my gaze. He looked like he hadn't slept in a month. His eyes were heavy and bloodshot. He stared at my injured but healing face, and then back at my eye. It unnerved me a little, before I realised that what I saw was empathy. Without saying a word, he turned and left.

'Jess. Hi. Sorry, I didn't know you were here,' Becky said, once the man was gone.

'I should have waited. I was having a cuppa with Geoff.'

'No, it's fine.'

'Is he OK? Tim, wasn't it?' I asked.

'He has a long way to go, but he'll get there. He'll find peace, one day.'

I nodded, unsure what else to say. Peace with being a victim? I wasn't sure how anyone could find peace. 'Want some help?' I asked, wanting to move on.

'Would you mind?'

Putting my tea down, I helped arrange chairs in a small circle, and then sat down next to Becky.

'You don't mind me being early?'

'Of course not. How's your week been?'

'Up and down,' I said, not wanting to dump my shit her way.

Voices came from down the corridor, and I looked round to see several women walk in. I tried to come up with their names, only remembering Kelly and Madison. I'd get there with the others.

The women first greeted Becky and then said hello to me. I was shocked when Kelly came over and offered a hug.

'Glad you came back.'

'Me too,' I said.

Geoff then offered to make everyone a hot drink, and as he got to work, more arrived, until eight of us, nine including Becky, were sat around the circle. Geoff delivered the teas and coffees. I noticed he didn't ask anyone what they wanted or how they took it, but knew everyone's drink order, which made me like him even more. Once he had placed a cup in every woman's hand, he said goodbye and made his way out of the room. As soon as the door was closed, Becky spoke.

'Good morning, ladies. Shall we talk about Tuesday?'

There were some sharp looks from women in the group.

'You know?'

'Of course I know. And I know it's on your minds. Remember, the elephant in the room is the one we face head-on.'

I looked around. They all nodded. I didn't have a clue what she was talking about.

'Has anyone spoken with Hannah?' Becky asked.

'I have,' Kelly replied.

'Is she OK?'

'She's OK.'

'Ladies, I don't think we should overthink this thing. It's weird, granted, but it's not for us to wade in with our pennies' worth.'

'Sorry,' I interjected. 'What happened?'

'Hannah's ex was attacked,' Madison said matter-of-factly.

'Oh.'

'Does anyone want to say anything about it?' Becky asked, looking around the group, but I could see that whatever people were thinking, they knew it wasn't for them to say.

'I think this is the healthiest response,' Becky said. 'Let's focus on us, the things we can control, and leave everything else to everyone else.'

A series of nods.

Something caught my eye and, looking outside, I saw Geoff walking to his car. His limp was less pronounced than before, but still there. I felt sorry for him; it seemed bad things happened to good people far too often. He paused by his car and Tim stepped around it. The two men spoke, just for a moment, then Tim nodded, stuffed his hands into his pockets and walked away. Geoff watched him until he vanished, then opened his car door. Just before getting in, he turned, looked back and saw me. He waved, and I waved back.

'Last week,' Becky said, 'we talked about triggers. Today, I'd like to have an open conversation around the things people don't see when they know we are survivors. They see the physical damage. They see us as victims. But I want to know, what is it people don't know? What don't they see about you?'

The room fell silent as the women thought about the question, and I found that, without being aware of it, I was speaking.

'How lonely I am,' I said, and then regretted it, as all eyes turned to me.

'Yes, that's a big thing,' Becky said, then patiently waited for me to continue.

I took a deep breath, and then spoke of Lewis, of how, slowly and quietly, he gradually altered my life and my routines. He didn't like my mum, and so over the course of two years we saw her less and less. When I spoke of how he didn't like my friends, some of the women nodded as if they understood, as if they had lived it too, and when I spoke of how I had to make excuses to blow them out when invited to do something, I received understanding smiles.

'Some of my friends have stuck around, sending the odd message every now and then, but most have moved on with their lives. I don't blame them; life is life. We all get busy and if people aren't making the effort then...' I trailed off, feeling suddenly a little teary. 'And now he's out of my life, I can see, without that chaos, that constant state of eggshell-treading, my life has become very quiet. Almost invisible. I don't want to be that person, you know? Does that make sense?'

'Yes,' Madison said. 'Complete sense.'

'Really?'

'Absolutely. Jess, I think we have all felt like this in one way or another in the wake of our trauma.'

'It sucks,' I said.

'Yes, it does. And I know it feels like it won't change, but I promise you, it will,' Becky said.

'I hope so,' I whispered.

'It will. It's important to not get hung up on that. It's too big – the small victories are what we all need to see. The little wins, they are quiet, easily overlooked, but if we focus on them, the bigger things come quickly. The little things have more power, in the long run.'

I nodded and wiped a tear that had ashamedly escaped.

'Thank you for opening up, Jess,' Becky continued. 'It's great that you feel safe enough to.' Then one by one, everyone echoed it, and I smiled, feeling somehow a little better, a little more like I was a part of something bigger than my small life.

After my sharing, the others shared too and I was surprised how alike we all were. They spoke of fear, embarrassment, feelings of failure. They talked of isolation, regression, self-loathing. All of the things I could relate to. As we shared, Becky spoke of how most of what we felt we were programmed to feel, of how we'd been gaslit to think it was our faults, our wrongs, our imperfections that had caused life to play the hand we had all been dealt. Our exes fed on that power. I wanted to believe her, but I still wasn't there. The little voice that told me I was just as responsible as he was kept talking. It told me I fucked things up just as much as he had.

As the session began to wrap up, Becky started to clear away, and the group chatted quietly, the conversation moving back to Hannah.

'Kel,' Vija said. 'Any updates?'

'Not really. He had to have surgery. I think he's been discharged now, but from what I heard, he'll be scarred for life.'

'Good,' Mads said. 'Hannah showed me some of her scars. He deserves nothing less. Surely Hannah was a little happy when she heard.'

'I mean, she wasn't not happy,' Kelly said, a wry smile creeping onto her face.

'I would be happy too,' Mads said.

'I know I was after New Year,' Baheela added. 'As bad as that makes me sound.'

'I'd be happy as well,' I said, and Kelly looked my way and smiled. 'Karma, right?' I said as a way of justifying my thoughts.

'Exactly. Whoever did this, I kinda wanna buy them a pint,' Kelly said.

'Kel, how do you know about his surgery?' Vija asked.

'I've worked in law for a long time. You get to know people in all professions. I've got a friend who is a head nurse at the hospital he is in. She shouldn't have told me, but she knows the kind of man he is.'

Becky returned and the session ended. Whereas last week I only hugged Becky goodbye, now I was hugging everyone in the support group.

'You'll be back next week?' Mads asked as we left the building and headed back into the cold winter morning.

'Without a doubt,' I said. 'Will you?'

'No, I'm going away, with my little one.'

'Aww, that's nice.'

'Just a cheap week in Spain. He's never flown before.'

'How old is he?'

'He's two. I'm nervous, but going with my sister and her family, so I'm sure I'll manage.'

'You'll have a wonderful time. Not at all jealous.'

I smiled, hugged Mads, noticing how strong she felt, and then, waving to the other women as they drove away, I made my way home. Halfway back, I became aware, that for the first time since New Year, I wasn't looking over my shoulder every five seconds.

Chapter Seventeen

THE CARETAKER

11th January 2025

Finishing the coffee he had bought from a bubbly young server at a local Costa, The Caretaker threw his empty cup in the bin and then sat on a public bench. He turned his face up to the weak but bright winter morning sun and sighed. He rarely got to sit and do nothing, but then, he wasn't really doing nothing; he was waiting. In his pocket, the knife he carried was heavy and hot, and comforting. It gave him power to have it close to him, where he could use it at a second's notice. Feeling untouchable, he closed his eyes. He almost imagined it wasn't below freezing, in the dead of winter, but a mild summer's morning. He wasn't sat on a bench by the side of a busy road, but somewhere peaceful, tranquil, quiet. The woods he played in when he was young. The trees, ancient and all-knowing. It made him feel small, and yet a part of something bigger. Something more important. It was almost close to how he felt now. Almost.

He couldn't wait for the sun to come, the ground to warm,

the new life to pop out of every dead tree and tired patch of grass. Birdsong and gentle breezes and soft cloud. He couldn't wait for summer. By summer everything would be different; the world would be green and bright, people would be out again, enjoying limitless skies. And his next target, the one he waited to see, would have been dead a long time. He would be forgotten by everyone besides his own mother. He would be rotting, or ash that had been absorbed into the soil to become nutrients for the next mighty tree to grow. He and his actions and the trauma he had caused would be a fading memory, obliterated within a generation.

The Caretaker could have stayed, eyes closed, face towards the sun, all day. But even though the morning was crisp and bright and wonderful, he wasn't there to enjoy some time with nature. So he stopped himself being lost in the moment, and refocused. Pulling out the blue book, he turned to his target's page. At any time after 9am his target would leave the gym across the road from where The Caretaker sat, and he would walk to the same coffee shop The Caretaker had just been in, and order himself a macchiato. A small, pointless coffee. He would then sit there, drinking it, legs widely spread, enjoying his post-workout pump, probably trying to find a woman he could lock on to and make his latest conquest.

The Caretaker didn't mind waiting. He enjoyed it; the stillness allowed him to think, to reflect on the road that led him to this place. The world had gone to shit, accountability was lost. Once, people paid for their crimes. Once, men were better. They cared, nurtured, they didn't wander or stray. The Caretaker grew up knowing that hitting your partner was the worst of the worst. He grew up knowing that men like that were hated. Loathed. Known. Now, they could go to the gym and right-swipe on new targets once old ones were used up.

Men like the one he was waiting for were now anonymous. The world was too busy, too loud for their crimes to be heard. Now, they could drive nice cars and strut around like they were untouchable. Now, these men behaved like they owned everything they saw. They might have always had that belief, but the world was once large, too large for just one person. Now, it was getting smaller and smaller, and their poison could spread without anyone being aware of it.

The Caretaker had to remind some of them, the few that he could, life was never supposed to be like that.

As he thought about men strutting, owning, spreading their toxins, the doors to the gym on the opposite side of the street opened and out stepped his target. The way he waved behind him to the receptionist, the way he bounded across the road, barely looking for oncoming traffic, made The Caretaker want to get up and hurt him. But this morning wasn't about that. It was too public, too busy. The Caretaker had to be patient. The cocky cunt's time would come.

Today was about research, about listening to his voice, about looking closely at the man he would kill, when the time was right.

His target passed so close he could have pulled his knife and plunged it deep into his chest, scraping his ribs as it embedded itself in his cold heart. A heart that used a baby as fodder, to gaslight and abuse an innocent young woman. He promised her the world, until she began to grow his baby, then she was fat, past it, used up. She was a whore. And after she broke free from him, he made sure everyone knew. Their private videos, made in the heat of passion, made with her blindly trusting him, became casual watching amongst his friends. They had all seen her, at her most vulnerable, at a time when she should have been made to feel the safest. He had shared it all and he made sure she knew. He had told her she had it coming for being the whore she was.

The Caretaker wanted to puncture his heart with all of his might, to watch the light in his eyes fade. It was so tempting, but he refrained. Instead, he watched as he walked by, oblivious to his existence. Then, as The Caretaker's target opened the door of Costa and stepped inside, The Caretaker put away his book, got up and followed him.

Back in the warm, noisy coffee shop, filled mostly with young mums and their children enjoying Saturday morning time together, The Caretaker joined the queue directly behind his target. Again, he had thoughts of taking out the knife, thrusting it deep into him. He looked at his back, broad and strong; the man was a lot taller and stronger than he was, but he knew that small space between his shoulder and neck would be soft, easy to penetrate. If he drove the blade down into that gap, he would be dead before he hit the ground. Knowing he could, and refraining, made him feel good; the tingle it caused was like electricity. Besides, he didn't want Jake to die without knowing. What he had planned was far more appropriate to the kind of man he was.

True to form, his target ordered his small drink and, finding one of the few free tables, dropped his gym bag on the floor and sat heavily, trying to attract as much attention to himself as possible.

'Prick,' The Caretaker said to himself, but a little louder than intended, as the same bubbly barista who served him before smiled knowingly.

'Americano? Am I right?' she asked.

'Well remembered,' The Caretaker said. 'Thank you.'

'No problem.'

She made The Caretaker's drink, a takeaway cup again, and

The Caretaker looked round for somewhere he could sit, where he could see Jake and take in the man he intended to kill. His first kill.

The only available table was the one next to his. As casually as possible, The Caretaker walked over and sat within touching distance. He smiled at Jake, but Jake didn't smile back.

'Busy in here today,' The Caretaker said.

'Yeah,' Jake replied, lifting his tiny cup, his elbow wide, flexing as he did, and taking a sip. The Caretaker had to wonder: did he know he looked like a fucking idiot? The Caretaker didn't know why, but he wanted to hear more of his voice. He wanted to engage with him more. Maybe it was because The Caretaker knew a lot about the man, besides how he sounded. He knew Jake was a financial abuser first, but later took up gaslighting. He knew the awful things he had done, and how he had betrayed a woman in the worst way. Those videos would outlive him; he had scarred her for life.

The Caretaker knew that, to Jake, the word 'no' didn't mean a thing, however often it was said. He knew Jake's intentions, he knew Jake's fate, and he wanted to revel in it a little. It was self-indulgent, but, he reasoned, if he couldn't enjoy what he was doing, the pressure would become unbearable. What he planned to do to Jake, to others like him, was huge, and it would ruin him if he didn't find joy in the work.

So he let himself savour the moment. He knew, if you wanted people to like you, to want to talk to you, you had to talk to them about something they were interested in. It was almost too easy.

'Still, I don't mind the yummy mummies,' The Caretaker continued. Surprised by the comment, Jake looked at him.

'Did you just say what I think you just said?'

'Well, bit of window shopping.'

Jake laughed, loud and obnoxiously. 'Window shopping.'

The Caretaker took a sip of his coffee, and Jake did the same, before continuing, 'OK then, tell me, which is top tier?'

The Caretaker scanned the room, looking at all of the people enjoying their quiet morning, oblivious of his scrutiny. On a table to his right sat three women with their toddlers. One looked a little like someone he knew.

'Her, the slim one with the dark hair.'

Jake looked, nodded. 'Yeah, she'd get it,' he said, and even though The Caretaker laughed, he wanted nothing more than to slit his throat, open it up like a yawn, and make him choke on his words.

'To be honest, the mum thing ain't for me,' Jake said.

'No?'

'Nah. All used up, you know.'

'Yeah, yeah,' The Caretaker agreed.

Jake finished his drink, stood and began to walk away. 'See ya.'

'See ya,' The Caretaker replied, watching Jake walk through the busy coffee shop and out into the crisp morning, knowing full well that Jake saying 'See ya' meant nothing at all. But for The Caretaker, 'See ya' wasn't a pleasantry, it was foreshadowing. For in just over seventy-two hours' time they would meet again, and the cocky little shit would be begging for his pitiful little life, before he was, to quote him, all used up.

The Caretaker drank his coffee in peace after Jake left, and then, once he had finished, he too stood to leave. He had one more stop, one more thing he needed to do before he could carry out his plan. He needed to see an old friend, one who had access to a plethora of recreational drugs. The Caretaker needed one in particular, something that would help him do what he had to do.

Chapter Eighteen

JESS

13th January 2025

T*he little things mattered.* That became my mantra, and since Friday, whenever I felt overwhelmed, or afraid, or like I was failing, I reminded myself of Becky's words. The little things had more power in the long run. It became my focus, my reason to get up, my courage when it failed.

The little things, for me, meant remembering what I wanted to do with my life before Lewis, and having the strength to wonder if I could try again to achieve it. The little things were the two children I worked with, Eva and Will. With their needs and personalities and ceaseless joy, even on the hard days. They were people who needed me to be strong, positive, unafraid. They needed me to be the fun Jess I have always tried to be for them, and acknowledging that my fears and trauma weren't for them to know, or to live vicariously, meant that at least when I was with them, I was something like the Jess Pendle I wanted to be. Even if I knew, deep down, I was faking it and a complete fraud. But maybe that was what I had to do. Fake it, until maybe, one day, I could make it?

Faking it or not, it helped, and for the eight hours I was with them, I coloured, watched films, played, went to a park. I cooked and sang and cleaned. But mostly I smiled more in that short spell of time than I had in a week. Their innocence was contagious. They made me feel like the world could be better, one day. That I could be better too, if I kept doing and enjoying the small things. Maybe, just maybe…

When Jenny came home, and it was time for me to leave, I was sad. I knew as soon as I was alone, I wouldn't be convincing in faking it anymore. I knew that when the world returned to its quiet, lonely state, no matter how hard I tried, the heaviness would return. The doubt, the sadness that seemed to leak out of every pore. I needed to make sure, as hard as it would be when the middle of the night came, and the world fell silent, that I had a little thing, even if I couldn't sustain it yet. My mind drifted back to that course I'd started. It was on a Monday evening at a local college, and for a few hours I was learning, growing. Lewis took that, along with many other things. But what if I re-registered, started again from the beginning? Monday would be the course, Fridays, the group. With that and work… Maybe, just maybe.

By the time I got off the bus and was walking towards my flat, night had taken hold. Although my neighbourhood was usually quiet and safe, I felt on edge. The little things had already gone. The lifeless tree branches buffeted in the cold wind, casting shadows that caught the streetlights, making them look like long tendrils grasping and clawing at the frozen leaves and dead ground. I felt that one might try and grab me, pull me into the darkness. I was also aware that although I hadn't heard a peep out of Lewis since he drew on my bedroom window and waved at me on my security camera, he could be somewhere, watching, waiting for me to arrive home to have that chat he demanded. He could step out of anywhere, grab me, and I knew that I would be too afraid to act and help myself. If Lewis turned up now, I would be powerless to do anything.

And I hated that.

As I turned onto my road, I saw in the distance a person walking towards me and I felt my nerves begin to tingle. It didn't stop me walking, and I had to wonder why. In the face of fear, it seemed my need to not offend, or look stupid, was somehow stronger than self-preservation. My body was literally yelling at me to fly away, and I was ignoring it because of embarrassment. It made no sense.

Thankfully, as I got closer, I could see it wasn't him but a woman. And that flight instinct withdrew. As we passed one another, we exchanged a small smile, suggesting to me that she too was a little anxious at being out at night alone. Then, feeling safe, I carried on up the path to my front door.

As I pulled my keys out of my bag, I became aware of someone being close. The flight mechanism kicked in again, only, without the door open, where did I have to fly to? I turned around to see the woman standing on the footpath.

'Hello?' I said.

The woman spat in my face, hitting me just below the left eye. The shock sent me reeling. I stumbled, dropping my keys on the ground.

'You fucking bitch,' she hissed. 'Your lies are gonna come back to you. Don't you worry. You'll pay for the shit you are spreading.'

Wiping my face, I managed to compose myself enough to look her in the eye and speak as calmly as I could.

'I don't know what Lewis has—'

My words were cut off as she stepped forward and slapped me across the face so hard a white flash danced across my vision. The taste of blood filled my mouth.

'Don't you say his name. You've got no right. Your lies are gonna come back and haunt you. He's told me everything about you, Jess Pendle, the accusations you've made about him, the lies you've told the police, just for a bit of attention.'

'No, I—'

'He's told me all about how he was going to leave you, and you are trying to ruin him for it. Don't you worry. The truth will come back and get you.'

I wanted to speak, to tell her he was manipulating her, abusing her to get to me, but the words wouldn't come.

'Fucking skank,' she said, before she turned and walked away.

My hands were shaking so violently that I fumbled as I tried to pick up my keys, and dropped them twice. It took me three attempts to get my key into the lock. As soon as I had the door open, I fell into my flat. I scrambled to close it, and once I heard the lock snap, securing me in, I managed to pull myself to my feet. I stumbled to the mirror in my hallway. My left cheek was scarlet; the slap had been so hard I could see the shape of her hand on my face. Opening my mouth, I looked inside; the blood I could taste was from the inside of my cheek, where I must have bitten it. I was glad that she hadn't hit me on the side where my face was still healing from New Year's Eve; it would have hurt a lot more, and caused more damage.

Did that count as a little thing?

My face hurt like hell, but I was fairly sure I would be OK – a bruise perhaps, stinging when I ate or drank. But nothing like New Year's. Closing my mouth, I moved my jaw, and then I stopped and looked at me. My eyes filled with tears and I watched as they dropped onto my cheeks. I should have rung the police, but I didn't. I knew it would only fuel him now, make him think of new ways to get to me. That woman, she was a warning: be quiet, or more will happen. Be quiet or you'll regret it. I had heard Lewis loud and clear.

I was on my own. I was powerless. I needed someone to save me.

Chapter Nineteen

THE CARETAKER

14th January 2025

People are just like every other animal on this earth, in that they are creatures of habit. In the animal kingdom, it's much easier to identify habits, as species tend to act like the masses. Rising, eating, mating, building in the same patterns that particular species have followed for millennia, all dependent on the trajectory of their evolution.

Humans are different. No two humans behave the same on a microcosmic level. Sure, they all rise and eat and fuck, and when they are young they all cry for their mums, and when they are close to dying they all wish they'd spent more time seeing the world and taken more risks. But day to day they vary so much that it's as if every human was in fact their own species. Following their own evolutionary path.

But if you know someone's movements, seldom do they deviate, and once you understand someone's habits, they rarely let you down.

Tuesdays for Jake went like this: wake at 6am. Out of the door by 7am to the site, where he would put in a shift until between 4pm and 5pm. He would then go straight to the gym and would be home anytime between 7.30pm and 8pm. There he would eat, take his supplements, shower and sleep. Tuesdays were always like this. Always.

Jake was also one for preparing meals in advance, in line with his need to look spectacular. And he did look spectacular, of that there was no doubt. Strong, muscular, defined. It was a commitment, and The Caretaker knew Jake would prepare his meals and supplements before leaving his house, his meals perfectly calibrated so he had the right amounts of carbohydrates, fats and proteins. It was almost impressive, the level of commitment and dedication. But The Caretaker didn't let himself feel impressed.

Tuesday was a seafood stir-fry. It would be in his fridge, sealed in Tupperware, so all he needed to do was heat and eat.

Knowing what he was going to do, The Caretaker had barely slept. In a café near Jake's flat, he sipped a strong coffee and watched Jake leave his front door exactly on time. Once he was sure he wasn't coming back, The Caretaker got up and, using the key he had acquired, casually walked up to Jake's house. He skirted around the back and let himself in by the back door.

After he did what he needed to do, he left, locking the door behind him, and walked away. He kept calm, casual, knowing that people might see him, but as he behaved like he should be there, no one would bat an eyelid. He was ready. He just hoped he was right, and his plan would work.

Back home, The Caretaker tried to sleep, but it wouldn't come, the adrenalin already too high. So he paced back and forth, recapped his plan, clock-watched until he knew it was time to leave. The day was long and difficult and, as it wore on, doubts started to creep in. Even though this had been a long time in the making, there were a few 'what ifs' attached. What if he didn't stick to his routine? What if something happened at work, or he had a date The Caretaker didn't know about? What if a neighbour thought The Caretaker was suspicious and rang the police after he left? The Caretaker fought with these questions all day, until his alarm sounded, telling him it was eight o'clock. It was time to finish what he'd started.

Double-checking his bag was packed and the things he needed were there and accessible in the correct order, he made the trip back to Jake's home.

The drive was tough, the adrenalin peaking, almost to the point of crashing, and several times The Caretaker felt like he could easily turn around, go home and forget the whole thing. But then he reminded himself of the desire he felt to kill. The need. Jake was a bad man, poisonous – he ruined lives, hurt people – and he had got away with it time and time again. The Caretaker knew the damage he had caused to one woman in particular. A sweet young woman named Madison. He had hurt her, possibly beyond repair, and he was making her life hell. He had made her look like a whore to so many others. She was a mother, her boy was his son, and he was hellbent on ruining them both. The Caretaker could end the suffering of two innocent souls by ending the life of one. It seemed like a fair trade-off.

Repeating it, he felt his resolve toughen once more, and by the time he arrived close to Jake's home, he knew he wouldn't back out. He would see it through, right until the very end.

The Caretaker arrived at the place he would leave his car, a quiet road, no CCTV cameras, half a mile from Jake's house. Turning off his engine, he looked at the time: 8:31pm. Jake would likely be where The Caretaker wanted him, but to be sure, he waited until 9pm.

'All right, let's do this.'

Getting out of his car, he walked towards Jake's. Once he left, Jake would be no more. The Caretaker knew it was going to be a long night, the longest of his life.

Chapter Twenty

Arriving at Jake's back door, The Caretaker hesitated before putting the key in the lock. Closing his eyes, he listened. Somewhere, far away, a dog barked, and closer a branch creaked as the wind blew. But from behind the entry to Jake's warped little world, The Caretaker couldn't hear anything.

It was time.

Taking off his rucksack, The Caretaker stepped around the side of the house and into the back garden. Safely in the shadows, he lowered himself to the ground and unzipped his bag. In it were a pair of latex gloves, gaffer tape, a pair of generic wellies, size ten, bought from a market, a balaclava, safety goggles, a surgical face mask and cheap but effective overalls. The Caretaker pulled the overalls on, slid into the wellies and gaffer-taped their tops, sealing him in. He then slapped on the gloves and taped them to his sleeves. Slipping on the balaclava, he raised the hood of the protective overalls and donned the glasses. It wasn't perfect, but if he was careful, it was likely he wouldn't leave any DNA at the scene.

Zipping the rucksack back up, he slipped it over his shoulders and then let himself into his target's home, gently pushing open the door, which squeaked as it swung open. He waited a moment – still nothing – and was satisfied Jake wasn't in a state to know he was there. He stepped in and closed the door behind him.

From the front of the house, he could hear the faint sound of talking. The voice was American and, The Caretaker realised after about twenty seconds, it looped. It was a reel playing through Jake's phone, likely Instagram, where Jake spent all of his time. It told him that Jake had started watching but then couldn't scroll onto the next. The first part of his plan had worked.

Feeling more confident, The Caretaker walked towards the sound, and when he stepped into the living room, he allowed himself to smile.

Jake was face-down on his floor, out cold, but still breathing. Picking up Jake's phone, The Caretaker locked the screen. The Instagram loop stopped, and silence took hold. He then tapped Jake with his foot. He didn't move. The second part of his plan had worked also.

Two for two. It was a good omen.

Ketamine was a brilliant drug, in the right circumstances – for anaesthesia, for its anti-inflammatory properties, for depression. It was used by hospitals all over the world. In the wrong circumstances, it was a powerful drug that could become addictive and ruin lives. In the worst circumstances, it could be used to sedate and immobilise a person against their will. Obtaining it was far easier than The Caretaker had thought. One phone call to an old friend, one exchange, one low price, and The Caretaker had enough of it to kill a person. But he didn't want Jake dead. It was tricky. The Caretaker knew a lot about the man, but not his exact weight. He had to make an educated guess, and the way Jake was moaning in his not comatose but not lucid state told him he had guessed right.

Knowing Jake so well, it had been easy to get the drug into him. Jake was a planner; his meal was ready to go. All The Caretaker had to do was mix the drug into his stir-fry, and wait for him to eat.

Creature of habit.

Taking his bag off his back, he pulled the thick black zip ties from the side pocket and, heaving Jake's dead-weight arms behind him, tied his wrists together. One tie should hold, but knowing how strong Jake was, The Caretaker looped three around. Just to be safe. He then heaved Jake onto his back and tied his ankles with several more.

All he could do now was wait, and stop Jake choking on his own tongue until he stirred.

It took four hours for Jake to stop moaning incoherently. As consciousness returned, in the moans and mumbles could be heard confusion and fear. The Caretaker knew it was almost time. So, taking the gaffer tape, he stood over Jake and wrapped it over his mouth. To be sure he couldn't slip it and scream – because there was no doubt he would scream – The Caretaker looped the tape three times round his head. There was no way he would slip out of that.

It took another thirty minutes for Jake to become lucid enough to take in his surroundings and try to understand why he was on the floor, why he couldn't move his arms and legs, why he couldn't talk. The Caretaker patiently waited, enjoying the fear, as he knew full well the fear Jake had caused in women during his short, vile life.

Jake looked at The Caretaker, who was casually sat on his sofa, and his breathing increased until he was hyperventilating.

The Caretaker smiled back, knowing that his appearance – balaclava, hazmat suit, gloves with taped sleeves – told a very interesting story. Jake flailed like a landed fish, desperate to run, to escape. But the zip ties held firm, and the ketamine still coursed. The Caretaker began to laugh. He didn't know why; he was almost as afraid as Jake was about what was to come. But, still, he laughed. This huge Adonis of a man was flapping and flailing like a dying minnow, and it was possibly the most ridiculous thing The Caretaker had ever seen. As The Caretaker continued to laugh, Jake stopped flapping, and the fear in his eyes turned to pure hatred, pure violent intent. The Caretaker stopped laughing, pleased with the reaction.

'There you are,' The Caretaker said. 'There's the man I've learned all about.'

Jake didn't try to move. Instead he stared at The Caretaker in such a way that The Caretaker knew if he got free, he would kill him.

'I don't have a lot of time, Jake. So let's get on with it, shall we?'

Jake started upon hearing his name. New confusion flashed across his eyes.

'Jake, I know everything about you. Well, most things, some things aren't important. Not for this.'

The Caretaker unzipped his bag, lifted out a litre bottle containing a clear liquid and placed it on the floor beside his feet. He then reached back inside and pulled out a small black case, around the size of one holding a pair of reading glasses. Opening it, he removed a hypodermic needle, the cap firmly on to prevent a scratch injury. When Jake saw it, anger again turned to fear.

'People talk a lot these days about toxic individuals,' The Caretaker continued, his voice hoarse, evidence of his humming nerves. 'Sometimes it's valid to call someone that, I think, but like all terms, it's got twisted, and all of a sudden everyone is toxic in one way or another. For me, being toxic means someone who is hellbent on causing harm to others. To hide their insecurities maybe, or their failings. To dominate, as it gives them a false power. I think toxic is when someone knows exactly what they are doing to another person. Toxic is abusing something that should be sacred. Someone like you, Jake. You are all of these things, and more. You, my muscular friend, are someone who is more than toxic.'

Jake didn't reply, but stared back, his breathing heavy, rhythmic, hypnotically pushing their exchange along. It was rapid, like a train close to derailment.

'You are a poison. You have ruined a young woman, Madison.'

Jake stopped breathing.

'Don't be so surprised, Jake. Why else would I be here? I know all about Madison. I know she is a good woman, kind. She is a glass-half-full soul. She has an innocence and sense of wonder about her; she sees the world in a way most don't, and you are poisoning that. Sharing what should have been sacred to you two. You are a real piece of shit. She will one day be completely ruined because of it, and in turn that will ruin any chance of your son growing up to be a man who is not like you. I can't let that happen.'

Jake started struggling again and The Caretaker stood and watched. His fighting meant he hadn't been listening to what was being said. And he needed to listen. The Caretaker needed him to acknowledge the truth. The Caretaker wasn't about sending anyone to hell; he wanted this man to atone, meet his maker, and perhaps be forgiven. The Caretaker just didn't want him to be forgiven in this world. He had had his chance in this world, and he had blown it. The Caretaker stood, and before Jake could shield himself, kicked him square in the face, most of the impact connecting with Jake's nose. There was a small snap, and blood began to pour. Jake instinctively rolled onto his side so he didn't choke. But after a few seconds, The Caretaker could tell, with his mouth taped he was struggling to breathe.

Picking up the hypodermic needle, he pulled off the cap. 'Hold still,' he said, but Jake didn't listen, and continued to struggle. 'Hold still, Jake, I'm gonna help you breathe.'

Still Jake didn't listen, and The Caretaker could hear him begin to gurgle the blood that was pouring down the back of his throat.

'Jake. You are going to die, unless you let me help you,' he snapped.

He listened that time and, looking at The Caretaker, did as he was told. The Caretaker grabbed his face, and using the needle, he perforated the tape binding his mouth, creating small air holes like you would find in a shoebox holding a hamster. Jake began to suck air. The Caretaker went behind him and heaved him into a seated position, his back to the wall, his hands tucked under his frame. His limbs were still dead weight from the ketamine. Jake continued to suck in air. His nose freely bled down his front, but after a minute began to slow. Jake's breathing, now calmer, more accepting, once again became the only sound in the room. The Caretaker sat back on the sofa, watching his target. Jake must have thought he wasn't going to die, that The Caretaker had saved him. He thought wrong.

'Now, where were we?' The Caretaker continued. 'Oh yes, poison. Now, Jake. I can't let you poison her, I can't, and even though, right now, you would say you would change, people don't. I suspect you're wondering what is in the bottle at my feet. I'll tell you. The clear liquid inside is something called potassium chloride.'

Jakes eyes flicked to the bottle. Once again, the fear was back.

'I assume you might know a little about what it is, given you are so into your fitness. Now, a small amount of this stuff is actually good for someone who is struggling to up their potassium levels. But too much...' The Caretaker trailed off as he picked up the bottle and unscrewed the cap. He then took the needle that had just helped Jake and lowered the tip into the liquid. He filled it up, 5ml in total, and then placed the bottle calmly on the floor again.

'I guessed you're around a hundred kilograms. About right?'

Jake's breathing became train-like again.

'Don't try and answer. I've already worked that out. That means, with two of these, you are likely to make it. Three, it will act just like poison, and you will die.'

The Caretaker stood and approached Jake, who, despite his best efforts, couldn't get up. Being bound and high on ketamine rendered his limbs all but useless. The Caretaker punched the needle into his upper arm, up by his shoulder, and stepped back. The reaction was almost instantaneous. Jake began to writhe, screaming under the tape that trapped his voice. For a second The Caretaker assumed he was having a seizure, but the convulsions soon slowed as Jake fought to manage the searing pain that was coursing through his body. The Caretaker had read that it was akin to fire flooding the veins. The pain was so excruciating, Jake looked like he would pass out. The Caretaker didn't want that, he wanted Jake to feel it all, so getting up, he walked to the kitchen, filled two glasses of water and carried them back into the living room. As Jake's eyes began to roll, The

Caretaker threw the first glass in his face. The cold snapped him back into consciousness.

'No sleeping now, Jake. That wouldn't be fair.'

The writhing slowed, but The Caretaker knew the pain was still excruciating. Jake lay staring at The Caretaker, who calmly sat and filled the hypodermic with another 5ml of potassium chloride. Without speaking, he reached over and shot another injection into Jake's body, this time in that space between his shoulder and neck where he had daydreamed of stabbing him in the coffee shop. Once more the pain caused Jake to convulse, and once more The Caretaker had to soak him to keep him conscious. But it wouldn't last long. Jake would pass out soon. And The Caretaker didn't want that to happen. It seemed like he was cheating if he wasn't awake for the final dose.

Heaving the semi-conscious Jake up into a seated position once more. The Caretaker filled the needle for the third time. Jake wasn't fighting anymore; his eyes rolled, his body limp. The Caretaker knelt down in front of him and slapped him across the face. Jake's eyes refocused.

The Caretaker then pulled up his balaclava and enjoyed the look of recognition that danced on Jake's face.

'That's right, motherfucker. You know me,' The Caretaker said. He took the needle and lowered it to Jake's neck, thumbed a vein, thick and inviting, and pushed the needle into it. He let it hang there for a second, as Jake's breathing thundered on. Then he pushed down the plunger and watched the clear liquid disappear into Jake's body.

The Caretaker returned to the sofa and watched as the light faded from Jake's eyes. He checked the time – it was almost one thirty. Satisfied Jake was gone, he stood and, to be sure, pressed two gloved fingers on the carotid artery. He didn't find a pulse. The job was done. Then, taken by surprise, he had to run to the toilet, where he threw up three times. One violent heave for each injection.

Once he was sure the heaving had stopped, The Caretaker grabbed some toilet bleach and scrubbed the toilet, removing all trace of him from the bathroom. He then retraced everywhere he had been, cleaning everything he had been in contact with. Then, once he was sure he had left everything as it should be, he stood over his victim, the sick feeling rising once more. For a moment, he wondered what the fuck he had just done. There was guilt – murder was murder, after all – but he thought about Madison, about her child, and how they would have been destined to have a shitty life without his intervention, and the guilt faded. Then he packed his bag, stepped outside, removed all of the protective clothing and walked into the night, like nothing had happened.

Chapter Twenty-One

SOPHIE SALAM

15th January 2025

Sophie Salam hadn't worked many murder scenes before. She had seen her share of dead people, accidents, the elderly, those who died of natural causes. But in her four years in CID, she had only been on one actual murder scene. From what she had been told in her brief, this was to be her second. As she approached the location of the victim, cordoned off by several police cars and a forensics van, she saw PC Edwards, the officer who had found the victim. She got out of her car and smiled his way. He didn't smile back, and she noticed he looked a little green around the gills.

'Hey, Edwards. You OK?'

'Yeah, I'm OK,' he said, but Sophie knew he wasn't. She remembered the first few times she'd seen a dead body, she too wanted to throw up.

'The call came in at just after noon,' Edwards continued.

'Take your time,' Sophie said. He nodded.

'Lad's employer was worried as he hadn't turned up for

work, and no one could get hold of him. It was unlike him, he said. He was usually diligent, never took a sick day. The usual stuff we hear. He seemed pretty concerned, so I came to do a welfare check, assuming the lad had been out, had a few and simply slept in. You know what lads are like.'

Sophie nodded. 'How did you discover him?'

'When he didn't answer the door, I looked around the property. The living-room curtains were closed, but there was a gap. I could see his foot, so I raised the alarm.'

Sophie nodded. 'You did well. Get a coffee or something, you look a little peaky.'

'Thanks, Ma'am.'

'What's the victim's name?'

'Jake Murray.'

'OK. Take a minute and then find out what we know about him.'

'You got it.'

Sophie turned her attention to the front door of the house. Another officer stood outside, ensuring only those with clearance entered the crime scene. Outside the house, in front of the window, was a white tent, and Sophie stepped inside. She quickly changed into a hazmat suit, ensuring that when she went into the property she didn't contaminate the scene, and then, saying hello to the officer on the door, she entered the house, following the sound of people working until she found the living room.

On the floor, sat against the wall, was Jake Murray. For a second Sophie recoiled – not because his eyes looked at her, glazed in the way only dead people looked, but because he reminded her of someone she used to know. A man she'd fought hard to forget, despite the daily reminder back home in the form of her daughter. She repressed the feeling of familiarity and focused. Hanging out of his neck was a hypodermic needle. As she stepped inside, the smell of faeces, strong and pungent, smacked her in the face. She was expecting as much – upon death, the bladder and bowel would have voided – but even expecting it, and with her face covered by a mask, the smell hit her hard, and she turned her head to one side for a second. When she had adjusted, she spoke to a forensic officer, a good copper and her friend, who had been working in the force for longer than she had been alive. He was on the floor, close to the victim, taking swabs.

'Hey, Clarke. What have we got?'

'Man, mid to late twenties. Time of death not confirmed, but anywhere within the last twenty-four hours.'

'His employer said he was at work as usual yesterday, so probably sometime in the night.' Sophie said, adding what she'd learned of the timeline in her briefing.

'That's what I reckon.'

'Cause of death?'

'We'll have to do some work in the lab, but my guess is, it has something to do with that,' he said, pointing to a bottle on the floor tucked behind the sofa. Sophie picked it up and looked it over.

'Potassium chloride?'

'Yep. Easily bought. Not confirmed, of course, but it seems our victim had a little overdose of this stuff.'

'Really?'

'Three different entry sites. Enough to kill him rather unpleasantly.'

'Three?'

'See here.' He pointed to the dead man's muscular shoulder. 'Bruising on the top of his arm, shoulder and, well, you can see where the last dose went in.'

Sophie nodded, looking at the needle hanging out of his neck.

'It seemed our killer either knew how much to give him, or just kept giving it to him until his heart stopped.'

'Would it have hurt?'

'Oh yes, it would have been torture,' Clarke said.

Sophie nodded, taking in the fact that he was bound, gagged and positioned upright. 'Have you seen anything like this before, Clarke?'

'This? Nope, never. Feels like a revenge thing, do you agree?'

'Yeah, it does,' Sophie said, and a niggle pulled at her, like an itch she couldn't quite reach. Before she could scratch it, her phone pinged and, pulling it out, she saw it was her mum.

MUM

> Call when you get this.

Her mum didn't message unless it was an emergency.

'If you find anything else, let me know?' she said, backing out of the room.

'Always,' Clarke said, returning to the victim.

As Sophie left the living room, more forensics entered, taking photographs, looking for prints, but somehow Sophie knew they wouldn't find any.

Stepping out, she pulled off her mask and took a deep breath. On the street, there was a small gathering of people wanting to see what the commotion was. In amongst them was a local reporter she had run into from time to time. Her phone pinged again, a new message from her mum.

> Ring ASAP. I'm struggling!!!

She was about to call back when the reporter shouted over to her. 'DS Salam? What's going on?'

'Nothing much. January blues. You?' she said, dismissing his attempted interrogation. She wasn't in a place to comment. They didn't know enough to even know where to begin.

'Don't be coy. Clearly this is big, looks like a murder. What can you tell me?'

She looked him up and down, noticing he was wearing a bright red pair of Converse. 'That you're too old to pull those off.'

'Stop flirting with me, DS Salam.'

'You wish.'

Walking back into the tent, Sophie removed her protective clothing, and as she adjusted her clothes, PC Edwards joined her.

'It's messy, isn't it?' he said.

'You got that right,' Sophie agreed. 'What can you tell me?'

'Jake Murray, twenty-eight. Works as a self-employed labourer.'

Sophie nodded. 'Any history?'

'A bit, has been cautioned a couple of times.'

'What for?'

'Fighting mostly.'

'Sounds like a lovely lad,' Sophie said. 'Do us a favour. The bloke out there with the hideous shoes, get rid of him, I don't have the energy for it.'

Her phone rang, and even without looking at the display, she knew it would be her mum. 'I gotta go. Can you deal with the reporter? I'll call you later, get an update.'

'You're leaving?' Edwards said, confused as to why the DS wouldn't stay.

'I'll be back.' Sophie said, lifting the phone to her ear as she began to move quickly back to the car.

'I need you here!' her mum said, shouted, over the commotion at home.

'Is she OK, Ma?' Sophie said, but she knew the answer. In the background, Lottie was screaming at the top of her lungs. Full meltdown. She heard a glass smash. More screaming.

'I can't calm her. She's breaking everything. She's tried to hurt me. She's been banging her head again. I can't get her to stop. Get home. Now!'

'I'm coming. Don't let her hurt herself, Ma.'

'I'll try.'

'Ma, don't try. Do not let her hurt herself. I'll be as quick as I can.'

Firing up the engine, Sophie began to drive home. She rang her boss, told him what was happening, and as always, he was understanding of Lottie's needs. She worked hard and would make up the time. But still, even with the blessing of her team, she felt she was letting everyone down. A good detective would have stayed on the scene, working out what that niggle was. A good mother would be at home, caring for her daughter who was struggling and needed her.

She was failing to do either.

Chapter Twenty-Two

THE CARETAKER

By the time The Caretaker had got home, it was almost three in the morning. Exhausted from the night's events, he assumed he would sleep. Only sleep didn't come. He expected it to railroad him into oblivion. He expected to want to curl up and die, much like his victim. He was expecting *something*, but nothing happened, no rush, no crash, just a vague numbness behind his eyes. A headache pending. The night's events were running on a loop in his head in high definition. The images that played were exciting, incredible, sickening. So, to cleanse himself from what he had done, he ran a hot bath and climbed in.

He practised the breathing techniques he had been taught back when times were tough. Breathe in, hold for four, out for eight… He felt his muscles begin to relax, and then ache as the tension was quickly replaced by lactic acid. His body felt like it had run a marathon. The hot water soothed him and then the vague numbness spread throughout his body, turning him into a dead weight. A bit like Jake at the end. Sleep did come shortly after, for when he opened his eyes again, the water was ice-cold and his skin had shrunk on his fingers and toes to resemble the skin of a Shar Pei puppy. He climbed out, warmed himself with a towel and looked out of his window to see it was day.

He checked his watch. It was almost one in the afternoon. It had been over twelve hours since his first kill, and he had slept for nine without stirring. Nine whole hours in a dreamless, weightless sleep. It had been years since he had rested so well, and it told him that what he had done, the suffering he had caused, was justified. He slept like a baby because a bad man had finally faced justice for his crimes.

Once dressed, The Caretaker made himself a coffee and then, going onto Facebook, he searched for any news about his work. It didn't take long; a local paper was reporting on a 'large police presence' at the house. It seemed his victim had been discovered only an hour before. It didn't give Jake's name, nor did it even say there had been a murder. It was simply a speculation post, but it had drawn attention, with dozens of comments below.

Soon the news would break. Soon people would talk about the man who had been killed.

Soon they would know this wasn't an isolated murder.

More would be killed before he was done.

Chapter Twenty-Three

SUPPORT GROUP CHAT

KELLY 10.43AM

I've had a week ladies, is anyone free for a drink over the weekend? Its only Wednesday and I'm fucking knackered.

HANNAH 10.44AM

I'm in. You OK?

KELLY 10.47AM

Fine, just him being a dick about things. Finally get the divorce I want, but he's trying to make it about him. He's now got a girl half his age dripping off him, and still the fucker won't just make it easy. Sorry. Don't wanna moan. I just wanna get drunk!

HANNAH 10.48AM

Right now?

KELLY 10.48AM

Its five o'clock somewhere.

😂

The Serial Killer Support Group

STEPH 10.51AM

I could get a sitter for the kids on Friday or Saturday. Count me in!

RACHEL 10.51AM

I never need a reason to have a night out!

KELLY 10.55AM

Great, let's get something planned. Sorry to moan, everyone else OK?

HANNAH 10.57AM

Ticking along, he messaged telling me he was attacked, like I wouldn't know, and as if I'd even care.

RACHEL 10.58AM

What did he say?

HANNAH 11.01AM

The whole woe is me deal. He does it sometimes, when he knows anger isn't working. I said, I've heard, and I hope he feels better soon and then I stopped messaging.

KELLY 11.02AM

Well handled Hannah, fuck him.

HANNAH 11.02AM

Yeah, fuck him.

BAHEELA 11.12AM

Hey all, sorry for just jumping in. Well done Hannah, but I gotta ask, and I don't want to freak anyone out, but, have you seen Facebook?

KELLY 11.13AM

No? What's going on?

BAHEELA 11.13AM

There is a rumour someone has been killed.

HANNAH 11.13AM

Who?

MADS 11.14AM

I think it's true.

KELLY 11.14AM

Mads? What are you doing here? I thought you were away.

MADS 11.14AM

I am. I've just turned my phone on to message you all.

KELLY 11.14AM

What's true? What's happened? Are you OK?

MADS 11.14AM

People are telling me Jake is dead.

😢 4

VIJA 11.14AM

What?

KELLY 11.14AM

Mads, I'm going to call you now.

RACHEL 11.14AM

Baheela's partner, then Hannah's, and now Mads' is dead…

STEPH 11.15AM

Let's not jump to conclusions… we don't know.

KELLY 11.19AM

Mads, I can't get through to you? Mads, are you there?

KELLY 11.24AM

Mads?

KELLY 11.32AM

I can't reach you.

MADS 11.36AM

Jake's mum just called me. Its him. It's true.

😦 5

HANNAH 11.37AM

What the fuck is happening?

KELLY 11.37AM

I don't know. Are we all there Friday? Want to meet early? Talk it over?

👍 ❤️ 3

KELLY 11.37AM

Mads, you gonna be OK?

MADS 11.39AM

I don't know.

KELLY 11.40AM

Ring me when you're back?

MADS 11.41AM

OK.

Chapter Twenty-Four

JESS

Right up until Lewis got the woman, no doubt a woman he was sleeping with, to spit at me and slap me on my own doorstep, I had hoped that maybe things could change. It was foolish, I know, but he wasn't all bad – he had his good qualities once, beautiful qualities – and I had secretly held on to them coming back, even at his worst. Even on New Year's Eve, I'd hoped.

But I knew hope wasn't enough. He had a woman attack me because he couldn't do it himself, and he knew that I knew if I called the police, not a damn thing would happen. So, after my assault, I locked my door, and pretended everything was fine. Fake it till you make it, right? I almost convinced myself too, apart from the horrible little cut inside my mouth that stung every time I ate. I was pleased about it though, I had got really good at sweeping things under the carpet, but the bulge in the rug from years of sweeping was now too big, and I kept tripping on it. It was time to clean up a little. So I decided it was time to tell the truth about it all. As shameful as it was. It was time to talk to my mum. I needed to own what my life had become, so I could move through it and find the old me, if she still existed.

When I rang Mum, asking if I could come over, as I wanted to talk to her about something, I could hear excitement in her voice. Lewis and I, in her eyes, had been happily together for a couple of years now, and I could see the conclusions she had drawn. Mum was expecting one of two things, for me to tell her either that I was engaged or that I was pregnant. When I arrived at her doorstep and she hugged me, I noticed that before she looked at my face and saw my fading bruise and red scar line, she looked first at my stomach, then my left hand.

'Jess? What happened?' she said, in shock when she finally looked up at me.

Steve appeared behind Mum and, being Steve, saw my face straightaway, and straightaway knew what had happened.

'Jess? Love?' he said in way that was angry, furious, but also deeply concerned, and even though I'd promised myself I would not cry when I opened up, I began to sob like a little child. Steve, the man I had come to think of as a father, wrapped me in his arms, held me and didn't try to stop me crying. Mum still hadn't worked it out and, as Steve pulled me inside, closing the front door behind him, she kept asking what was wrong.

'Just give her a minute, Sarah, let her cry it out,' he said softly, and not knowing what to do, Mum bustled into the kitchen and flicked the kettle on.

And still I cried. I cried until I felt dry, and after the sobbing stopped, Steve continued to hold me for another full minute before letting go.

'Come and sit down, love,' he said, so tenderly I almost cried again.

Taking my hand, he led me into the living room and sat me down. My still-bemused mum joined us with coffees.

'Jess? What's happened?' Mum said, calmer than before but still desperate to know why I was there, crying, without a ring on my finger.

'Give her a minute. Jess, love. No rush, we are here for you. You're our girl. We are always here.'

Even though I thought I had cried myself dry, a fresh tear formed, and as I let it fall I started talking about everything. I told them about New Year's, about all the other times he'd hurt me. About how he'd isolated me, how my friends have drifted away. How I dropped out of the course that Mum was so proud I had started. How the police were now involved. As I spoke, I saw Mum wanting to get up and hug me, but Steve gently took her hand, stopping her. If Mum interrupted with a hug, I'd stop talking.

Eventually, I ran out of steam, and looking at my mum, I could see the hurt in her eyes. Hurt that her daughter had suffered in the same way she had, but also hurt that I'd kept it from her.

'I'm sorry,' I said. And Mum leapt up, pulled me to my feet and squeezed me so hard I struggled to breathe.

'You listen to me, Jessica Pendle, you have nothing to be sorry for. Nothing. You hear me.'

'Yes, Mum,' I said, my voice muffled in her shoulder. But I didn't fully believe it.

Mum let me go, and as I lowered myself onto the sofa once more, she joined me. Steve did too, and for a long time we just sat, the three of us, me in the middle. We didn't speak. We just hugged, and when the tears came again, Mum whispered to me that everything would be OK.

I wanted to believe her, but I wasn't sure how. What I did know was that now my dirty secret was out, now those who were most important to me knew, there was no way back. It was almost like that first moment I walked into the support group. There was no undoing it, no denying it. I was who I was, and maybe now I had accepted it, I might be able to move forward?

Once our hugs began to loosen, Mum picked up the TV remote, no doubt feeling the same I was, that our hug reminded her of Sunday movies when I was young, and she turned it on.

'Let's find a Harry Potter film.'

'Perfect,' I said, smiling at her. She smiled back, a smile full of grief, before turning her attention to the screen. On the local BBC news, a reporter was outside a flat somewhere in town. Lots of police. A serious crime of some kind. Mum turned it over before I could hear what was going on.

Chapter Twenty-Five

SOPHIE SALAM

As soon as Sophie arrived home, she began to calm Lottie, who had banged her head so much she had a bruise in the middle of her forehead. She had to get hands-on, hold her little girl, and she had to shout. She hated doing both. But it worked: within an hour her little girl was sleeping, exhausted from the day. Her mum was exhausted too, for the same reasons, and she readied herself to go home.

'Ma, wait, are you OK?'

Her mum looked at her, then couldn't hold her gaze.

'I'm tired.'

'I'm sorry.'

'It's not your fault; it's not hers either, I know. But when she starts headbutting things, I just…'

She trailed off and began to well up, then, clearing her throat, she restrained her tears. 'She needs her mother, I know that much. I try, but I'm not you, Soph. I can't do what you do to help her when the world becomes too much. We need help.'

'We can manage.'

'We need her father, Sophie.'

'Ma, we have been over this. I don't know where he is.'

'You're a detective; you can find him.'

'No, Ma, no. We can manage.'

Daya considered her daughter for a moment, and when she spoke, it was Sophie's turn to look away. 'I know you're hiding something about him.'

'I'm not.'

'Don't lie, Sophie. We don't do that.'

Sophie didn't speak, and Daya, knowing she wouldn't, took a deep breath.

'She needs you more, Sophie. Something's gotta change.'

Sophie nodded, unsure what to say. Her mum was right, of course, but what could she do? It wasn't as if she had a magic lamp she could rub and ask for enough money to stop working and be a full-time mother. Even if she left the police, she would have to work somewhere, be away from Lottie, to earn a living. Life just didn't allow you to stop when it got tough. You had to keep moving, keep trying. It wasn't as if she had Lottie's dad to lean on either; he didn't even know Lottie existed. Men like him shouldn't be parents, and if he ever found out about her, Sophie wasn't sure how he would react. She wasn't sure if she or her baby would be safe. It was just her, Lottie and her mum, the three of them against the world.

Sophie wanted Daya to stay, to see Lottie when she wasn't overwhelmed, and for them to have a moment together that was calm and loving. She could see her mum was emotionally worn out, and she wanted the tonic of Lottie happy and settled to remedy it. But she didn't stay.

Lottie only slept for just over an hour, but it was enough time for Sophie to clean the mess she'd caused, so that when she woke, she didn't see the chaos and it didn't stir up any fresh feelings. Lottie needed to wake in a calm, ordinary house, as if to a completely new day. It seemed to work. For the rest of the day Lottie played, coloured, sang to herself and was cuddly with Sophie. Needing things to stay exactly like that, when it came to bedtime Sophie lifted Lottie in with her, and as her daughter slept, Sophie pulled out her laptop, logged into the police network and opened up the file on Jake Murray.

As Lottie gently snored beside her, she recapped what she knew, wondering if there wasn't something in that initial briefing that caused the niggling feeling she felt. Nothing leapt out. There was now more information in the file. His accounts, his social media details, his record with the police. He wasn't, for the most part, a bad man. He had a few minor interactions with the law, none of which interested her, but further along, something did catch her eye. In early 2024, almost a year ago, Jake was interviewed by the police, a DS Jones, about an accusation of domestic violence. Opening the file, she read about how his partner went to the police and reported that he had shared intimate things about her. The details weren't recorded brilliantly – she could tell they had rushed the interview – but it seemed Jake hadn't been charged and was released the same day.

Forensics were still working on the cause of death and there appeared to be no witnesses. Knowing she wouldn't get anything done, Sophie looked over at her sleeping daughter. She looked like her dad in so many ways. She went onto Google and typed in a name, his name. The man her mother wanted to be in Sophie and Lottie's life. The man she couldn't let close, ever. The man who could never know about his daughter. His image shot onto the screen, an old picture from a long time ago. Seeing his eyes looking directly at her through the image was enough to send a shiver up her spine. It took her back to that winter, when the lines had been blurred, the mistakes made. She closed her laptop, promising herself she wouldn't look again.

As she settled next to her daughter, breathing in her wonderful smell, Sophie thought about the niggle she felt, forcing herself to focus on that, a thing she could control. And then she realised she knew exactly what it was.

Exactly a week ago, a man had been attacked. She couldn't remember his name off the top of her head, but she did remember he had been attacked with a belt. One which not only was his, but also had someone else's blood on it. It told a story, and she wondered, could that story be revenge? Fast forward seven days, a man was found with a needle in his neck. It looked like revenge again.

Could they be connected somehow?

Sophie knew sleep wouldn't come, not now, so she logged back into the police network, pulled up the murder she'd been called to but hadn't properly investigated, and the case from a week ago. It didn't take her long to find a connection, one she was annoyed she'd overlooked.

Martin Goodfellow, the man who'd been beaten with a belt, and Jake Murray, her murder victim, had both, in the last couple of years, been interviewed by police about domestic abuse. She wondered, could it be the same attacker in both cases? Could the cases be linked?

'Oh shit,' she said.

Chapter Twenty-Six

JESS

17th January 2025

Telling Mum and Steve what was happening to me made me feel as if a huge weight had been shifted from my diaphragm. A tightness that had existed for far too long, a tightness that I wasn't even aware was living in my body, was gone, and that night, in my childhood bedroom, I slept the deepest and longest I had in years. I was safe, my mum was nearby, and I knew, with her close, no one could hurt me. I even had a dream, the first I could remember in years. I was on a beach, completely alone, the sands shifting as a strong wind swept inland from the sea, carrying the taste of the ocean, salty and clean. I was walking, barefoot, along the shoreline. My feet were occasionally soaked by the gently moving tide. In the distance, I could see someone. They were standing still, looking out into the ocean, and even though I was too far away to make out who it was, I knew it was a woman. Just as she turned her attention my way, just as I was about to see her face, I woke.

The sun was up, its milky light bleeding through the thin

curtains. Feeling rejuvenated, I joined my mum and Steve for breakfast. I knew that if I asked to move in, they would say yes – I could almost see the offer in the way they exchanged glances as we drank our coffee and ate the poached eggs Steve had made. But life had to go on, so, the next day, after a family meal, Steve drove me home. I could see he didn't want to leave me – he even offered to sleep on the sofa – but I needed to be alone. Besides, he didn't know that the sofa had become my new bedroom since Lewis had stood at my window. I needed to see if I could hold on to the lightness in my chest without Steve's help. He didn't understand when I tried to explain to him why I wanted to be by myself, but he respected it none the less. It was time for me to take ownership of my life again.

I didn't sleep as well as I had in my family home, my old bed, but I did manage to get some curled up on the sofa, and even though the fear had returned, I was at least able to acknowledge it, look it in the eye, even if it was only for a second, and flip it the bird. The night was long, quiet. Lewis didn't come over, and I didn't dream.

By morning, I was ready to leave the flat once more. It was Friday, which was quickly becoming my favourite day of the week, and as I left, the sun was shining, the morning crisp. It was deep in winter, and yet there was the faintest suggestion of spring – a false promise, but I allowed myself to enjoy it on my walk to the bus stop.

Normally, I was the type to either have just missed a bus or be waiting for half an hour for one, but as I reached the stop, I looked up and saw the one I needed rumbling towards me. Hopping on, I scanned my card, smiled at the driver and took my usual seat right at the front, where I could watch the world go by, and every time someone climbed on, or alighted, the fresh air swept on to me. Along the route was a row of flats, the end one having its front door covered in police tape. The news report Mum had turned off when I was on their sofa was about that door. Someone had been killed inside. Someone had been murdered. Seeing the door in real life sent a shiver up my spine. It was a few miles from my house, and I knew a few miles might as well have been a thousand, but still. The shiver lingered.

As the bus continued, I forced myself to be present. Within an hour, I would be with a group of women, just like me, who were friendly, understanding, and quickly becoming my reason to brave the world. I had no doubt that joining the group was the reason I had spoken to my mum, and I knew I would tell them about the woman on my doorstep who spat at me. I wondered if any of them had a similar story, or was this one for me alone?

By the time I thanked the driver and got off the bus, all thoughts of that front door and the police tape were gone. Ahead was the battered community centre, and the people who were becoming my friends. As I approached, I could see Becky's car was there, Geoff's too, as well as three others.

As I reached the door, I heard a car approaching. The car stopped and a woman got out. Dark-featured and slim. I didn't recognise her, but smiled. She might be an old member, returning after a break, or she might be new, newer than me.

'Hi,' I said, as she approached.

'Hi. Are you Becky?'

'No, I'm Jess. Becky will be inside. I'll show you to her.'

'Thanks.'

The woman followed me in, and I wanted to say some reassuring words to her, something about the group being kind, a safe place, but I was still so new myself, I didn't feel I had the authority.

As I opened the door into the main room, the conversation stopped. Most of the group were there, Becky too, as well as three men. One was Tim, one was the man I saw on the morning of my first session, the third I didn't recognise. Even Geoff was in the room, although on the outside of the circle.

'Am I late?' I asked.

After a beat, Kelly spoke. 'Hey, Jess. Sorry, no, not at all, we were just catching up.'

'Oh good, I was worried. This is...' I turned to the woman. 'Sorry, I didn't catch your name?'

'Detective Sargent Salam.'

'Oh, a police officer. That's cool. Hi,' I said, smiling, but I was the only one. The room felt instantly tense, and Geoff closed his hands into fists. I noticed the police officer saw it too.

'Who is Becky, please?' the detective asked.

Becky stood up from the circle and approached. 'Hi, I'm Becky.'

'Hi, can I grab a few minutes of your time?'

'Ummm, sure,' she said.

As Becky and the police officer turned and left the room, the other women collectively sighed. They looked spooked, uncomfortable. Geoff too, who, as soon as the door was closed and Becky was gone, said he was going to make everyone a hot drink. He left quickly for the kitchen, and I sat beside the others. No one was speaking.

'What's going on?' I asked.

'Have you heard about that murder?' Kelly said, her voice barely a whisper.

I looked around the room, trying to understand what I was being told. The women all held my gaze, but the men – none of them could look at me. Then, as if they had outstayed their welcome, all three got up, made their excuses and left.

Chapter Twenty-Seven

THE CARETAKER

Even though The Caretaker had meticulously planned the events that would keep him busy watching, stalking, executing well into the spring, plans that were so well conceived he was sure no one would ever be able to prove it was him, he still wondered, *What if?* He knew that it wouldn't take long for the police to arrive and want to talk to one of the group, in fact he expected it, but even so, seeing that police officer had sent him into a spin, and as the day wore on, he waited, expecting a knock on his front door, or for it to be lifted off its hinges by a battering ram, as the police exploded into his house.

Yet they didn't come.

They had come close, they had come eye to eye, and they didn't have a clue. They were blind. His crime was too perfect.

The Caretaker had to put his crazies back in the box, though the lid could barely be closed, and practising his breathing techniques, he forced himself to be objective. Madison's ex-partner had been murdered, but they hadn't linked the crime to the beating of Hannah's ex. If they had, Hannah would have been spoken to, interviewed, arrested even, and she hadn't. She came home from her mother's and continued with life as normal, her version of it at least. Uninterrupted. Baheela's ex, blind and miserable, wouldn't even occur to the police, ever.

It would have taken the police all of five minutes to find out that Madison was out of the country, with her sister and son. They might have suspected her, but her alibi was such that it would have been impossible for her to kill and catch a tan at the same time. That was why The Caretaker acted. These women had been through enough; they needed closure and to be left alone. That was as much a part of his planning as the actual attacks.

He suspected the officer coming to the centre and speaking to Becky was just a formality, and he had no doubt Becky didn't say much to them, partly as she wouldn't know anything that could help, and partly because she was bound by confidentiality – but she would have said something. The Caretaker could almost hear the conversation play out. Madison was sweet, couldn't hurt a fly. No, she didn't seem different. Yes, she was excited to be going on holiday.

The policewoman no doubt thanked Becky for her time, apologising for taking her away from the session. She might have even commented on what Becky did being so needed. Then she would have left, knowing it was a waste of time, knowing she was no closer to working out what had happened to poor Jake Murray. He could hear this conversation so clearly in his mind, it was almost like the two women were in the room with him.

It settled his nerves and allowed him to close the lid on his box of crazies airtight.

What that officer wouldn't have known was that The Caretaker was already planning the next, preparing for another man to face justice. He knew that that police officer was unaware that one murder was about to become two. The world would soon know he was out there, and why he was doing what he was doing.

Chapter Twenty-Eight

JESS

18th January 2025

After the police had left, Becky returned, telling us it was just a lead that they were following, and that they wouldn't be back. She asked where the men had gone – Tim, Pete and Alfie – and we told her they'd left. I added that they looked spooked, but she didn't comment. We spoke about it briefly, the murder, the fact that two of the group's exes had been targeted, and the third attacked with acid before that, and after that we settled into the session. It was a shaky start, almost a write-off, but we spoke, and I shared about the vile woman who spat and assaulted me, and I noticed that not one woman in the circle was surprised when I mentioned I didn't call the police. I then told them about going to my mum's and saying my dirty little secret aloud.

After the session, as we were wrapping up, Kelly said a few of them were going for a drink.

'It's been a weird few weeks. We need to blow steam,' she said.

I almost said no – I'd not been out for drinks with anyone other than Lewis for over a year – but then, if I did say no, it would be him winning again. So I agreed. Kelly could sense my indecision, and offered to come to mine to get me.

'We can get ready together, share a cab.'

I nodded, feeling more excited than anxious about the idea of going out with some girls.

Kelly knocked on my door at 6pm. We'd exchanged numbers and she'd said what time she'd arrive, but still, when she knocked, my first thought was that it was Lewis, coming for 'that chat'.

Kelly greeted me with a hug, like an old friend, squeezing me tight, and I was a little shocked at how strong she was. I was also taken aback at the closeness I felt, but then, we women had been to hell and somehow found a way to leave for the return leg, and even though our journeys had been quite separate, the road was one we both knew very well, her footsteps upon it preceding mine. That bonded us in a way that we didn't need to talk about.

'I bought wine,' Kelly said as she entered my flat. 'Rosé OK?'

'Perfect.'

'Great, I'll pour us a glass.'

Without invitation, Kelly walked into my kitchen and placed the bottle on the counter. I grabbed two glasses and rinsed them – as I'd not had a glass of wine since before New Year – and Kelly poured two generous helpings. We clinked and drank. I only sipped, but Kelly drank over half of the glass in one go. As she did, I took in her outfit: a green, long-sleeved dress that came down to the floor, and on her feet a pair of Converse.

'Needed that,' she said.

'Tough day?'

'Tough week.'

'You look amazing,' I said, sensing she didn't want to talk about it.

'Thanks. Best thing about this dress – pockets.' She put down her glass and stuffed her hands into them. I laughed, and she did too.

'What are you gonna wear?' she asked.

'I was hoping you'd help?' I said. 'It's been a while since I could wear what I wanted.'

'Fucking say no more!' she countered and then, before I could reply, she grabbed both our glasses and walked out of the kitchen.

'Which one's your bedroom?'

'Second door on the left,' I said pointing, trying to catch up. Kelly opened my bedroom door and then putting down our glasses, opened my wardrobe.

'I've not dressed up in a while,' I said. 'I've got things here that haven't seen daylight in, what must be two years.'

'About time they did,' she replied, looking through some of my clothes in my wardrobe, understanding my reasons. I didn't need to say Lewis had an opinion on what I wore. If my outfit was too tight, I was cheap; if it was too revealing I was 'gagging for it'. He called me a tramp, a tart, someone wanting it too bad. Attention-seeking was one of his favourite phrases. So I put away my favourite clothes, the ones that made me feel good and confident, and sometimes, I dare say, sexy, and opted for what he liked me in.

'What about this?' she said, holding up a black dress that I once loved.

'Sure.'

Ducking behind a door, I slipped it on, and then showed her.

'You look amazing.'

'I met Lewis in this dress.'

'Fuck that then. Burn it,' she said. I laughed again.

'This?' she offered, this time holding up a blue top with a lace trim. 'Would look nice with some black jeans. Some heels. Got any?'

'Yeah,' I said, riffling along the rail to find my Levi's.

'OK, try it on.'

Kelly picked up her wine and began to drink, while I tucked myself behind the wardrobe door once more and started to change again. As I wrestled myself into my jeans, I could see her looking over my room. Her attention was caught by something, and she got up. With my jeans up, I threw on my top and stepped around from behind the door. Kelly was looking at a picture on my wall: me, a few friends and Lewis.

'It's from when I first got with my ex,' I said.

'Why is it still up?'

'I forgot it was there,' I lied. Kelly looked at me knowingly. 'It reminds me of a time when things made sense,' I whispered by way of explanation.

Kelly took the picture off the wall and, sitting on the edge of my bed once more, she looked at it. 'You look happy.'

'I was.'

Kelly nodded thoughtfully, then turned her attention to my outfit.

'This OK?' I said, feeling as if my jeans were too tight, my top showing too much cleavage.

'You look amazing.'

'Not too much?'

'No way! Do you feel good in it?'

'Yeah, I do.'

'Then it's settled,' she said, before turning her attention back to the picture. 'He ain't what I expected.'

'What did you expect?' I said, picking up my wine.

'I dunno, someone more handsome.'

I laughed for the third time. 'Not your vibe?'

'Nah. But what do I know? Duncan, my ex-husband, has a forehead you could land a jumbo on.'

'I must admit,' I said, 'he looks better in that picture, at the start of us, than he did by the end.'

I pulled out my phone and, scrolling back, I found a picture of me and him on Bonfire Night, and showed her.

'Sweet Jesus. He beefed up.'

'He did gain a few pounds,' I said, taking a sip of my wine.

'A few pounds? Looks like he ate the whole of NatWest bank.'

I spat my wine all over the floor.

'Oh shit, sorry,' she said, getting up.

'No, it's fine.'

As I went to get a towel, Kelly stood looking at the picture.

'You know you'll be this happy again, right?' she said as I began to wipe the carpet.

'I hope so.'

'You will. Perhaps not rehanging this might help.'

'You think?'

'Can't move forward if you're always looking back.'

I nodded.

'And trust me, he isn't going back to looking like this.'

'No?'

'No way. He'll always be a fat bastard now.'

'You know what?' I said, standing up. 'He is a fat bastard!'

'First time saying anything bad about him?'

'Yep.'

'Say it again.'

'He's a fat bastard.'

'Shout it.' Kelly said.

'Lewis, you are a fat bastard!' I shouted. 'You fat fucking bastard!'

'What else is he?' she asked. She sensed I had never spoken poorly of him.

'He's stupid, like completely fucking dense. And has the emotional intelligence of a dry roasted peanut. His teeth are awful. He thinks he's funny, but he's not at all.'

'Anything else?'

'He's a waste of oxygen. Like a tree has struggled for eighty years to grow and produce oxygen for him to steal it. A worm deserves it more.'

'One more?' Kelly said, laughing.

'Yeah, he was shit in bed. Like so shit! I had to fake faking it.'

Kelly put down her glass and clapped and cheered me. I was laughing. I'd not been able to be angry at him. In the weeks since New Year's I'd not raged against him. Kelly dragged it out in me within half an hour. And she was right: I was better than what he had to offer.

'Helps it sting a bit less, doesn't it?'

I nodded.

'How do you feel now?' she asked.

I didn't reply. Instead I picked up the photograph and dropped it in the bin.

'He should have loved you going out wearing things like this,' she said, pointing at my outfit. 'But then, everyone would have seen you were way out of his league.'

'Thank you,' I said, reaching for my glass, and she clinked hers against it. 'God, I've only just realised what a wanker he actually is.'

'An oxygen-thieving, fat wanker!'

'I'll drink to that,' I said, and we both drained our glasses.

'Right, shall we get an Uber?'

The cab journey took ten minutes, and when we arrived, we walked into The Lion pub and met up with some of the others from the support group. Madison wasn't there because she was still in Spain, but Hannah, Baheela and Rachel were. No Vija or Steph, they had other plans, and I got the feeling they weren't as close as these were to one another. I felt lucky to be included in what appeared to be a tight group of friends, survivors, warriors. At first, I was aware that Lewis might be there, or turn up, and Hannah saw me looking for him, and took my hand. Her grip made me feel secure.

'First time out since?'

'Yep.'

'Try not to worry, you're safe with us, we got you.'

I smiled, trusting her, and as the evening went on, I relaxed. I felt safe with these women. If he showed up, caused any problems, I suspected that at the very least Kelly would kick his ass. We drank, we laughed, we overshared, and as the evening wore on and the alcohol took its hold, we talked of our journeys, our healing. It was like a therapy session, but on the rocks.

Chapter Twenty-Nine

To get home, Baheela, Hannah and I shared a cab. Kelly went alone, but we made sure she was in the cab OK. She'd had a lot to drink, more than anyone else. We didn't ask why. We all could see her awful week had been really awful. Sometimes you just had to forget, and sensing that was the case with her, no one asked. She'd have one hell of a hangover. But sometimes a hangover was the best remedy.

I was the last to be dropped off, and because of the friendships I was forming, the wonderful evening I'd had and the alcohol that flooded my system, I felt fine being alone in the taxi for the five or so minutes between Hannah's place and mine. The driver, a kind older man, spoke mostly about his grandkids, and in my drunken state I eased into his stories and his gruff London accent. He doted on them, and hearing such love made me feel warm inside.

When we arrived outside my flat, I thanked him for the journey and climbed out. He pulled away as I took my keys out of my bag and, once he was gone, I turned to walk to my front door.

'Jess?' a voice called out, and the softness in the tone meant I didn't immediately place it. I turned and saw Lewis approaching.

'Lewis?'

'Sorry, I didn't mean to startle you.'

'Go away.'

'Wait.'

'I'll call the police,' I said, hurrying to my front door. I wanted to be in control but my hands started shaking and I struggled to get the key in the lock.

'Jess, please, that woman … I didn't tell her to come here.'

'Lewis, go away,' I said, managing to get the key in the door at last. It swung open and I stepped inside.

'Jess, just hear me out.'

I hesitated. I shouldn't have, but I did. And he sensed it.

'She and I, we are old friends, I told her we had separated and she… When she told me what she did, I was so angry.'

'Did you split her lip open as well?'

He paused. 'I deserve that.'

'She spat in my face.'

'I know.'

'Slapped me.'

'I know, I'm sorry. I didn't expect her to do that.'

'She said that I was telling lies, Lewis.'

'I swear I didn't say that to her. Jess, please, hear me out.'

I turned to him but kept my feet behind the threshold of my flat, holding the door so I could close it if I needed to. 'Lewis, what do you want?'

'Nothing, I just want to say I'm sorry. You were right to talk to the police; you were right to leave, to change the locks.'

'You came into my flat without my permission.'

'I know, I know, I wasn't thinking, I was so ashamed, so angry at myself.'

'You came to my flat in the middle of the night, drew on my window.'

'I'm so sorry, Jess, I am. I didn't just let you down; I let me down too. I hate the man I have become. I do.'

'I can't help you deal with your feelings, Lewis.'

'And I'm not asking you to.'

I hated that a tear fell onto my cheek. I hated that even though I was in my flat and could easily close the door, I didn't.

'Lewis. You shouldn't be here.'

'I know. I do,' he said, his voice, body language, tone, so different from New Year's. So much more like the man I fell in love with. 'I just, I needed to tell you that since New Year's, all I've done is thought about what we once were. Do you remember how good it was?'

I hated that I nodded.

'I know I fucked up. I know. I've been in a dark place. But I'm getting help now, I'm getting better. I'm seeing someone, a doctor. You know about how I grew up, how my mum's boyfriend was… I vowed to not be like that, but it's all I know. I don't want that. I'm learning to be better. I am.'

'I'm happy for you,' I said quietly, my voice losing its power to push him away.

'I don't expect you to forgive me; I don't even forgive me. I can't forgive me. I did the worst thing imaginable to you. Things that the younger version of me would beat the shit out of me for.'

Lewis started to cry. I'd never seen him cry before. 'I'm so sorry. I really am. I love you, Jess.'

I nodded. No words came.

'Can I come in?'

'I... No, Lewis, I can't let you in.'

It was his turn to nod.

'I'm going to close the door now. Are you going to be all right?'

'Please, let me in. I miss your place. I miss you.'

'No, Lewis,' I said, but my assertiveness wavered, and he sensed it and came closer.

'Just for a cuppa? I want to see how you are.'

'Lewis, I'm glad you are getting help. But I will not let you into my flat.'

He took another step closer, and panicking, I stepped back and began to close the door.

'No, please don't. I just want to talk,' he said, the tears still falling.

'Goodnight, Lewis.'

'Don't you care? Look at the state I'm in.'

'I do care, Lewis, that was never the issue.'

'I've changed, Jess, can't you see?'

I went to close the door fully, but before I could, he sprang forward and pushed it open. If it wasn't for my foot behind it, he would have burst into my flat.

'Let me in,' he said, his tears now stopped.

'Lewis, back off.'

'Just let me in, Jess. I used to be here all the time.'

'Lewis. Stop!'

'Is there someone else? Is that it?'

'What? No, but it's none of your business. Back off.'

'Fucking open the door,' he shouted. 'Let me in. What are you hiding?'

Lewis had been talking loudly and from the flat above a man shouted down.

'Hey. Some of us are trying to sleep!'

Lewis was spooked. 'Fucking bitch,' he whispered.

The pressure on the door slackened, and it slammed shut. I quickly bolted it and then ran to the front room window and looked outside to see him walking away, head down. The man I remembered from the beginning of the year was back.

Sinking on to the sofa, I forced myself not to cry. I was so angry that I had almost believed what he was saying. I had almost allowed myself to be swept up in his 'I'm a changed man' routine. For all of my life, I wanted to see the best in people. Especially him.

But no more. No fucking more.

I vowed I wouldn't be that woman ever again.

I pulled out my phone. I knew I should have called the police, but I didn't. Instead, I looked into my security camera and saved the footage of our exchange, just in case, and then I messaged Kelly.

> Hey, Kel. He was just at my front door.

She messaged back straight away.

KELLY

> Fuck, are you OK?

> I'm fine. He just scared me.

> Want me to come over?

> No, it's OK. Kel, don't judge me, but is it wrong that right now, I kinda wish what happened to Hannah's ex happened to him?

> No, not at all. Secretly, this thing that's happening with Baheela's ex, and Hannah's, and even Mads' – I kinda hope it happens for me too… Jess, you sure you don't want me to come over?

> No, no, I'm OK.

> OK, call the police now. You need to have a record of it. xx

Chapter Thirty

SOPHIE SALAM

20th January 2025

Sophie stepped into the mortuary, weary from a challenging couple of days, both at work and at home. Her mum had come down with Covid, and although she was going to be fine, she was wiped out, and not wanting Lottie to get sick, even though it probably came from Lottie in the first place, she was at home, recovering. Sophie did wonder, was she really sick, or just sick of how hard things were? With her mum out of action, it meant Sophie had spent the weekend when she was on shift working from home, caring for Lottie as well as trying to solve a murder inquiry. When Lottie was awake, she was a mother; when she slept, a detective. But for almost two days she had only slept a handful of hours herself and was doing neither job as well as she should have been. She was so tired that as she slapped on a mask, then some gloves, she barely acknowledged Clarke had spoken.

'Sorry?' she said, once she realised he was looking at her over the corpse of Jake Murray.

'I said you look like shit. You OK?'

'Charming. Yeah, fine, just tired. Tough weekend with Lottie.'

'You know what you need…'

'I swear to God, if you're about to say I need a man in my life, you're gonna end up on a slab.'

He laughed. 'Need to talk about it?'

'No, thanks though. So, what have we got?' she said, yawning out her question. He caught it, yawned himself, then smiled.

'At least I'm not a psychopath,' he said.

'You work with dead people all day, Clarke; I wouldn't be so sure,' Sophie said, making him laugh again.

'So, our boy here did die from a potassium chloride overdose, as we suspected.'

'OK?'

'He also took a blow to his nose before he was killed.'

'That explains all the blood.'

'Yep. Busted. One hell of a kick. We managed to get a shoe imprint from his face.'

'And?'

'Size ten, the tread is a generic welly. Would be impossible to trace back.'

'OK.'

'Besides that, and the bruising from the cable ties, there was no other suggestion of physical torture.'

'He willingly let himself be bound?' Sophie asked.

'Nope. This is where it gets more interesting.'

'Don't tease me, Clarke.'

'I also found ketamine in his system.'

'Ketamine. He didn't strike me as someone who was on ket.'

'Nope, nor me,' Clarke said. 'It does explain though how our killer managed to tie our lad here without there being too much of a ruckus.'

'A ruckus, really?'

'What? I like the word.'

'You think our killer drugged him?'

'That's my guess. Just enough to knock him out, but not kill. We tested his meal, the food that was at the scene half-eaten. Ketamine was found in it.'

'So, our killer drugged our victim. So not to cause a ruckus?' Sophie said, smiling playfully.

'Piss off.'

'Then ties him up, and then what?'

'Waits for him to wake.'

'So he could torture him with potassium?'

'Yep. that's about it,' Clarke said, sighing. 'World's gone to shit, kid.'

Sophie ignored his comment. 'This tells us our killer planned meticulously.'

'Yeah, it also tells me they are clever, Sophie, really bloody clever.'

'Great,' Sophie said. 'Did they find any DNA at the scene?'

'What do you think?'

'Well, this is worrying, isn't it?'

'Yep. Sorry to say this, Sophie, but it gets worse.'

'How?'

'Come look at this.'

Clarke approached the victim lying on the table, and Sophie joined him.

'What are we looking at, Clarke?'

'At first, I almost missed it.'

'What?'

'That,' Clarke said, pointing to a small mark on the victim's chest. A little cross over his heart.

'What am I looking at?' Sophie asked.

'It was cut into him post death. The blade is so fine it's almost invisible.'

'Our killer cut this into his chest after he killed him?'

'Yep.'

'Oh, shit,' Sophie said, knowing exactly what she was looking at. She thought back to her niggle, the revenge thing that played on her mind, and knew, because of this little cut, she was right about it being the same person. What she was staring at was a calling card, a mark left by a killer who intended to kill again.

'Sophie Salam,' Clarke said without a hint of mirth, 'it looks like you might have the makings of a serial killer on your hands.'

Chapter Thirty-One

THE CARETAKER

21st January 2025

They say no news is good news, but for The Caretaker that wasn't entirely true. It had been a week since the life of Jake Murray ended. Seven whole days of the world being a fraction better than before. One hundred and sixty-eight hours since The Caretaker had found out what he was capable of. The world was different, but somehow, aside from a large picture of Jake on the front page of the online edition of the local paper, a picture of him smiling, looking handsome, looking kind, with no more than a hundred words underneath about his 'remarkable and short life', nothing had been said. There was no mention of his heavy hands. His abusive ways. There was no reference to his refusal to pay support to his own child. One he didn't see and didn't love. Nothing about showing Madison in a compromising position.

Soon, that would change. Soon they would know the man he really was.

Soon they would all know about what The Caretaker was doing.

And they would know, because of a man named Duncan.

Duncan Miller, forty-three. Soon to be divorced from his wife. Corporate attorney, working for a top London-based law firm that specialised in businesses mostly in India. The large firms that power that massive third-world nation, building all of its highways and city buildings.

Everything about Duncan was in the little blue book. Comfortable mid-six-figure salary, enjoyed running, prostitutes and demeaning his ex because she's grown sick of his wandering ways. A smoker, a heavy drinker, with heavy hands once he had had a few. Whisky was his poison, whisky made him rage.

He preferred red wine to white, savoury to sweet, was an olive eater, allergic to bee stings. Financial abuser, gaslighter and, from what The Caretaker had researched, seen and heard, soon to be engaged to a woman almost twenty years younger. A woman called Clara, who had no idea of the dog this man was. The Caretaker knew, because The Caretaker understood these men. He was going to ruin her life too, and The Caretaker wouldn't let that happen.

Duncan worked from home three days a week and in the office for the other two, and accessing his diary wasn't difficult. The Caretaker had spoken several times with his receptionist, a lovely woman by the name of Maggie. The Caretaker had built up a rapport with her, and through her he'd come to know Duncan's comings and goings. The Caretaker posed as a potential investor in the firm who wanted to set up a meeting with Duncan, and understood that next week, the week The Caretaker wanted to know as much as possible about, was busy for Duncan. The two days he was in the office, Monday and Tuesday, he had back-to-back meetings. On Tuesday he had a client dinner at seven, and then a Zoom to colleagues in the US at nine-thirty. He would conduct his meeting from his office; it was pencilled to be two hours long and he would be entirely alone. Meanwhile, Kelly, his soon to be ex-wife, the woman who had, from what The Caretaker had heard, taken his abuse for fifteen years, would be in Edinburgh, at a work conference. The Caretaker's notes said she would leave Sunday night, returning the following Thursday.

It was perfect.

She would be left alone in the wake of what he planned to do.

All of the details of Duncan's week were in the blue book, and as The Caretaker sat enjoying a spot of lunch, a panini with salad, he read all the notes he'd taken, making sure he was ready. To anyone in the café who happened to glance his way, he looked just like one of the many remote workers, sipping his latte, keeping the coffee trade thriving. No one knew his book was full of plans for murder. No one knew that soon, because of this book, everyone would be talking. Taking a bite of his panini, he looked up from his book and saw Duncan leaving his office. He looked around, beamed a crocodile smile at the young woman approaching, kissed her, and then they walked away. It wasn't his soon-to-be bride, but another young and pretty woman.

The Caretaker made a note of it – the time, the date – then, closing the book, sat back and enjoyed his meal, his mind fully set on the task at hand.

Next Tuesday Duncan had a late-night Zoom in his office.

Next Tuesday he would die where he worked.

And then, the morning after, everyone would know why.

Chapter Thirty-Two

JESS

24th January 2025

Lewis being outside my flat again had shaken me to my core. I blamed myself for letting my guard down, for being a little drunk, and when I called the police, as Kelly said I should, the same officer, Jones, arrived at my house. His first question was about how much I had drunk. Like it was my fault I came home from a night out and he was there. I told him I was tipsy but in control and even though Jones wrote down what had happened, I could tell he wasn't going to do anything about it. He looked at me like it was my fault for not being sober, like Lewis's actions were a result of my intoxication.

Lewis hadn't hurt me and he hadn't got into my flat. He'd left without causing any criminal damage. In Jones's mind, I could tell, it was one of those 'it is what it is' things, a waste of his time. Especially when there was a murderer out there.

I barely slept, and, because of my exhaustion, I called in sick at work.

As I did the next day.

And the next.

Then, calling the doctor, I self-certified for the rest of the week.

Jenny was understanding, and when I said I was simply unwell, flu probably, she bought it. I felt guilty, but really, I knew I couldn't work. Will and Eva, they were intuitive, they would see straight through my fake smiles. And until I knew otherwise, I had to be concerned for them. Lewis was out there – the police weren't acting – and I didn't want him to follow me again, like he had before, and cause a scene. I'd never forgive myself if he scared those children like he'd scared me.

I needed to feel safe first, and having no help from the police, I found myself online, Googling where I could buy pepper spray, or a taser. Something I could carry and use, if I had to.

The week felt long, the longest of my life, and I was counting each day down to Friday, when I would see Madison and Hannah and the others. Being with them I felt safe. Kelly had offered to come over several times since I messaged her in a state of panic, but I said I was fine. I didn't want to be a burden. I couldn't be that friend who always had baggage that they were desperate for others to hold. I'd not let myself.

So I hid in my flat, waited, lied to my boss about my health, until Friday arrived. I was so anxious and excited to feel safe, I was awake and drinking my morning coffee at just after 5am.

After the group, I was due back at work, and knowing I wouldn't be able to, I waited until seven, when I knew she would be awake, and rang Jenny. She picked up on the third ring.

'Hey, Jenny.'

'Hi, I'm guessing you're still not OK to come to work?'

'I'm so sorry,' I said.

'It's OK.' In the background I could hear Eva laughing. It broke my heart.

'How are they?'

'They are good, missing you.'

'I miss them too.'

'Jess, can I be frank?'

I swallowed, thinking I was about to be sacked. 'Ummm, sure?'

'That cut you had on your face. I don't think you fell.'

I didn't reply.

'Listen, Jess, if something is happening, we can help, Samuel and I.'

'I'm OK,' I said, but my voice betrayed me, and the way it came out sounded anything but OK.

'Jess. I'm gonna guess something? If I'm wrong, stop me?'

I didn't reply.

'Lewis hurt you?'

Still I didn't reply.

'OK, I hear you. Jess. Is he with you now?'

'No,' I said, my voice barely a whisper. 'The police are involved.'

'OK, good. Jess, has he hurt you again?'

'No, but I'm afraid he will,' I said, and knowing she knew, the door opened and my fear flooded out. 'He followed us to the seaside that day. I don't want to get Will and Eva mixed up.'

'We understand. Jess, Samuel is good at what he does. One of the best solicitors in the region. The police will take care of this, I'm sure, but if you need help, he wants to.'

I almost asked if he knew Kelly, because if he did, he would know she was a strong woman, and still, she had lived like I was now. But I didn't.

'I'm sorry I can't face work at the moment.'

'As always, you are thinking of my children. Jess, you take whatever time you need, and don't worry about signing on. You've done so much for us; it won't affect your pay.'

'No, Jenny I can't—'

'It's done. I won't take no for an answer on this. I can't imagine what you're going through, and I want to help. This is the only way I know how.'

'Thank you,' I said, choking up.

'You ring me if you need anything, OK?' Jenny said, and I agreed I would, even though I knew I probably wouldn't. I didn't want to bring my work into this, the shame was almost unbearable.

I thanked Jenny once more, and then, having hung up, I forced myself to get ready for my day. I still had two hours before I needed to leave. In that time, my imagination began to run wild, and I had visions of Lewis standing outside my flat, waiting for me when the door opened. To be safe, instead of catching the bus, I'd get an Uber, but still, I needed something more. Again, it was going to cost me money trying to be safe from him, but I had to.

Going online on my phone, I looked at my bookmarks and clicked through to a page which I found where I could buy pepper spray. I'd be breaking the law by buying it and carrying it. But then, if Lewis could get away with so much, couldn't I?

Clicking through to the payment page, I hesitated, then, knowing it would give me a little power back, I hit buy. I waited for it to confirm payment, but it didn't. Instead, it stated there was something wrong with my accounts.

Opening my banking app, I logged in and looked at my balance. My account was hundreds of pounds overdrawn and I didn't know why. I looked at my transactions list and saw that an automatic payment had gone from my bank account to my credit card. I had a direct debit to pay the balance every month, as I only used my credit card for a few subscriptions, to keep it ticking over, and for emergencies if they arose. Several hundred pounds were missing.

Leaving my banking app, I logged onto the one for my Virgin credit card and saw several contactless transactions for things for which I hadn't paid. A meal at Nando's, something from John Lewis. Petrol from Tesco. All of them on the same day, the day after Lewis was at my door.

And when I realised what had happened, my stomach dropped.

I ran to my bedroom, and looked in the top drawer of my bedside table, where I kept my credit card, already knowing I wouldn't find it.

Lewis had it. Lewis had taken it, probably on the day when he'd entered my flat to leave me his note.

For the fourth time in just a few weeks, I rang the police, and for the fourth time, I knew they'd likely do nothing.

Chapter Thirty-Three

My call was short, my crime number generated, and then I spoke to Virgin, who were actually really good; my account was frozen and they said they would no doubt be able to help with what had happened. The fraud team would be in touch and would advise me about my options. I felt optimistic I would get my money back, but because I didn't have any right now, I couldn't get the Uber I wanted, or the pepper spray I had hoped to buy. I didn't feel safe taking a bus, but I didn't want to miss my session; it was the only thing that was getting me from week to week. The journey was tough, the constant looking over my shoulder, both for him but also for strangers, as I knew he wasn't above getting someone to do his dirty work in his absence. Everyone who looked at me was a potential attacker; everyone who stood close was someone who could hurt me. The bus was crowded, dozens of threats, dozens of sets of eyes. I kept my keys in my hand the whole journey, my front-door key protruding through a gap in my closed fist. By the time I got off and walked to the centre, I felt frazzled. I needed the women of the support group to make me feel safe once more.

As I entered the building, I could hear the group chatting. I joined them, doing my best to smile naturally, hugged my friends and offered to make hot drinks.

'Morning, Jess,' Geoff said when I stepped into the kitchen. He was standing over a row of cups. 'Coffee, white, no sugar?'

'I should have known you'd beat me to it,' I said. 'Yeah, thanks, Geoff.'

'Pleasure. I see Madison is back,' he said.

'Yeah, but no Kelly?'

'She said something about a work thing?'

I nodded. She did mention it on our night out, but a lot has happened since. 'I've not had a chance to ask if Mads is OK, have you?'

'No, no, I try not to ask those type of questions. Not my place.'

'I think it is. You know these women better than I do.'

He nodded thoughtfully. 'Maybe by name, or conversation, or by how they like their tea. But no, I don't understand these women. How could I?'

I smiled, then turned to look through the door at the group. Madison was sat being supported by Hannah.

'I suspect once the shock has passed, Madison will be all right,' Geoff said, looking over to her.

'I hope so,' I said, but I had to agree. If it was me, I know I would be all right.

Helping Geoff with the teas and coffees, I rejoined the group, and after Geoff left, his foot still causing him a little discomfort, our session began. As expected, everything was focused on Madison, rightly so, as she had had the most stressful time of it. A winter break with her family and a murder, all within the same week, meant that when she started to open up, she didn't stop talking.

'I feel terrible he's gone. I do, but…'

She trailed off, and Hannah took her by the hand. 'It's OK, we understand.'

'I can't stay long. His mum has asked to meet to discuss funeral plans. I know it will be weeks yet, maybe even a month, because of the way he died, but…'

She trailed off again. Vija asked if anyone, his mum, her mum, knew what had happened between her and Jake.

'No, we said that we just unravelled, drifted. No one knows.'

We all nodded. Our stories were mostly the same. I wanted to tell her that speaking to her mum, telling her the truth, would lift a weight, but I didn't. It wouldn't help now.

'Guys, am I the only one who has questions about what's happening to us?' Madison continued. 'Baheela, Hannah and now me? What are the odds?'

'Almost impossible,' Steph said.

From behind me, movement caught my eye, and turning, I saw Geoff walking away down the corridor. I wasn't sure if he was simply doing one of his jobs or listening.

'The police came last week too,' Vija said.

'What?'

'It's OK,' Becky said. 'They just wanted to ask me a few questions, about the group.'

'Why?' Madison asked.

'I guess to tick it off their no doubt horrendously long list,' Becky said, smiling. 'Have they been to you yet?'

'They came when we got home, on Tuesday. A woman, I forget her name.'

'DS Salam?' Becky offered.

'Yeah, that's it. She had a tea, didn't stay long. She obviously knows he was bad to me. But she didn't say much.'

The Serial Killer Support Group

'Did she ask anything?' Hannah asked.

'No, not really, just when I last saw him, did I know anyone that would want to do this. I didn't know how to answer. I've never had the police in my house before.'

'Just ticking boxes,' Becky said. 'Try not to overthink. It's been a traumatic, shocking time. The priority is to try and make sense of it somehow, and make sure your little boy is OK.'

Madison nodded and wiped her eyes, and then Becky moved us on, sensing that was what Madison needed. She went around, asked us all how we were feeling in light of the recent events. Angry, afraid, confused, relieved. It was a full mixed bag.

Halfway through the session, on our break to grab a drink, have a wee or a smoke (for those that did), Madison's taxi arrived and she said her goodbyes. I couldn't imagine what she was feeling. Her ex, whom she still, in some way, loved, had been murdered. He was a bad man – we were all there because of bad men – but still the father to her boy. Would she see her ex in her boy? What would that do to her moving forward? Would she ever be rid of the feelings associated with him? It was almost too much to bear.

After Madison left, I could feel a collective relief wash over us all. There was no right or wrong thing to say, and she was dignified in expressing herself, but still, the tension was palpable, and as Becky picked up the session, we all had time to talk of our weeks. Vija had cried more than usual. Hannah had spoken with her ex, who was at home resting from the assault. And he hadn't changed a bit. Steph had met someone new and was cautiously optimistic. Then, Becky asked how I was.

I told them that he had been in my flat. All were outraged, supportive, but none were shocked. I told them of the missing money, then I told them I found out it was missing because I wanted to buy pepper spray.

'Jess, lovely, I know it might not seem that way right now, but no good can come from that,' she said.

'I don't ever want to use it. I just… I don't know… Having it will make me feel safer.'

'We understand that,' Hannah said. 'I've been there too, wanting something to protect me. But it's not worth it.'

'So what do I do?' I said, my voice rising slightly with the frustration, the exhaustion of it all. 'Do I just wait for him to go away? Wait for the police to act? What if he doesn't leave me alone? What if the police don't stop him? What then?'

Becky took my hand and spoke calmly. 'Jess, it will get easier.'

'What if it doesn't?' I asked, aware that everyone was looking at me. 'What if I become yet another woman who is hurt, or worse, at the hands of her ex. You know, I've done some reading. One woman every eight or nine days dies at the hand of their partner or ex. I don't feel safe anymore, and I need someone to do something about it.'

'Jess…' Hannah started.

'I need my power back,' I said.

Becky started talking about how I will get my power back, that knowing it was missing was the first step, and that the group will help me, but I was struggling to hear her. I didn't like being afraid, but that was exactly what I was. I nodded as Becky spoke, and watched as, outside the centre, Geoff got into his car. He caught my eye through the window and I wondered, had he just heard my plea?

Chapter Thirty-Four

THE CARETAKER

28th January 2025

From across the street, sat in the same chair that he had occupied exactly a week before, The Caretaker looked up at the office of Duncan Miller, watching him smooth his greying hair as he spoke animatedly to his partners in the States. His profile was captured by the light from the screen and a single lamp just to his left. The man oozed charisma, even from afar, and through two glass windows The Caretaker could tell, whatever he was talking about, whoever he was talking to, he had them in the palm of his hand. Duncan liked those around him to be putty; it was easier to mould them as he saw fit.

The Caretaker checked his watch: 9:45 pm, time to move. Finishing his drink, he stood and stepped out into the night. Rain hung in the air, tiny particles that silently soaked the world, making it glisten, making it otherworldly. When it passed through the channels of unnatural orange glow cast by the streetlights, it seemed almost as if it were travelling backwards, as if time was moving differently somehow.

The Caretaker pulled up his coat collar, and then, crossing the road, he stepped into an alley beside the building where his target sat alone. Hidden away in the shadows of London's ancient buildings, he prepared. Gloves, wellies, overalls, tape, balaclava, then finally the face mask and eyeglasses. All traces of him were tucked away, unable to contaminate, as far as possible.

From the notes in his little blue book, the fire door was located at the end of the alley, and although it was closed, it wasn't alarmed, and with a little force, a little effort, The Caretaker could get inside, and no one would know. The building was like many in this part of the city, looking glamorous, sophisticated and expensive from the front, but the backs were rat-infested and decaying. London, in parts, was like a crackhead that had been given a Hollywood smile. For The Caretaker, it said so much about the world and the state of it. But it presented the opportunity The Caretaker so desperately needed. The world liked shiny things, so much so that it didn't look anywhere else. There was one lonely CCTV camera, pointing down from the upper right corner of the building, but it didn't cover the door, so as long as The Caretaker stayed close to the wall, all anyone would see would be the door swinging open – but not who had opened it. Duncan was at the front of the building, and behind was another office set-up – an office hub where freelancers could rent a pod. On his scouting missions, The Caretaker had never seen anyone inside after seven in the evening.

Kelly was out of the country, Duncan on a call alone, and there would be no one who would see him.

It was planned.

Perfected.

And now it was time to perform.

Removing his rucksack, the same rucksack he'd used for Jake, The Caretaker pulled out a crowbar, and forcing the straight edge into the door frame, leant against it. The door creaked, groaned, but didn't give.

'Shit,' he said quietly under his breath, pausing to stretch before trying again. The door cried angrily, and The Caretaker's hands began to hurt. He paused once more.

'Fuck, come on.'

One final, all-or-nothing tug, and the door snapped open. The Caretaker had been pulling with such force, that when it did give in, he fell to the floor, landing heavily on his side. The wind was knocked out of him and, scrambling to his feet, he looked at where he had landed, making sure he hadn't fallen into the view of the camera. If he had, he would leave, and they would just assume it was a botched break-in. But, thankfully, he hadn't. He was still on.

Struggling to suck air in, The Caretaker listened to the night, which was playing as a night should. Distant thrum of cars. The sound of faraway sirens. Static in the air from a thousand wires and screens.

There were no voices speaking, no questions. No people. The sound of the door snapping open had been fully absorbed into the orchestra of night.

Composing himself, he put his crowbar back in the rucksack and stepped inside, gently closing the door behind him.

The building was cooler than the wet winter air outside, and so silent that The Caretaker felt intrusive by just breathing. It almost stopped him. But then, he had to finish what he'd started. Jake had paid. Duncan had to as well.

The Caretaker began to move, slowly placing one foot in front of the other like he was a tightrope-walker. He travelled down the long corridor, past the kitchen and toilets, until he reached reception, where the streetlights illuminated everything in a sepia glow. Beside him were the stairs, and at the top, the muffled voice of Duncan. Slipping the bag off once more, The Caretaker pulled out what he would need first and stood looking at it, fascinated that something so small could do so much harm. He began to quietly ascend, the voice of his target, his prey, becoming louder with each step.

Closer.

Step.

Closer.

Step.

Closer.

Chapter Thirty-Five

At the top of the stairs, The Caretaker pressed himself against the wall and began walking towards the light. Duncan was laughing at something one of his attendees had said, their voice mechanical through the small speaker on his laptop. The Caretaker wondered what was funny. What was it that made Duncan laugh so heartily? Was it worthy of the moment? It was likely to be the last hearty, head-thrown-back-without-a-care-in-the-world laugh he would have in his life. Was it real? Or was it like him, all for show, all what he wanted people to see, all fake, like his smiles and his promises and his actions?

The Caretaker stood by the wall, patiently waiting for another thirty minutes, practising the breathing exercises, calming his inner thoughts, making himself feel present, and then, as if jolted from his meditative state, he heard Duncan begin to wrap up the meeting. He thanked everyone for their time and said he would see them all in four weeks.

'No, you won't,' The Caretaker mouthed, tightening his grip

on the item in his left hand as he peered around into the office. Duncan was sat rubbing his eyes, then he reached into a drawer and pulled out a bottle of whisky, followed by a glass.

The Caretaker knew he would pour a big drink and throw his head back as he swallowed it greedily. He knew because The Caretaker had watched him do it before. It would expose his neck, and The Caretaker needed that to happen.

As The Caretaker quietly approached in the shadows, enjoying Duncan's unawareness that his fate was about to be sealed, the man opened the bottle and poured himself a glass. He put the bottle down, and as he began to swig, The Caretaker shook the item in his hand, a small clear vial, and the bee inside became angry. He dashed to his target, pulled off the lid and pushed the vial into his neck.

The bee, in a buzzing rage at being violently shaken, tried to escape the tube, and with Duncan's flesh in its way, it thrust its sting like a hypodermic needle into his neck, just beside his Adam's apple.

'What the fuck?' Duncan said, leaping out of his chair. The bee was still stuck, and as he grabbed it to pull it from his body, his shock turned to realisation.

Most people with severe allergic reactions, those who needed an EpiPen, usually had around five minutes to get the lifesaving drug into them, but a small minority would only get seconds, and Duncan was one of those few. So, instead of dealing with his attacker, Duncan staggered backwards and, falling onto his desk, struggled to get his top drawer open, where the Epinephrine was. As he flapped, The Caretaker walked behind him and closed the blinds. Just in case anyone was interested in the commotion. Turning to his victim, The Caretaker found it remarkable how quickly his face began to swell, how quickly his body began to shut down. He knew, from research, that Duncan's immune response, the thing that was designed to keep him alive, would be flooding his body with chemicals, which would send him into a state of shock, closing his airways, covering his skin with hives – but he didn't expect it to be so visceral, so immediate. The handsome man had morphed into something that was almost non-human right before his eyes.

Duncan managed to find his pen, and with shaking hands he fought to pull off the cap. The Caretaker stepped down to help. He took the pen, and then removed the cap.

'Please,' Duncan said in a strangled voice.

The Caretaker looked like he was going to administer the drug but stopped and just held it close to Duncan's contorted face.

'P-please... help me,' Duncan managed to rasp out.

The Caretaker threw the pen away.

'You have stung someone badly with your ways, Duncan Miller. It was time you understood, actions have consequences. Right now, this is ... I can only think of one word for it, serendipitous.'

Duncan, confused and fighting for his life, tried to get up and retrieve the pen from across the office, but it was no use; he fought to move, but The Caretaker pushed him back. His tongue was so swollen, it forced his mouth open.

'Shhhh, Duncan, stop fighting, this is it. This is how you go,' The Caretaker said. It was the last thing Duncan Miller ever heard.

Once he was sure he was gone, The Caretaker opened Duncan's shirt and, using the same scalpel as before, carved a small cross on his blotchy chest. Then, instead of leaving, The Caretaker sat in Duncan's chair, opened his rucksack, set up what he needed to set up and prepared himself for the next step in his plan. Before he began, he looked down at Duncan Miller, whose face was unrecognisable, and stared into the one eye that hadn't quite swollen closed.

'They won't mourn you like the last. They'll know exactly who you are,' he said.

Chapter Thirty-Six

SOPHIE SALAM

With Lottie lying prone across her torso, Sophie tried as best as she could to work. But she struggled to focus on her computer screen. Her attention kept coming back to the pale yellow bruise across her daughter's forehead that didn't want to go away, from her panic attack almost two weeks before. Parenting was hard, parenting a little one with severe autism harder, and doing it alone was almost impossible. But she knew things could be worse. Things could always be worse. And her being alone with her baby was better than the alternative, better than the life she almost had. Sometimes she tried to imagine what life could have been like with Lottie's father on the scene. It was unbearable. She and Lottie would be in some hell-hole, probably alone anyway. So she ploughed on, knowing she would make it work, because she had to. The life she had was the life she had. She had made her choices, right or wrong, and she had to live with them.

Rubbing her eyes till they focused again, she continued. On her screen were the details of the Murray investigation, and also the Goodfellow one. If her instincts were right, which she had to believe they were, because Clarke also believed it, the killing of Jake Murray was the start of something. Somehow it was linked to Martin Goodfellow, and as Lottie gently snored, she wondered, was Martin a test? A trial of some kind? People killed all the time. Many of those who kill did so in the moment; some had never committed a crime before – it just happened, passion, rage, lust. But Jake Murray's case wasn't like that. His death had been planned, meticulously planned, and the killer was smart too; he knew how to sedate and torture. As for the small cross carved into his chest, nothing about it said crime of passion or rage. Those types of killers, serial killers, they didn't leap into a kill. They planned, tried things. Worked their way to the ultimate prize. She wondered, was there anyone before Martin Goodfellow, people who had been hurt, that she didn't know about? She made a note to see if there were any other assaults or attacks that might link with this. But if she searched through the database for assaults on males, there would be hundreds, thousands probably.

She wouldn't find the answers, not from home, so Sophie closed her laptop and turned her attention to her girl. Her deep breaths were calm and relaxed, and Sophie did all she could to mimic them until her own rhythm settled. Stroking Lottie's hair, Sophie started to hum 'Everything's All Right' from the musical Jesus Christ Superstar, like she did when Lottie was tiny, before she knew of her autism. She hummed the same song during nappy changes, during tired or hungry tears. When Lottie was younger, the song comforted her, and now Sophie was humming it in the hope that it would have the same effect on herself. As she hummed, and stroked her daughter's small, precious head, she felt her body begin to sink further into the mattress, and smiling, she carefully rearranged her pillows so that when she began to fall asleep, Lottie wouldn't be disturbed.

Wrapped in a makeshift cocoon of daughter, pillows and duvet, Sophie closed her eyes and continued to hum, and the world didn't seem so bad after all.

Then, her phone pinged and in her sleepy, warm state, she chose to ignore it. It pinged again, and again, and knowing it must be important, she carefully reached over for it, Lottie stirring momentarily in her lap as she did so.

'Shhh, it's OK,' she whispered, and sensing her mummy was close, Lottie drifted into her deep sleep once more.

As her eyes focused on the bright screen on her mobile, she was expecting to see it was Ma, but the messages weren't from her, and her stomach dropped. Clarke had messaged.

Something was going on.

Opening the messages, Sophie prepared herself, and then read.

> **CLARKE**
>
> Sophie, sorry to message, I know you're at home.
>
> Just had one come in, a man, mid 40s.
>
> Call if you can?

She didn't know what to do. If she called, she knew it would send her into a spiral, but if she didn't, she wouldn't sleep anyway. She looked at Lottie; she might stir, but if she was quiet, she wouldn't wake. Sophie had a choice, call or not call, but really, as she knew and Clarke knew, you seldom had a choice in their job.

'Hi, Clarke,' she began, her voice barely a whisper. 'Lottie is asleep on me, so I gotta be quiet. Can you hear me OK?'

'Yes. Sophie, I'm sorry to message you. But I knew you'd want to know.'

'What's going on? You said there was another murder?'

'Well, at first, we didn't think it was one.'

Lottie stirred, and Sophie stroked her hair again. 'What do you mean?'

'I've been working in this job for thirty years now; this one might be their weirdest.'

'Clarke, stop teasing me.'

'Our man died from a bee sting.'

'A bee sting. In January?'

'Yep, stung on the side of his neck. Turns out some bees hibernate alone; it could have been in his office; our man disturbed it, paid the price. But I don't think it went down that way.'

'No? Why?'

'Looks like the poor sod tried to get to his EpiPen, but instead of administering it, and likely saving himself, it ended up on the other side of the room.'

'He could have panicked, dropped it maybe?'

'Maybe, but it doesn't explain what else I found,' Clarke said, and Sophie could hear something in his voice. It wasn't fear, but it was close.

'Clarke, I'm too tired for games.'

'Our man has a small cross carved into his chest.'

'Oh, shit,' Sophie said, loud enough that Lottie jiggled, before resettling.

'Yeah, shit.'

'Clarke, can you send over what you know? I need to find what links these three men.'

'Three?'

'The belt beating, it's linked, I can feel it. Send what you can. My laptop is beside me. What's his name? I'll start digging.'

'Duncan Miller. He works at MCF Law.'

'Got it. Clarke, you did the right thing messaging me, thank you.'

'I'll send over what I know right now.'

Clarke hung up and Sophie carefully rearranged her pillows so she could sit up. She reached for her laptop and, twisting so she didn't wake Lottie, she logged in and, using Google, searched for Duncan Miller. A few leapt on to her screen, so she edited her search to include MCF, and his image appeared, handsome and no doubt charming. She scrolled down the page, seeing his LinkedIn, Facebook and Twitter handles as well as the MCF website. Before she dug into him professionally, she wanted to see his personal life, so opting for Facebook, she loaded his page. His profile was closed, but Duncan had been tagged into a video, and Sophie could see that although it was only an hour old, it had many views and shares, far more than any of the other videos on his partially visible page. The video had a one-word title, Serendipitous. She tried to watch it, but it needed her to log into her own Facebook profile to do so, and Sophie didn't have Facebook. She didn't have any social footprint.

Back in Google, she typed 'Duncan Miller – Serendipitous' and waited as the page loaded. Lottie twitched and shifted her leg, dreaming, and Sophie turned to her daughter to make sure she didn't wake. Once she knew it was just a muscle spasm in her sleep, she looked back at the screen. Serendipitous was everywhere, the video was going viral. She clicked on a YouTube link, it loaded, and, without restrictions, she pressed play.

On the screen sat a man wearing a full hazmat suit, a face mask and dark glasses so his eyes couldn't be seen.

'Oh, shit,' Sophie said, knowing exactly what she was looking at. Duncan's killer, Jake's killer, had gone public.

When the man spoke, his voice had been filtered through some software that distorted it. It reminded her of a serial killer from 2019, one who called himself The Host, who over a period of eight days forced strangers to play a deadly game where they had to fight and only one of them could live. The city had slipped into chaos; good people died and good people became killers. His crimes shocked the nation and ruined the career of a good police officer. Sophie knew that whoever this man was, he was inspired by those crimes. She couldn't let what happened then happen now. The man on the screen began to speak and Sophie turned up her phone, just enough to hear.

'You can call me The Caretaker, but my name isn't important. What I represent is. Duncan Miller stung; he injured; he wounded. And now he has been stung in return.'

The phone he was holding turned and showed the bloated dead body of Duncan Miller.

'He is not my first.'

The camera moved from Miller back to the masked face. 'Jake Murray poisoned two people's lives with his violence, hatred and gaslighting. He was poisoned in return only two weeks ago.'

'These men were not good men; they were not pillars of the community; they were bad, toxic, damaging. They hid behind their charm and smiles whilst they ruined the lives of the women who loved them. The police have failed to protect these women, so now I look after them. Their ex-partners have been held to account.

'But my work is not finished yet. I have only just begun.'

Chapter Thirty-Seven

SUPPORT GROUP CHAT

Hannah added Jess P to the chat

HANNAH 1.37AM
> Ladies, what the actual fuck is going on?

Chapter Thirty-Eight

JESS

31st January 2025

All anyone could talk about was the man in the face mask who had told the world he had killed, and would kill again. The one who was calling himself The Caretaker. Before YouTube and Facebook and X could remove it from their platforms, millions had seen it. Discussions around it were focused on him, who he was, who he would target next. The video had been analysed, discussed on forums like Reddit and Quora, with so many, from all parts of the world, throwing their opinions into the ring. Some were for his actions, some against. People claimed to know the Caretaker or be The Caretaker. His victims had also been discussed, villainised.

However, even though the discussions hadn't referred to the support group, me, Madison, Hannah, Kelly and the others, we knew it wouldn't stay that way. A storm was coming, and we had to be prepared. Hannah's ex-partner and now Kelly's were dead. The one who called himself The Caretaker had been clear that he wasn't finished, and it made me wonder, who might be next? Would he go for Lewis?

Would I even care?

I hoped – we all hoped – that we had more time before a link was found between the two murders, but sadly that wasn't the case. When I arrived at the centre to see my new friends, my Friday not feeling like a good day without them, the press were outside. Eight, maybe nine of them, waiting for us to arrive, to talk, to answer their questions. Somehow, they knew that both Madison and Kelly were linked to the charity that Becky ran. I assumed our information would be kept private, but then, is anything private these days?

With the reporters waiting hungrily, I didn't stop walking but continued along the main road, away from the one place I was beginning to feel safe. I decided that although I would feel shit about it, going home was a better idea than facing the torrent of questions I would be asked, questions I wouldn't know the answers to. As I passed from their line of sight, I saw Hannah approaching in her car. I waved her down, and she pulled into a parking space beside me.

'Jess? You OK?'

'There are loads of journalists outside the centre. I didn't want to walk towards them.'

'Shit, didn't take them long.'

'That's what I thought. They are going to think we are involved somehow.'

'Hop in.'

Walking around the car, I opened the door and jumped in.

'We'll drive straight to the door. I've no doubt Geoff will see us coming and help us get inside. He'll probably get them to back right off.'

'Yeah, I hope so. This is freaking me out.'

'They won't be allowed in, and we've done nothing wrong. I reckon Becky has let the police know and they will be moved on. This group is supposed to be private.'

She was right, and it settled me. Hannah put the car in gear and turned into the lane. The reporters turned to face us, lusting for some inside information from a member of the support group that was somehow in the middle of this. As we drew closer, they didn't move, hoping that their human shield would pin us in, but Hannah didn't stop; she slowed to a crawl and kept going until we were directly outside the door. Sure enough, as she'd said, Geoff stepped out, as if he'd been waiting for our arrival, while behind him Becky looked on anxiously, and we quickly dashed inside the centre. Questions were fired our way, phones filmed and took photos, but they didn't get much, just our backs and Geoff's voice telling them to go away. Nothing that would add to their story, nothing their editors would approve for print or website.

Once in the building, we tucked ourselves out of the way of prying eyes, and Geoff stepped in, locking the door behind him.

'Bastards,' he hissed before catching himself. 'Sorry, ladies. I don't like their kind, sticking their noses in, making up stories.'

'It's OK.' I said. 'Thanks for coming to get us.'

'Ladies, shall we go inside? Let's make a cuppa,' Becky said. 'Geoff, can you stay here, for the others? They might not come, but if they do…'

'Don't worry, I'll look after them,' he said.

'Thanks, Geoff,' Becky replied, before leading me and Hannah into the main room of the centre. We weren't the first; already sitting there anxiously were Claire, Vija and Steph. There were no men though. And when I looked to Becky, she understood my question without me needing to ask.

'Everyone knows the link to us; none of them turned up today.'

I nodded, and then understood why. The killings were linked to us, this centre. I had only seen three men at the sessions, but they all knew the lives the women had lived. They all knew the ex-partners' crimes.

'Shit. You don't think...' I trailed off.

Becky didn't reply.

The session was quieter than usual. Kelly wasn't there, as expected, but Baheela and Madison hadn't come either. They had no doubt seen the crowd and bailed, as I would have if Hannah hadn't arrived. Becky tried her best to keep us together, and she rang 111 twice to find out when the reporters would be moved on. She hoped it would be within minutes, but we all knew that wouldn't be the case. So, as a group, we drank tea and tried to quietly process what was happening in our small but quickly growing lives, in a state of pseudo-shock. Eventually, half an hour into our session, thirty minutes of barely talking, a car began to advance up the narrow lane towards us, a solitary police car.

'About bloody time,' Vija said.

We all watched through the window as the car pulled up beside Hannah's and two officers climbed out. I recognised Detective Jones straight away. He wore the same 'this isn't what I signed up for' expression he had when in my flat, after Lewis left his note. And even though the others seemed happy about his arrival, I wasn't sure I shared the sentiment.

Behind, another police car arrived, and then, immediately behind it, a third.

'Seems like a big response for a few reporters?' Vija said.

The two new police cars stopped, and six officers climbed out and began to move the journalists back. They protested, but complied until they were back on the main road. We could see that another police car was on the road, blocking the entrance, to stop anyone else coming up the drive.

'Becky?' I asked. 'What's going on?'

'I don't know,' she said.

No sooner had she replied than more police ran up the lane. These weren't ordinary uniformed or suited officers, these were dressed for conflict: stab vests, tasers and riot shields.

'What's happening?' Claire asked.

Instinctively, we gathered closer together, moved away from the doors and windows.

'Stay here. OK?' Becky said, removing herself from the group.

'Becky. Wait,' I said, but my voice was drowned out by the sound of the centre's front door crashing into the wall as it was flung open. We all jumped, unable to see what was happening, but able to hear as the crash was immediately followed by voices, several voices, loud and intimidating.

'Stop, get to the floor, get on the floor right now.'

'Don't fucking move.'

'Get down. GET. DOWN!'

Becky backed away from the door, and staying close, we stared towards where the sound was coming from, hearing the struggling and swearing and then a cry of pain that sounded like it came from Geoff.

We listened as Geoff was taken from the building, and looking through the window, we watched as he was forced into the back of a police car. From inside the car, he gazed back at us inside the centre. His look was one of regret, sorrow, maybe shame.

Chapter Thirty-Nine

After the police had taken Geoff away, the reporters stirring into a frenzy as they pulled out, DS Jones walked into the main centre.

'What the hell?' Becky said.

'You need to go home,' he replied.

'Why have you taken Geoff?' Vija asked, her voice shaking.

'You need to go home,' DS Jones said again, this time with a little more force, a little less compassion. 'We will keep the reporters back, but you all need to leave. We'll be in touch.'

'But…' I began.

'I'm not asking you,' he snapped at me. It made me flinch, and I hated that I did. Before we could challenge him any further, he turned and left, almost walking straight into a police officer behind him. She entered the room and I recognised the female detective who had already been to our group.

'Sorry about him,' she said. 'But he is right, you need to go home. We won't be able to keep the circus away from you, and I know that this place, and what you are doing here, isn't about attracting attention.'

'DS Salam, isn't it?' Becky said.

'Well remembered.'

'Why have you taken Geoff? There is no way—'

'He's only being brought in for questioning,' she said, cutting Becky off.

'You think, he is The Caretaker…?' Hannah said. Then she realised what she was saying. Geoff was, in fact, exactly that. 'Oh, shit.'

'We just want to ask him some questions. I can't say anymore, OK? But you really do need to leave now.'

'Ladies. You heard the detective. Let's pack up,' Becky said, and Salam nodded, turned on her heel and left the centre. Outside, she stopped beside Jones, and I watched as he spoke to her. There was something in the way he did so that I didn't like, and I saw Becky notice it too. He stood too close, leant over her too much. But to her credit, she didn't step back. She held her ground, and then, with a small shake of his head, he got into his car and left the centre. The police car at the end of the lane let him out, then quickly blocked it again.

'Becky? You don't think Geoff is…' Claire asked, her voice trailing off before she could call him a murderer.

'I … umm,' Becky faltered.

I nearly said that I wasn't completely shocked, that Geoff knew our secrets, that he was someone who wanted to protect us, someone who cared, someone who knew how to do such a thing, someone who had likely killed before, for a living, but I didn't. I didn't know him as well as the others, and although it was upsetting for me, the fact that he had been arrested made Hannah sob. As we consoled her as best we could, Becky tidied, and once the centre was clean, no longer our space but a children's centre once more, we left. I got into Hannah's car again and in convoy we all drove away.

I assumed that would be that. We would go home. Then I had the sickening thought that the support group might now fold. It was designed to keep us safe, tucked away; it was supposed to be a place where we could hide and deal with our traumas and perhaps even find a way out of it all, to begin again. The centre would now be under scrutiny, especially if Geoff's arrest was for what we all assumed. I wanted to talk to Hannah about it, but my words didn't come. They were trapped, buried by the overwhelming shock of the morning. I looked at her as she drove, fat tears falling down her face. Where would I even begin to try to make her feel better?

Thankfully, I didn't need to. Steph had messaged Kelly in the group chat and she replied, asking if everyone was OK. Then, a second message came directly to me, Hannah and Madison in a separate, smaller chat. It started with an address, her address, then a simple message.

> Tomorrow night, come to mine, let's talk this through.

I read the message to Hannah, and she nodded.
'OK,' she said. 'OK.'

Chapter Forty

SOPHIE SALAM

1st February 2025

Watching through the small monitor in the office, Sophie observed how still their suspect was. After a night in the cells following an interrogation by Jones after his arrest, he was back in the chair, and it was Sophie's turn to talk to him. They wondered if a woman's approach would be better, considering the type of man The Caretaker was. He had been escorted to the room, told to sit, and for an hour Sophie had watched. In that time, Geoff Brown had barely moved a muscle. He was patiently waiting, cuffed hands on the desk. He was either a man without a care in the world or a man who was very, very dangerous.

'What do you think?' Clarke asked.

'I think he's waited long enough. I need to go talk to him.'

'Want me to come?'

'Clarke, two things with that. One, you're off shift and I know you're not getting overtime for this. And two, is this even part of your job?'

'No, but—'

'Just hanging around for my good company?' Sophie joked.

'You wish, kid.'

'Piss off.'

'I'm curious,' Clarke continued, waving off her banter. 'If he is The Caretaker, I want to know how he thinks. I want to hear his justifications. I'll stay here and watch, that OK?'

'Yeah,' Sophie said. 'Wish me luck.'

Sophie headed along the corridor and then into Interview Room 2. She smiled as she walked in. Her suspect didn't smile back, but looked at her keenly. Like he was trying to work her out. It unnerved her, until she remembered: The Caretaker was helping women, not hurting them.

'Mr Brown.'

'Geoff,' he said, softly.

'Geoff. I'm DS Salam. I wanted to talk to you.'

'OK.'

Sophie looked at his wrists. The handcuffs were tight, no doubt uncomfortable. 'If I take off those, are we gonna be OK?'

He nodded his head slowly and Sophie looked back to the camera, knowing she was being watched. If he did decide to kick off, help would be with her in seconds. But she didn't think he would. Even so, she was cautious removing them. Once she had, Geoff sat back in the chair and rubbed his wrists.

'Thanks.'

'I want to ask you a few questions.'

'About The Caretaker,' he said matter-of-factly.

'Yes, about The Caretaker.'

'OK.' He nodded,

'What can you tell me?'

He exhaled, rubbed his face, his stubble sharp. 'Only what everyone knows.'

'Which is?'

'He is killing bad men.'

'Are they bad men?'

'Do you think they are not?' he asked, looking into her eyes for the first time. And Sophie could see that despite his soft voice, his calm demeanour, there was violence in the man. She almost replied saying yes, she agreed with him, they were bad men, but the interview wasn't about her views. Only his.

'Tell me about your time in the forces,' she asked and noticed a twitch in his eye. Intentionally shifting the focus meant her suspect would be taken by surprise, his defences weakened.

'What has this got to do with anything?' he asked.

'Did you serve on the front line?'

'I suspect you know the answer to that.'

'Adjusting after must have been difficult. I can't imagine it was easy in the fallout of that war.'

'Nope. It wasn't.'

Sophie considered him. His resolve was strong. He looked back, but not in a way that intimidated her at all. He appeared calm, controlled, but then, psychopaths were, weren't they?

'Mr Brown.'

'Geoff.'

'Geoff, can you tell me where you were on the night of the 14th January?'

'At home.'

'Can anyone confirm that?'

'I live alone.'

'What about the night of the 28th?'

'At home.'

'You seem so sure. Don't want to consider it?'

'I work, I go home, that's what I do.'

'Don't go to the pub?'

'Nope.'

'Out for a meal, see a movie?'

'I live alone, DS Salam.'

'No friends? Family?'

'I have grown-up children back near Edinburgh.'

'See them often?'

'When I can.'

Sophie nodded. 'Geoff, why do you think we arrested you?'

'Someone is attacking the men that are linked to the support group where I work.'

'Killing them. He is killing them.'

'And you think it's me.'

'Is it?'

'I can see why. I look like I do; I'm ex-service; I know these women. I would assume it was me too.'

'So, are you The Caretaker?'

'I hate those men, I do. And I won't lose sleep over them facing justice for what they have done to those women.'

'Murder isn't justice.'

'Karma then. But did I do it? No. I've seen death before. It's not pretty.'

'You don't mind they are dead?'

'Why would I? Death happens every day, DS Salam. Good people die every day. A few bad men dying isn't going to bring anything but peace. The law doesn't help those women. Not really. If someone is going to, then who am I to think badly of them? But did I do it? No, DS Salam.'

'But you know who did?'

'I waived my right to a solicitor when I arrived, but I think I would like to speak to one now.'

The way Geoff sat back in his chair told Sophie that he was

done talking. She said she would get him a solicitor as requested, then left the room. Back in the office, she stood beside Clarke and watched the monitor. Geoff was just as still, just as unrattled as he was before they spoke. If he did kill those men, he was as cool as they come.

'What do you think?' Clarke asked.

'He knows something, I'm sure.'

'But is he The Caretaker?'

'Maybe. But I doubt we've got enough to charge.'

'What now?'

'We'll lean on him a bit longer, once his solicitor is here. Hope he cracks. Doubt he will.'

'Soph. What he says, about karma.'

'Do you agree with him?'

'No, the way those men died couldn't have been pleasant. But, if these women were really let down this badly, then...'

'Then what?'

'I understand, I guess. What about you?'

Sophie didn't reply, but turned her attention back to the monitor, where she watched Geoff calmly sip from his glass of water. She stared, trying to work out if she was looking at a double murderer, and as she did, she silently answered Clarke's question. Yes, she understood. If she was looking at a murderer, if that man sat calmly sipping water was The Caretaker, she knew she wouldn't hate him.

Chapter Forty-One

JESS

For over twenty-four hours I sat glued to the news, waiting to hear more about Geoff. It was being reported that there had been an arrest, linked to the double murder that had started 2025 with a bang, a firework of public anxiety. There was speculation about who had been arrested, but as nothing had been confirmed, the BBC kept his name out of their reports. The *Mail Online* were not so considerate of a person's reputation, and as I scrolled on Facebook, one of their articles leapt out, the title damning.

Arrest made in the 'Caretaker' Killings

I dared to read on.

At approximately 10.30am yesterday (1st February) police arrived at a community centre in the city and arrested a 67-year-old man in connection with the double murder of Jake Murray and Duncan Miller.

The man, named as Geoff Brown, works for the council as a handyman or caretaker for the community centres in the area and has been described as a quiet and mild-mannered soul.

Brown served in the army, and was posted front line in the Falkland wars, where he received medals for courage under fire. It is speculated that during his tour he killed people.

Detective Sophie Salam, who is leading the investigation, has yet to comment on the arrest, or whether Brown will be charged for his crimes.

More details about the victims are emerging too. Both had run-ins with the law regarding domestic violence and neither were charged, which poses a bigger question – not if Brown will be charged, but should he?

War hero, city villain – we'd love to know your thoughts. Get in touch in the comments below.

They had not only named Geoff, but showed a picture of him in the back of the police car, looking bewildered. The thread underneath the article had dozens of comments from readers, their opinions matching the article's energy, some thinking he should be locked up, some hailing him a leader in a world gone to shit. I still didn't know if Geoff was involved, but what I did know was that I liked him, and I didn't hate him if he had done what they think he'd done. He'd stopped bad men doing bad things, and maybe, just maybe, he would scare others into stopping. Maybe Lewis would be scared straight. But somehow I doubted it. And if Geoff was The Caretaker, any fear Lewis might have felt would be gone.

I wondered how the other women felt.

With Kelly insisting we all meet up in the wake of Geoff's arrest, Hannah picked me up at just before seven, and using her phone's satnav, we drove to Kelly's house in the outskirts of town. I expected it to be big – sometimes you can just tell by a person – but I gasped when I saw it: a huge detached property with at least four bedrooms and a drive large enough for six cars.

'Jesus, it's like the McAllister house from *Home Alone*,' I said, and Hannah laughed. It wasn't quite the same size as the one from the 90s hit film, but it wasn't a million miles off.

We parked on the drive, behind Kelly's car, and climbed out. As we did, another car approached, a taxi, and Madison got out. She gave us both a hug and then tried to smooth out her top.

'I feel underdressed,' she said, her voice small and lost. I wanted to tell her she would be OK, that everything would be OK, but I didn't feel I had the right.

'Not at all,' I replied.

We walked up to Kelly's front door and rang the doorbell, and a few seconds later Kelly opened it. I could tell she had been crying – her eyes were heavy, tired – and it was only then I realised that, with all the chaos around us, the murders, Geoff's arrest, it was still her ex who had been killed. She looked politely at me and Hannah, then stepped and pulled Madison into a long embrace. The two women cried and I suspected it was both grief and relief in equal measure. After she let Madison go, she wiped her eyes and smiled at us.

'Come in, come in,' she said, as we each hugged her.

Her house was just as beautiful inside as it was out. The hallway was wide, with a small table, a lamp and a luscious green plant. We took our shoes off and followed her to a massive kitchen/hosting space, with two large couches towards one end, a kitchen island, and skylights in the ceiling. This space alone was probably the same size as my entire flat. We could all see that Kelly was struggling, so we gathered around the kitchen island. Seeing a bottle of wine standing there, I asked where her bottle opener was, opened the bottle and poured us a large glass each.

'Are you OK?' I asked. She nodded, but we could see she wasn't, not really.

'He was a prick, but still, you know?' She paused. We didn't interrupt. 'I guess I'm still trying to process it all. Mads, are you holding up OK?'

'Better. Since that video came out, my mum has had a lot of questions about mine and Jake's relationship, and I've had to answer them. It's actually made things a lot easier.'

'Well, that's positive,' Kelly said, though her smile was twisted by grief.

'Yeah, Mum has been great, and I no longer feel trapped. You'll start feeling the same too, soon, Kelly, I have no doubt. I still feel guilty but—'

'There is nothing to feel guilty for,' I cut in. 'Either of you. You've done nothing wrong.'

They both nodded, but didn't say anymore.

'So, ladies,' Kelly said, clearing her throat, wanting to move on from her grief. 'Tell me about yesterday.'

We filled her in as much as we could about the reporters, the police, and Geoff being dragged away in handcuffs. We speculated about what we had read in the newspapers, and maybe it was because I was with women I had grown to trust, maybe it was the fact that I had drunk an entire glass of wine too fast, but I told them how I wasn't shocked that he was a suspect.

'Really?' Kelly said.

'I mean, he has a violent history because of the army; he knows everything about you and your pasts; he really cares for everyone in the group. And when that Salam police officer first came in, he looked really uncomfortable.'

'Maybe,' Madison said. 'But didn't we all?'

'Yes,' I said. 'And the men from Becky's first session, they didn't turn up yesterday.'

'None of them?' Kelly asked.

'Nope. None,' I said, thinking about them, how damaged they were, how angry, how guilty. None of them came to the session, but Geoff did. Geoff was there, and he didn't appear any different when he helped me into the building.

'If it is him, if Geoff did it,' I continued, 'Kelly, Mads, would you hate him?'

They looked at one another and both shook their heads.

'No.'

'No.'

'Hannah, do you think maybe your ex being attacked was him too? I mean, it has to be connected, surely?'

'Yeah, I think so,' she said.

'Girls, is it awful that I wish he'd got to Lewis before he was caught?'

Kelly looked at Hannah, who nodded, and then at Madison, who also nodded.

'Do you mean that?' Kelly said.

'Yeah. Maybe. I don't know. I hate him, you know. He has ruined me for too long, and gets away with it. I've had to change my locks; I'm the one the police frown at; I'm the one with the scars. And what happens to him? Nothing. It's so fucking unfair. And I'm sorry if that sounds insensitive. I can't imagine how you are both feeling. But I fucking hate him.'

The women looked at each other once more.

'Sorry,' I said. 'Shit, I'm sorry. I'm being a bitch.'

'I'll get another bottle of wine,' Kelly said. 'Shall we sit on the sofa?'

Again, Madison and Hannah nodded.

'Kelly?'

'Jess, you might wanna sit down. You'll thank me for it soon.'

I was confused, but Hannah began guiding me to the sofa. Kelly quietly opened a fresh bottle and, bringing it over, topped up all of our glasses. Madison didn't look at me, and whenever Hannah and I made eye contact she looked away.

'What's going on? Kelly?'

She sat directly opposite me, between Hannah and Madison, and I felt like I was at a job interview. Kelly considered me for a moment, then began to speak.

'Geoff didn't hurt anyone.'

'Sorry?' I said.

'He didn't kill Duncan,' she said.

'Or Jake,' Madison added, finally looking at me.

'And he didn't attack Martin.'

'I-I don't understand?' I said. And even though I was confused, there was something in the way all three women now held my gaze, trying to weigh me up; it was like I was being judged on how I reacted to what they were telling me.

They knew something I didn't; they knew something no one did. I swallowed hard, then took another big mouthful of wine.

'Duncan abused me for a long time,' Kelly continued. 'For years, and even though I reported him to the police, they didn't do a goddamn thing. I filed for a divorce, and he threw it in my face for far too long, and yes, even though he agreed, I knew he wouldn't ever let me go. Men like him don't; they hang on, come back, like a cancer. I survived him, but I knew, deep down, he would always end up killing me.'

'Kelly, what is it you are telling me?'

Kelly paused, considered me again, and then she too took a sip. Whatever it was she wanted to say, I could tell it was on the tip of her tongue. She knew. She knew who was killing these men. They all did, I could feel it. It was one of the others from the centre; it was one of the three men I had seen. I remembered Tim and Geoff talking – maybe they were both in on it. Working together?

'Jake,' Madison continued when Kelly didn't speak, 'posted things about me everywhere, made me look like a slut to all his friends. Everyone he knew saw me at my most vulnerable.'

'Oh, Madison.'

'It's OK, it is. I could live with that; my ego died when he did what he did. It's not about that. It's about the fact that, one day, he would take interest in his little boy, as he got bigger. He would want something out of the relationship. He poisoned my mind, made me feel like I wasn't ever going to be good enough or smart enough or beautiful enough, and I don't know if I'll ever unlearn that, but I couldn't let it happen to my child.'

I opened my mouth to say something but stopped myself.

'You've worked it out, haven't you?' Kelly said.

'I….' I trailed off, piecing it together. 'You know something? Don't you?'

'We weren't ever going to be helped. We weren't ever going to feel safe,' Hannah said.

I stood up and walked away. What they were saying couldn't be true – it didn't make sense – but panic flooded into my body regardless. They knew who had killed their exes. They were involved somehow. I walked back to the kitchen island but stood on the other side, creating a barrier between me and them. They didn't move, only looked back at me, patiently waiting.

'Kelly, what are you telling me?' I eventually said.

'Geoff didn't kill them,' Hannah said quietly.

'But you know who did? You know who The Caretaker is?' I asked.

'Yes,' Madison replied.

'Who? Who killed them?'

'We did,' Kelly said. 'Jess, we are The Caretaker.'

Chapter Forty-Two

'What?' I said, my mind unable to connect the dots. I couldn't make it make sense. 'What do you mean, you are The Caretaker?'

'Jess.'

'Kelly, what the fuck do you mean, you are The Caretaker?'

'Jess,' Kelly said again, more forcefully. She walked over towards me and reached for my hand, but I yanked it away.

'No, don't touch me. What is this, some sort of sick joke? I thought you were my friends?'

'We are,' Madison said, standing up.

'Stop fucking with me. I want to go home.'

'We're not messing with you,' Hannah said, her voice soft, calming, joining the others around the kitchen island. Hannah started to move around to me, and I stepped back. Feeling trapped. 'Jess, we are telling you the truth.'

'The Caretaker is a man,' I said, my voice wavering as fear crept into my marrow.

'That's what we want people to think,' Kelly continued. 'Jess. Just listen.'

'Please,' Hannah added.

'Are you going to hurt me?' I said, a big tear escaping.

'No, Jess, no. The opposite. We want to help,' Hannah said.

I didn't dare speak, didn't dare move. The intensity with which they stared at me told me they were just as vulnerable as I was.

'Jess, let us explain.'

The women I had bonded with, the women I was now beginning to call my friends, were the killer everyone was talking about.

'Jess?' Kelly said quietly.

'I... Fuck,' I managed to say, looking away from them, focusing on a small scratch on the island's otherwise immaculate countertop. 'How?'

'Come, sit, we will tell you everything.'

I felt paralysed, my fight or flight response having left me entirely. I was frozen like a rabbit, a deer, waiting to be hit.

'Jess?' Madison said, reaching over and placing her hand on mine. 'No one was going to help us. No one was going to help my little boy. Or me, or Kelly, or Hannah. And, no one is going to help you either. You think Lewis will back off, move on. He won't. He just won't. He will always find a way to try to own you. He will always try to find new ways to ruin your life. These men, they only want to possess. You'll never escape that.'

I looked up, and the three women I had come to like, to trust, looked back.

'We all did the right thing by speaking up, asking for help, asking for justice, but they failed us. Speaking up made it worse. We didn't want this. We just wanted to be freed, we wanted to be saved,' Kelly said, approaching me. She took my hand and guided me back to the sofa, this time choosing to sit beside me.

'But you seem so upset?' I managed to say, my voice as fragile as a butterfly wing in a thunderstorm. I knew, through the fog of what had just been revealed, I should have asked a better question, but none came.

'I am upset, upset that to feel safe and like I could move forward, I had to act. I'm upset because I've had to take matters into my own hands. I never wanted Duncan dead, not really. But in a world where I would always be a victim to him, what other choice was there? I wasn't going to let myself be that woman anymore.'

'But you were in Scotland until today?' I said.

'I was.'

'And, and, Madison, you were in Spain? When Jake was killed?'

'Yes.'

'Then how?'

'I didn't kill Duncan,' Kelly said.

'But you just said you did?'

'I said we did. I didn't kill him. Hannah was The Caretaker that night.'

I looked at Hannah, sweet, kind, polite Hannah, and she nodded at me. 'Kelly had the perfect alibi. There is no link between me and Duncan other than Kelly, but the night he died, I was with Madison,' she said.

'You were?'

'In a way.'

'She came to mine and stayed the evening,' Madison continued. 'I have ring doorbell footage of her entering and leaving the following morning. If the police came, we could prove she was with me. All night. As for Jake, as you said, I was in Spain.'

'So who killed Jake? Who was The Caretaker then?'

'I was,' Kelly said, holding my gaze, no doubt trying to gauge my reaction.

'You killed him?'

'Yes. I killed him.'

I felt sick, but somehow weirdly comforted too. Being with these women made me feel safe. Now I knew why.

'Hannah. Who attacked your ex?'

'Madison did.'

'You have done this for each other?'

'We have, and remember Baheela's ex was burned with acid, on New Year's Eve? Remember, at your first session it was briefly talked about.' Kelly said.

'Yes?'

'That was all of us. We created a scene where he was attacked; we wanted to see if we could be invisible. We then followed. I threw the acid. It worked; we knew it would. No one came for us. No one suspected a thing. Until yesterday, we have been invisible for years.'

'Who was the one who made the video?'

'Me,' Hannah said.

'Fuck.'

'Jess, are you OK?' Kelly asked. 'Am I wrong to put my trust in you?'

I hesitated. I was with three women who had killed people. They were murderers. They were my friends. They were acting when everyone else had let them down.

'Jess?' Kelly prompted again.

'No,' I said quietly. 'No, you aren't wrong. It's just a lot to process.'

'We've planned for over a year, creating The Caretaker. We have watched, learned, and when we decided it was the only way. We readied ourselves, mentally and physically. We work out in a gym. We lift weights. We are strong, stronger than the men who once hurt us.'

I nodded and thought back to when Kelly had hugged me, and how tight it was, how when Hannah took my hand, her grip was strong. These women had lifted weights, grown muscle, ready to take revenge.

'And we created The Caretaker. He is all of the things we hate about our exes amalgamated into one man. He is cruel, calculating, vengeful. He enjoys watching men suffer. He hurts; he dehumanises. He is everything Duncan and Jake and Martin and, I'm gonna guess, Lewis is, rolled into one.'

'They all think that a man is the killer.'

'Yes, because The Caretaker is a man,' Kelly continued. 'Don't you see, we made him to be a confident, determined man. A woman couldn't be doing this. Imagine what the news would say? She would be deranged, dangerous. She would be sexualised in some grotesque way. If The Caretaker was a woman they would want to burn her at the stake. They always want to burn women at the stake, even now. The Caretaker being a man means people will talk about the right things to do with this.'

'Right things?'

'That men who hurt and abuse need to be held accountable. There are thousands, maybe even tens of thousands of us out there. We don't want them all dead. We just want the laws to be on the side of the victim, not the perpetrator.'

'The Caretaker', Hannah took over, 'is the worst kind of man, and he's bringing justice to those men who are just like him.'

'No one would never suspect it was you,' I said quietly.

'That's the plan,' Kelly said. 'But, to be safe, we have made sure that all of us are accountable for at all times.'

'We all have airtight alibis. The only link is the support group, which is why the police have gone to Geoff,' Hannah added, sadness back in her voice.

'Why him?'

'As you said, he has a violent history because of the army, he knows everything about us and our pasts, and he really cares for everyone in the group.'

'Does he know what you are doing?'

'No.'

'What about the other men?'

'No, no one. We suspect they will be questioned too. And we feel bad, really bad, for them, for the fact that Geoff has been arrested, but soon he will be released without charge. Geoff will never know it's us. We love that man, and we feel really awful. But they can't charge him; a few days in a cell and he will be out. They might investigate the other men in the group too. But they won't be charged, none of them, because there is no proof. Geoff will be home soon, and able to get on with his life once more.'

'How can you be sure?' I said, and then I remembered the video that The Caretaker posted, the video I now knew was Hannah's. 'Oh, shit. You are going to kill again, aren't you?'

They didn't reply.

'Am I right?'

'Yes,' Kelly said, her voice steady.

'Who?'

'Since his hospital release,' Hannah said, 'Martin hasn't changed. He tried to get into my house the other night. I rang the police – they came out – but I know they won't do anything to stop him.'

'So you are going to kill him?'

'Yes, we are,' Kelly said again.

'When?'

'Tuesday.'

'Who? Who will do it?'

'It's my turn,' Madison said in a way that told me she was nervous but ready to do her part. 'Hannah is going to go to her mum's again.'

'I leave in the morning,' Hannah said.

'Shit,' I said, and then, reaching for my glass, I drank a large mouthful of wine. As it washed down, I sat back, unable to look at them, trying as best I could to process what I had learnt.

'I've watched him for months,' Madison continued. 'I know his comings and goings. I know he doesn't lock the gate to his back garden, and thanks to Hannah, I know he keeps a spare key in the eaves of his shed roof.'

'He often locks himself out,' Hannah said quietly. 'I suggested he kept a key there, just in case.'

'Are you sure he still keeps a key there?' I asked.

'Yes.'

'How?'

'Because I check twice a week.'

'You are going to go into his house?'

'Yes, I am.'

'Shit,' I said again.

'We aren't messing around with this, Jess. We mean to do it and to never be caught,' Kelly said.

'Does anyone else from the group know?'

'No, it's just us three, and now you,' Hannah said.

'But what about Baheela?'

'She is a scared woman. We wanted to see if The Caretaker could work. We like Baheela, and God knows she needed the win after her ex did what he did, but we don't trust her.'

'But you do me?'

'We weren't sure whether to tell you, but a few times, including tonight, you have said you wish someone would do something to Lewis. You said you wished Geoff got to him before he was caught.'

I nodded. I had said those things, but I didn't know if I meant them, deep down.

'Jess. When we started this thing, we weren't sure we could go through with it. However, as sad as it is, and scary, and uncertain, and damaging, we are sure now. Our question is, did you mean what you said? Do you really wish The Caretaker would deal with Lewis?'

I thought about my year, of how it'd started in a hospital, my face battered by my partner. I thought of the note, the security footage, the fact that he let himself in, I thought about the woman he got to attack me, the credit card he stole. I thought of how I couldn't even sleep in my own bedroom anymore. I thought of how it made me feel knowing the police wouldn't help, not really. Of DS Jones and his unsubtle not giving a shit. The police could scare him off, give him an injunction maybe, but Lewis could get to me at any point, any time. At any time, he could hurt me, or worse.

'Jess?' Hannah prompted.

'Yes,' I said. 'Yes, I meant it. I wish The Caretaker could deal with him.'

'And are you willing to help us with this?'

I nodded. 'I am.'

'OK,' Kelly said, raising her glass. Madison followed, then Hannah, and then me.

'Well, then,' Kelly said. 'Welcome to the serial killer support group.'

Chapter Forty-Three

3rd February 2025

Two sleepless nights visited me, nights where I tried to process the secret I now kept about the identity of The Caretaker. Nights where I wrestled with my own moral compass, wondering what I should do with the truth. I felt sick with the knowledge. Weighted down with the burden. These women had killed. These women had murdered. They were, in the eyes of the law, the worst offenders that society had. But I knew these women too. They weren't evil; they were good, good people.

They were like me.

Learning that the women I had come to know, to like, to care for, were involved in murder played heavily on my mind. I wondered if I had made a mistake in allowing myself to be complicit in such heinous crimes. Murder was murder. Right? It was always wrong.

Unless, of course, it wasn't.

Kelly was my friend, Madison and Hannah too. When Lewis

tried to get in, it wasn't the police I went to first, it was Kelly. It was Kelly I needed to help me feel safe. Now I knew why.

But still, the argument between right and wrong played out in my mind. Yes, it was wrong, so very wrong. The pain, the fear Jake and Duncan must have felt before they died would have been intense, cruel even. I struggled to see my friends doing it. I couldn't imagine Hannah pressing that bee into Duncan's neck. I couldn't see her being the one under the mask in the video. Despite Kelly being fiery, I didn't know how she managed to drug Madison's ex and watch him die. What they had done was so very wrong.

But at the same time, they were right in doing it. They didn't want to kill. They wanted help and when they'd asked for help, it hadn't come. If the world backs you into a corner, is it not right to try and get yourself out of it? If you were drowning, would you not kick to the surface to survive? That was all they were doing, just kicking up. I wondered, if Lewis tried to hurt me, would I be worried about morality and ethics, or would I try and survive? The age-old question that many had had to face throughout human history looped in my head, a question that until now I hadn't ever asked myself. Could I kill a person? Most would say they couldn't, but I was beginning to understand that most people lied to themselves, and I concluded I could, and if I had to, I would. If Lewis tried, I would want him dead. But I knew if he tried, I wouldn't have the strength to overpower him. Will was one thing, but if he attacked, will wouldn't be enough.

I saw that Geoff had been released, the *Mail Online* saying that there wasn't enough evidence for a charge, and he had left the station. I felt awful for him, spending days in a holding cell for a crime he hadn't committed. If he ever found out, I hoped he could forgive.

With Geoff released, and me realising all my friends were doing was trying to survive, sleep was no longer an issue.

Even loaded with this knowledge, I knew I had to continue like I didn't know the truth. Life had to go on, as it always had, because the truth was a fragile thing, and if I didn't protect it, as the others did, it would crack. So, by Monday, I was up, dressed and ready for work as usual. Jenny was thrilled when I said I was coming back, and looking at my schedule, I saw I was needed for wake-up time until just after lunch.

Being back at work again made me feel close to normal. To her credit, when I arrived at just after six to a quiet house with two sleeping children, Jenny didn't try to talk about how I was feeling, or if I was safe – she just welcomed me back – and I got on with caring for her two beautiful children. In the back of my mind, I was still worried about Lewis turning up, trying to get to me through them. But it plagued me less. Lewis was bad, awful, but I knew those who were worse, I knew those who were as dangerous as they come, and even though it was a secret, just knowing was enough.

As the weather was bright and crisp, a perfect winter morning, after breakfast I didn't hesitate to take the children out to a park, and for a few hours they played in the fresh air. Jenny insisted I call her if I felt unsettled at all, but I told her not to worry. The park was full of families, and not just mothers, fathers were with their children too, and I had to hold on to the fact that most men were good men. If Lewis came, someone would help. But he didn't come, and those few hours, knowing I was safe, knowing that I could keep a terrible secret and not have it affect how I presented myself to the outside world, were reassuring. I would not slip; the serial killer support group and its secrets would stay safe in my hands.

I also realised that when I said I would want them to deal with Lewis, I meant it.

I was in.

And there was no turning back.

I think.

When I returned from the park with Eva and Will, I cleaned them up and prepared their lunch. Jenny arrived home and, after a quick coffee together, I said my goodbyes, telling Will and Eva I would be back tomorrow morning. As I went to leave, Jenny stopped me.

'Jess, if you need anything, just let me know?'

'I will, I promise.'

'OK, don't feel like it's a burden. Both Samuel and I can help make him leave you alone.'

'Thank you, Jenny, but I'm OK. Lewis is backing off now, and it won't be long until he's gone.'

'Good, I'm pleased to hear this, but still, you need anything, you let us know. We see you as family now.'

I nodded, feeling myself well up a little. I loved Jenny's children, loved them like I was their aunty. For Jenny to think of me in the same way meant the world. She pulled me in for a hug, and then, shouting another goodbye to the kids, I left and began to make my way home, wiping a big fat happy tear.

After work, I usually walked to the nearest bus stop and then hopped on for the ten-minute journey, but the day was bright, a hint of spring in the air, so I decided I would walk. I loved walking; it was my way to switch off, to feel settled and at ease. I'd often wrap up and walk for miles and miles, and I realised that it was now February, and I hadn't walked so far in 2025. Lewis had taken that from me too. So, I slowed to a gentle stroll, enjoyed the moment, and even though the fear of Lewis lingered, as it always lingered, I forced myself to suppress it. It would return, of course, but I needed to hold on to the peace of the moment.

A mile or so into my walk, I was winning the battle between my fear and my tranquillity. As I headed through the town centre, I saw my favourite coffee shop. Before Lewis, I would go, sometimes twice a week, to read or to catch up with a friend. Or simply have a coffee and watch the world go by. Then, when we were together, I went less and less. It had been maybe six months since I'd stepped inside.

I slowed as I approached, and looked in. It was busy, but there were free tables dotted around, and behind the counter was the familiar face of a barista who had been friendly with me.

'Fuck it.'

Opening the door, I walked in and joined the queue of four people. When it was my turn, the barista, a tall, rotund man named James, smiled my way.

'Oh, hi! It's been so long. We thought you had moved.'

'No, I'm still around.'

'Nice to see you, what can I get you?'

I ordered myself a latte and a teacake and then found myself a little table where I could sit and look out to the High Street. I knew a window seat meant that there was more opportunity for Lewis, if he was around town, to see me. But I sat next to a window anyway. Because fuck you, Lewis. Fuck. You.

As I drank my latte, which tasted better than any latte I had ever tasted before in my life, I saw that across the street, in the window of a newsagent, there was a large tabloid heading, *Serial killer on our quiet streets.* Beside it, another. *Infamous 'The Caretaker', hero or villain?* I read, but tried not to show any reaction to the words I was reading. I knew what was coming. Kelly told me The Caretaker would strike again in just over twenty-four hours' time. I had to look away from the questions posed and instead I focused on those in the coffee shop. Young mothers with babies in prams, those working remotely with headphones on. Older couples sitting in silence with their coffee and cake. I wondered, were any of them talking about my friends, about The Caretaker? I sat, knowing all the answers, completely invisible.

Across the café, in the far corner, I heard a young voice begin to sound distressed; they were calling out, moaning, and it caught the attention of everyone. I looked to see a mother struggling to calm her daughter. The little girl thrashed in her mother's grip, knocking a coffee off the table. The woman's bag ended up on the floor, its contents scattering. People looked away, embarrassed or disgusted, and no one was going to help, so I got up, and made my way to her. Hide in plain sight, right?

'Here, let me help,' I said, bending over to pick up the woman's belongings. The barista came over with a mop and helped to clean up whilst the mother did all she could to calm her daughter.

Once I had collected her things, the mother, still dealing with her daughter, looked at me. I was startled. I could tell she recognised me too.

Sat before me was the police officer who'd been there when Geoff was arrested. Struggling to calm her daughter was the woman investigating the murders I knew everything about. Looking into my eyes was Detective Sophie Salam.

Chapter Forty-Four

As soon as I locked eyes with the detective who was trying to find The Caretaker, I knew I should have walked away. However, I could see in her eyes how tired she was. I had seen it on Jenny's face a thousand times. I knew how tough it was, and I knew I could help. The little girl was struggling, wanting to hurt herself. She was pulling at her hair, wanting to bang her head, completely frazzled. I had seen Eva do the same more times than I could count. So, before I stopped myself, I asked if there was anything I could do.

'No, it's OK. She's just overwhelmed. I stupidly left my iPad at home.'

'I can help,' I said.

Going back to my table, I picked up my bag, and as I opened it to grab my headphones, I took a deep breath. Here I was, complicit in the serial killer support group yet willingly talking to a detective.

Pulling out my headphones, I went over and handed them to DS Salam. 'Put these on her.'

She did as I said, and I connected them to my phone and

began to play birdsong. The little girl stopped fighting, and within a minute she was sat, cradled in her mother's arms, feeling soothed. Detective Salam looked at me, shock and relief etched into her face.

'I've never had her calm so fast. What is she listening to?' she asked, looking down at her daughter, who was mesmerised by what she heard.

'It's birdsong.'

'Birdsong?'

'Yeah, birds chirping.'

'How did you know it would help?'

'I work with a little girl who is on the spectrum and struggles when overstimulated.'

'You're a life saver.'

'Hardly,' I said.

'Jess, isn't it?'

'Yes,' I said, feeling myself tense up. Maybe I had made a mistake, wanting to help her little girl.

'I shouldn't really be talking to you but—' she continued before being interrupted by James.

'Here you go, ladies,' the barista said, setting down two fresh coffees.

'Oh, sorry, I didn't order another,' I said.

'It's on me, both of them,' he said, first smiling to us, then looking at the little girl, who was daydreaming, her blinks long and sleepy. 'Is she OK?'

'She's fine now. I'm sorry about that.'

'It's OK,' he said, walking away.

'Detective Salam,' I said once he was out of earshot.

'It's Sophie, right now, anyway.'

'You shouldn't apologise to anyone about your daughter's needs.'

'I know, it's just… It's a scene and—'

'It doesn't matter. If people can't see what's happening and understand, that's on them, not you. You and she have nothing to say sorry for. Ever,' I said, fired up by the countless times I'd known I was being judged when Eva was overwhelmed.

'You're right. Thank you, Jess, for helping.'

'It's OK.'

I lingered, unsure what to do. Her daughter was drifting off, and seeing me look, Sophie looked too.

'She's not slept well for days,' she said quietly.

'I'll leave you to it.'

'No, it's OK, sit. My daughter has your stuff after all.'

I hesitated again, wondering if I would slip up if I stayed with the police officer. I didn't know her, but she seemed smart, switched on, a pro at stopping criminals, and I was a complete novice at being one.

'Please? I want to know how you knew how to help,' she said, imploring me with her eyes, and I saw she wasn't a copper at all; she was a tired, overworked, stressed, sad mother. And besides, what I knew, the secret I had been burdened with over the weekend, was just a secret. I was good at keeping them; I had done so for years.

'I'll just get my things.'

Walking back to the table in the window, I grabbed my bag and then rejoined the detective, who was looking down at her daughter in her arms. 'She's asleep,' she said.

'Sounds like she needed it.'

'She did.'

'Looks like you needed it too,' I said, sitting opposite her, thinking of the many times I had seen Jenny looking just like she did. She nodded and looked down at her daughter once more, and I could see her holding back her tears. She then looked up, through me, and I turned to see an older couple looking back. The woman shook her head. I moved my chair, to block their line of sight.

'Hey, don't worry about them.'

'It's just—'

'No, fuck them,' I said.

She laughed quietly, and a tear dropped.

'I don't have my own kids, but working with them, I can empathise with how hard this is. But you're doing OK. Children with autism, they just have meltdowns. It's not because of you.'

'I hope you're right,' she said quietly.

'I am,' I said.

She looked me in the eye and gently nodded before picking up her coffee. I picked up mine too and we both drank.

'So, Salam?' I said, changing the subject. 'It's an unusual surname.'

'It's Indian. My mum is from there; she married an English guy. But I kept her name.'

'I like it,' I said.

'It's unfortunate, you know, the Salem witch trials. Growing up, kids were mean.'

'Hello, my name is Pendle.'

'Oh yeah,' she said, smiling.

For the next twenty minutes we talked about her daughter, Lottie, and I talked about Eva. I shouldn't have named her, but I figured, I was with a detective, so it was safe. We shared some of the challenges, the rewards, the strategies for coping, and I helped her find the soothing sounds playlist her daughter was now listening to in her sleep. As we chatted, I realised that although she was a woman who would, if she knew the truth, arrest me and my friends, I liked her. She was a little like the woman I set out to be, maybe the woman I once was, before Lewis.

After we had finished our coffees, Sophie dared to remove the headphones from her daughter, who slept on, and gave them back to me.

'Jess, thank you for helping today. I was stuck.'

'It's OK,' I said, getting to my feet. 'See you, Detective Salam.'

'See you, Miss Pendle.'

I picked up my things and walked out of the café. On the street once more, I looked back and she nodded, then I made my way home.

I felt bad for Salam. As a woman, she had a lot going on, and I saw she struggled. I didn't ask about her daughter's father; I could sense he wasn't on the scene. But I didn't feel bad about that, nor because her daughter was quite severely autistic. I felt bad because she believed she had figured out the killings, and that the man responsible was out on bail, though no doubt still their prime suspect. I felt bad because in just over twenty-four hours, she would discover she was completely wrong.

Chapter Forty-Five

THE CARETAKER

4th February 2025

Four weeks had passed since Madison, dressed as The Caretaker, had stood outside Martin Goodfellow's house, waiting to follow him and beat him with the same belt he had many a time hurt Hannah with. Four weeks, and so much had changed. She was now complicit in two murders. Two men, bad men, would no longer be able to hurt, to control, to manipulate. She was free from her ex's grasp forever.

It was time for Hannah to be freed also.

Madison didn't need to consult the book as she had before, because she remembered every detail of his routine. Tuesday: work, gym, pub. And sure enough, as she waited in the same place she had four weeks before, Martin kept to his routine. At three minutes past eight, he was out of his front door, on the way to his local to play darts. He walked in the same way as he did before she attacked him, and it told her everything she needed to know. Martin Goodfellow hadn't changed. He was still cocksure, confident; he still believed he was invincible.

As she watched him walk away, she reflected on the last time The Caretaker was there. That night he'd followed Martin, stalked him, until he was alone and down the dark alley that ran alongside the secondary school. And then he pounced and beat him unconscious. And even though he had done it for Hannah, really, it was Jake he had been thinking of.

Madison remembered she'd been unsure of when she would attack that night: before or after he'd been to the pub. She'd opted for before, so there was no chance of alcohol diluting the pain. Now, she knew it had to be after. She needed him at home, where it was quiet, where no one would be able to see. So she didn't move from her hidden spot, but watched as Martin limped down the road towards the pub where he would laugh, drink, and feel like he was 'the man'. When he rounded the corner, she crossed the road and nipped down the side of his house, towards his back garden. The gate wasn't locked, as usual, and closing it quietly behind her, she made for the shed, where she knew a key would be hanging under the roof eave. She removed it from its hook and unlocked his back door, then wiped the key and replaced it. Once she was inside, she could lock the door and wait for him to arrive home. But before she went in, she needed to get ready, so, hiding down the side of the shed, a space she knew was tight but manageable, she pulled off her rucksack, squatted and prepared.

It was the same as what Kelly and Hannah had worn. Overalls, wellies that were five sizes too big, to leave what would look like a man's footprint, gloves, hair inside a hood, and face mask. She taped her cuffs, both wrists and ankles, and then, zipping up her bag, she entered her target's house, locking the door behind her. Madison was no more – not for a while, at least. Now, the man they had created, the amalgamation of all of the bad men in the world, the one they called The Caretaker, was in charge.

Even though there had been extensive research, detailed and lengthy conversations with Hannah about her life with Martin, and the kind of man he was, The Caretaker had no idea what the inside of his house would look like. It was minimalist, clean. Almost proudly so. He wasn't expecting that.

Quietly The Caretaker made his way through the house and up the stairs. There were two bedrooms, the master and the guest room, which doubled as office space. He first walked into the main bedroom and went straight to the wardrobe. Hanging, just as he had been told, was a row of belts. He looked at them all, examining the thickness of leather and the sturdiness of buckle. He looked, not to choose a weapon – he knew, from before, it would take a lot to stop Martin, even more to kill him – but to reaffirm his motivation, his reason. Any number of the belts could have been used against Hannah. Any one of them could have caused her pain.

Leaving the bedroom as he found it, The Caretaker went into the office and, sitting at Martin's desk, waited for the clock to pass eleven and for Martin to come home. As he did, he thought through how he expected the night to play out, and visualised how he would end the life of Martin Goodfellow.

Chapter Forty-Six

Despite all of the planning, all of the preparation, waiting for Martin Goodfellow to return home was the hardest thing The Caretaker had had to do during this campaign. With each passing minute, doubt crept back, the what-ifs loud and strong. What if he didn't come home? What if he knew The Caretaker was there? Maybe Martin Goodfellow had changed, become more wary, and had installed cameras somewhere. What if the police were coming for him? The questions played out so loud, they obscured the vision, the reasons for doing what must be done.

Hour after hour ticked by, until at just after eleven-thirty, The Caretaker heard voices from the street. He wanted to look out of the front window, but stopped himself. Instead, he moved behind the office door, and waited.

A key went into the lock, the door opened, and then two voices were heard.

Two.

The other voice was female.

The Caretaker hadn't planned for his target to have company.

He didn't know what to do. The plan was to wait quietly until Martin went to sleep, and then attack him. He was supposed to be alone. All The Caretaker could do was wait some more, and hope she didn't stay the night.

For over an hour The Caretaker stood behind the office door, listening as Martin and the woman talked, laughed and then fell into silence, punctuated by the odd quiet moan. She expected them to come up to Martin's bedroom, but fortunately they did the deed down in the living room instead. The Caretaker had to listen as he climaxed, noting how she hadn't, and then another twenty minutes passed before the front door opened again.

She was leaving.

The plan was back on.

The Caretaker listened as Martin's deep voice mumbled something to the woman, she replied, and then the door closed. Footsteps clipped down the street, then faded into nothing.

Straining to refocus his ear on the inside of the house, The Caretaker heard a tap run in the kitchen, followed by steps coming upstairs. He held his breath and prayed Martin wouldn't find a need to come into the office. Thankfully, he heard him enter the bathroom and then the sound of an electric toothbrush. He wanted to ready himself, to act, but stopped himself. He needed to be patient, to see it through the way the whole serial killer support group had planned.

Martin Goodfellow was a beater, but more than that, he enjoyed creating fear in Hannah. Sometimes he would wake her up forcefully to have his way, whether she liked it or not. Hannah spoke of how he once woke her by hitting her, because she had embarrassed him in public. She hadn't agreed with something he'd said amongst friends about immigration in the

UK, because his views were bordering on extreme, and even though she was afraid of him she hadn't wanted people to think they were her views too. For retribution, he'd struck her with his belt whilst she dreamed.

When Hannah told that story in session, it was hard to not be shocked, angered and afraid.

Martin would know the fear he had caused, the pain he'd inflicted. So The Caretaker had to wait for silence to fall over the house. Martin needed to be asleep when the first blow came.

The toothbrush stopped and then The Caretaker listened as he urinated. He didn't flush, he didn't wash his hands, and then he walked into his bedroom. Silence came quickly. And then, fifteen minutes later, The Caretaker could hear Martin's gentle snores.

It was time.

Chapter Forty-Seven

The Caretaker moved from behind the door, rolling his ankles to help the blood return to his feet from standing still for so long. He moved onto the landing, and then, slowly, padded in the direction of Martin's room. Daring to look, he saw his target in a state of catatonia, face-down, spread-eagled, wearing only his underwear. The Caretaker could tell he wouldn't wake, but to be sure, he stepped back out of sight before removing his rucksack.

Slowly he unzipped it and pulled out the two items he would use. And then, leaving the bag on the floor, he prepared to bring long overdue justice.

On a dark alley on a Tuesday night a month before, a belt had hurt this man, but what The Caretaker held in each hand was heavier than a belt. What he held wouldn't hurt; it would kill.

Gripping the handles of each hammer, knuckles white, The Caretaker stood over his prey, who was snoring deeply, oblivious of what was about to happen. The Caretaker felt his heart rate increase, the adrenalin and anxiety peaking so high his hands felt numb. But he knew he wouldn't back down, not now. This man had hurt someone he had come to love. He had scarred her for life. He needed to pay.

Raising the hammer in her left hand high above her head, Madison forgot for a moment where she was and who she was being. This man, this man she hated, just as much as she hated Jake, her Jake, who had to die because he was as he was. She'd wanted to help him, to change him, to show him that she was loyal and loving and everything a good man could want, but he wouldn't listen, and now the man she had imagined in her life for ever, the man who was her son's father, was dead. The grief and rage took over, and as she fought to stop herself crying, she focused on the middle of her target's back, right between the shoulder blades. Then, blinking away a tear, she swung down hard as she could.

The hammer missed its mark but still caught him square on the shoulder blade, and a half gasp, half cry came from Martin's mouth as he was violently jolted into consciousness. He tried to move, his body trying to help him escape. But the hammer had wreaked havoc, and Madison was sure the blow had both broken his shoulder, and perhaps, because of the way he was breathing, punctured his lung.

Martin instinctively rolled away from the attack and fell onto the floor, a strange glugging noise coming from his mouth. When he rolled over, Madison enjoyed the whites of his eyes glaring back at the image of his attacker, dressed in a hazmat suit, wielding two hammers. Only her eyes visible, but they told Martin all he needed to know. Tonight, he was going to die. She had no doubt. The whites of Hannah's eyes had glared many times before, and she had no doubt hers had too, and she felt her rage morph into something else, a red quiet, as silent and calm as fog.

'Please. Don't,' Martin begged, his voice small and wheezy. He struggled to speak, which told her two things: his lung had indeed been punctured, as she thought, and he didn't have the strength to cry out.

'Too late for that, Martin,' she said, enjoying the flash of confusion that danced across his face at hearing that The Caretaker was a softly spoken woman.

'Why are you doing this?' he said, trying to move away from her, but in his state of shock, all he did was squeeze himself further into the space between his bed and the window. The tight space that would be his coffin. 'I-I can change,' he said, but Madison didn't hear his words; all she saw was her ex, lying there, and she needed him to pay. Her mind left for somewhere else, a quiet space that was safe, as her body took over, and unconscious of what she was doing, she raised the hammer in her right hand.

'Please, please,' Martin gasped, but it was too late, and she swung the hammer. He tried to defend himself by raising his left arm, and the hammer impacted with it. The cast from his surgery a month before exploded and something snapped. His forearm and hand flopped as if broken. Madison impassively swung the left hammer, and Martin again tried to defend himself. This time it hit his hand, pushing it back into his face with such force that his nose shattered. She swung the right again, catching him on the collarbone, and white bone punched through his skin. The left caught him in the ribs, the thud echoing around the room. The right, the jaw. He spat out teeth so hard they hit the radiator under the window, the sound like pebbles being dropped on a stony beach.

Then, in a daze, Madison unlocked herself from that safe space in her mind and came back into the present. She was panting, and both hammers were covered in blood, as was the front of her hazmat suit. She looked down to see what she had done. Martin was broken, bone and blood leaking everywhere. But, to her surprise, he still had fight in him, and although his face was swinging like the pendulum of a grandfather clock, because his jaw was so badly smashed that it had detached at his ear, he tried to struggle, to survive. Madison took a small step back so Martin couldn't reach her, and looked at him. He must have known death was close – both lungs were damaged badly, and he could barely breathe – but still he tried to retaliate. As blood from his unhinged jaw poured onto the floor, he tried to speak, but all that came out of his mouth was a wheezing guttural noise. Something no longer human.

He tried to sit up and then fell onto his left side.

Madison, blinded by hot tears of rage and vengeance, stepped towards him and raised the hammer once more, this time with the claw facing her target.

'Fuck you, Jake,' she spat, and Martin, even close to dying, looked confused, the whites of his eyes so large she was sure they would pop out. She swung. It struck him on the bone above his eye, and the claw buried itself deep in his face, penetrating downward so that it smashed through the roof of his mouth and into the void where his jaw once sat. She pulled it free, tearing out a chunk of bone and eye from, and staggered back.

She caught her breath, and before she allowed herself to absorb what she had just done, pulled the scalpel out of her pocket, unsheathed it and left the mark on his heart, a cross because he had broken someone else's. Then she pulled out her phone and recorded the video, relaying in a neutral voice the message she knew everyone would hear. Then she saved it, ready to edit later.

Madison looked at the mess that was once her friend's abuser. His twisted body, the epitome of violence.

Then she cried.

Chapter Forty-Eight

JESS

5th February 2025

Knowing what was happening, I couldn't sleep. I paced to the soundtrack of BBC News 24 in the living room: looping stories over and over about a flood in India, the cost-of-living crisis that was now sweeping North America, a rigged election somewhere in the Far East. Every hour, it reset and retold, over and over, endlessly presenting loss and fear and doom. I thought about Madison a lot, wondering how she must be feeling, doing what had to be done. I worried she would be caught, or something had gone wrong, and the hours dragged slowly. Then, at just after four in the morning, the news had something fresh to say, and as the loop had been broken, it lifted me from my tired state.

An update was coming in.

There had been another murder.

Picking up my phone, I jumped online. The news would only show so much; somewhere The Caretaker's video was out there. It didn't take me long to see it. The Caretaker, or rather

Madison, looking down the lens of a camera, her face covered. And behind, the body of Hannah's ex. The state he was in made me feel sick to my stomach. He hadn't just been killed – Madison had destroyed him.

Turning up the volume on the side of my phone, so I could hear everything she said, I listened. Her voice was so distorted it didn't sound like Madison; it didn't sound like a woman at all.

'There has been talk of me being a bad man, an evil man, but I am not. The thing that is bad, the thing that is evil, is a world where victims are punished instead of those who wrong them. Women who speak up against violence must be protected by those who pass laws, by those who are paid to keep the community safe. If anyone is to blame for what I have done, it is those. I am not the one who is wrong; I am the one who is turning a wrong right again. As you can see behind me, another man has paid for his crimes. A man who beat and called it love. A man who had been warned and failed to change. The police have the wrong man under suspicion. The ex-soldier has nothing to do with what I am doing, and I haven't finished yet. Not until those things that are wrong are made right. Not until the change needed is realised.

'You men out there, who hurt and call it love, who lie and call it protection – do not turn your back, because I might be there, waiting for you.'

Locking my phone, I sat on the edge of my sofa in a state of shock. Despite knowing about the serial killer support group, and that my friends had killed twice before, I still couldn't believe Madison had done what she had done. The effort it must have taken to see it through, the images that would haunt her for ever – I couldn't get my head around it all. I wanted to talk to someone, Kelly or Hannah, especially Hannah, to make sure she was OK. But it was the middle of the night, and I suspected everyone would be asleep.

I was wrong, for my phone pinged in my hand, and I was shocked to see a new message in the support group chat. I was even more shocked that the message was from Madison herself.

My hands shaking, I opened the thread.

Chapter Forty-Nine

SUPPORT GROUP CHAT

MADISON 4.17AM

Ladies, I'm sorry it's so late, my little one woke up and I've just seen on the news there has been another killing.

😦 3

KELLY 4.19AM

Hey. I'm up too, I've just seen it. Jesus.

VIJA 4.19AM

You mean it's not Geoff?

KELLY 4.19AM

That's what he said

😦😢 3

CLAIRE 4.22AM

Shit! I've just seen the video.

RACHEL 4.22AM

Where?

The Serial Killer Support Group

CLAIRE 4.22AM

TikTok. Search #TheCaretakerkiller.

RACHEL 4.22AM

I can't find anything.

KELLY 4.24AM

It's been removed already. Did anyone see who it was? Is it someone linked to us.

MADISON 4.24AM

Yeah, I saw. I think it was Hannah's ex.

😢 4

RACHEL 4.25AM

Shit, another one connected to us? Who is doing this?

KELLY 4.25AM

I don't know.

KELLY 7.04AM

Guys, Becky just called me, she thinks we need to call off this week's session.

RACHEL 7.17AM

What?

CLAIRE 7.18AM

No way. I need this more than ever. I am freaking out about all this, I can barely sleep.

RACHEL 7.18AM

Same, I already have nightmares, they are really bad at the moment.

VIJA 7.18AM

But it will be a circus. Maybe we could meet elsewhere? Thoughts?

JESS 7.19AM

I need it too. Good idea.

KELLY 7.19AM

OK. I'll put it to Becky. Hopefully see you Friday?

MADISON 7.20AM

Has anyone rung Hannah?

KELLY 7.20AM

I'll do it now. Ladies, it might be a good idea if we stop using this chat, just until they work out what's happening.

👍😢🖤 4

VIJA 7.20AM

You mean this group is being disbanded?

KELLY 7.20AM

No, just quietened. We still have each other's numbers, we can still call. I'm here for all of you.

CLAIRE 7.22AM

Same.

MADISON 7.22AM

Ditto

RACHEL 7.29AM

🖤

JESS 7.29AM

🖤

Chapter Fifty

SOPHIE SALAM

Sophie stretched, her body stirring into wakefulness, and then, with a jolt, she shot up and looked at the time. It was just after seven thirty, and she couldn't hear Lottie. The house felt completely still. Like she was gone. She jumped out of bed, panic flooding her bloodstream, wondering if the thing she had feared all these years had come true, that somehow Lottie's father knew she existed. She raced towards her daughter's room, only to see she was still asleep. She smiled, took a deep breath, silently berated herself for being so paranoid and backed away, returning to her own room.

Lottie had settled well, and in her own bed. It was the first time she had managed to do either in weeks. And the only explanation Sophie could find was the calming sounds of nature that Jess Pendle had shown her in the coffee shop. The sounds had played on the Alexa in the living room the whole evening, and then again in Lottie's room whilst she got ready for bed. It might not last – Lottie might desensitise to it – but for one blissful night both mother and daughter had slept.

Putting on her dressing gown, Sophie padded quietly past

Lottie's room, checking in once more. Downstairs, she made a coffee and then stood by the kitchen window, watching the winter morning. The wind was blustery, bending branches of the dead trees at the back of her garden, and there were a few signs of life, like a white dove sitting on the back fence, its feathers buffed by the wind. Sophie often saw doves – there must be a nest nearby – but she couldn't remember the last time she had had the time to look at one properly. The white of its plumage was crisp, highlighted against the greys and browns of the rest of the world. She understood why it was a symbol of hope. It was too pure to be anything else.

Behind her, the front door opened and Daya walked in. Sophie raised a finger to her lips, and Ma understood. She closed the door quietly and made her way into the kitchen. Sophie looked outside again. The dove was gone.

'Hey, was it a rough night?' Daya asked.

'No, the opposite. She went to bed just after nine, and she's still asleep now.'

'She slept through?'

'Not a peep, and in her own bed too,' Sophie said, grabbing a mug and switching on the kettle again so Daya could have a coffee.

'Did you drug her?'

'Very funny, Ma.'

As the kettle popped, Sophie heard footsteps above, and a minute later, Lottie walked into the kitchen.

'Morning, lovely,' Sophie said, giving her daughter a squeeze and a kiss on the head.

'Morning, Mama,' Lottie said, wriggling free and taking her usual seat at the kitchen table. Sophie made her some cereal and poured an orange juice, and Lottie ate like it was any other morning.

The Serial Killer Support Group

'She looks so chilled,' Daya said, leaning in to kiss her granddaughter on her head.

'I was introduced to a new way to help her stay calm. Nature sounds.'

'Nature sounds?'

'Honestly, Ma, it might be a game-changer.'

'How did you stumble on this?'

'A stranger helped me in a café,' Sophie said, wondering how she would go about thanking Jess without using her information, obtained by the police, for personal use.

With Lottie eating, and Daya sat opposite talking about her morning, Sophie left them and went upstairs to get ready for work. It was refreshing not to wake up thinking about the case she was working on, but it was time to focus, so, as she showered, brushed her teeth, dressed and applied a little makeup, she thought about the double murder, and about Geoff, who had been released pending investigation. Her day would consist of digging further, trying to find the smoking gun so they could charge him.

As she dressed, she turned on her mobile phone, and within seconds messages began to ping. Clarke had tried to call and then followed up with texts. She had a voice message, and she knew what it would say.

'Sophie, there's been another kill, same mark cut into the chest. The ex-soldier we have been watching all this time, it's not him. He's in Scotland with his daughters. It's been confirmed by Edinburgh police. We are looking at the wrong man. He sent another video, uploading from an unknown source onto YouTube, Facebook, TikTok. It's getting removed now, but you know how these things are. They have no doubt been downloaded onto a million private servers and will find their way back. I'll send it to you now.'

Sophie stood dumbstruck for a moment. The wrong man? They'd been so sure. He had the skill, opportunity, information, motivation. If it wasn't the ex-soldier, then who the hell was doing this?

Picking up her TV remote, she turned on the news and saw that the case was out there, a crowd gathered around a house, police tape outside, just as before. Reporters mingled, hoping for something. All of that she expected. What she wasn't expecting, what worried her the most, was the small crowd that had gathered, one of whom held a sign for the camera to see. It read, 'Hey, caretaker, wanna help me?'

A serial killer was out there, and he was becoming a celebrity. Again, she thought of the case in Peterborough a few years back: The Host, and his game, and the players, and how bad things had got. The legacy of those days lingered. His message and ideology were still being discussed. Serial killers once left calling cards, clues to tease those investigating; now, they were profiling publicly, with agendas and statements and ideologies and a platform to be heard. The Caretaker, whoever he was, believed that what he was doing needed a large audience, and conversations around it. But, with murder at the heart of it all, those conversations would quickly turn to violence. She could already see that some, like the woman holding the placard, would agree, and some would not. The court of public opinion was not a good place.

Chaos would come, unless they stopped it, and stopped it now.

Turning off the TV, she opened the message from Clarke with a video attached. When she saw the scene, it shocked even her. The other kills had been brutal, cruel, yes, but nowhere near as blatantly violent. This one was different. Their killer's modus operandi was changing.

And she knew that could not be good.

Running downstairs, she kissed Lottie goodbye and, as soon as she was out of the front door, was on the phone to Clarke.

'I wondered when you would see my messages,' he said.

'Is the body with you?'

'I'm just processing him now. This one is a mess.'

'I saw. You're sure it's the same killer?'

'The cross is there on his chest. That information hasn't been released. I'm sure it's the same guy. Also, Sophie, you were right, the belt attack is linked.'

'How do you know?'

'Because the man on the slab with me right now is Martin Goodfellow.'

'The belt man?

'Yep, the belt man.'

'Shit. I'm on my way into the office. Ring me if you have something.'

Chapter Fifty-One

The drive to the office was agonising. They were so sure that the ex-soldier was their man that even Sophie had felt confident they had stopped what was happening. But with the new murder and the world knowing, and their soldier being hundreds of miles away in Scotland with his daughters and therefore, clearly not The Caretaker, everything had changed. Not only would the police look incompetent, but public interest would be fuelled by The Caretaker's ability to escape capture. The conversations would deepen. Is he good? Is he evil? The opposing camps would fracture further. There would be chaos. A shit storm.

Arriving at the office, Sophie walked into the beginnings of that shit storm. Every available officer, detective, even Police Community Support Officers was at the station, and everyone was looking for the same answers. She sat at her desk and got to work. First, she looked at the details of the assault she had investigated a month before. The man had been assaulted on the way to the pub, beaten with his own belt. She saw she had circled that detail in her files. Then she read what was known about his murder. Blunt force trauma was the cause; he had sustained horrific injuries to his arm, hand, ribs, back, jaw and skull. Beaten to death, just as he'd been beaten unconscious that night in early January.

She dug deeper into the life of Martin Goodfellow, looking at his social media presence, his family tree. She dug up the phone numbers of his brother and mum. Then, while scrolling on his Instagram, she saw a post from the summer before. He was standing in a pub garden somewhere, his arm around a woman Sophie recognised.

She hovered over the picture, and another account was tagged. She clicked on it to see it was for a woman named Hannah S. The account was private, so, going back to Facebook, she looked at his friends list and saw there was a Hannah Smith.

She knew the face and she knew the name. She had written it down within the last couple of weeks. With that familiar feeling of excitement when she was on to something, she looked through her notes, flicking through the pages until she saw Hannah Smith's name.

'Oh, shit.'

Hannah Smith was listed as one of the women from the support group.

On the same page was a number for Becky, the woman who ran the group, and punching in the number, Sophie rang.

'Hello?' Becky said when she picked up.

'Hello, Becky, it's DS Salam.'

'I wondered when you would call.'

'You did?'

'Yeah, I've seen the news. I know the victim. It's the ex-partner of one of my clients.'

'Yes, it seems so.'

'Did Geoff do this?' she asked, her voice close to cracking. 'I haven't heard from him, no one has. He's completely disappeared.'

'I cannot comment on that at this stage, but I was wondering, could I ask, do you keep a record of users of your group?'

'Of course. I've got the name of every man and woman I have helped in the last three years, since we got our funding. I have to, GDPR and all that.'

'Sorry, men?' Sophie said, and then heard Becky sigh at the other end.

'Yes, men. Most of the people I help are women, but I have worked with lots of men too. I have a session before the one you have visited, for men in the area.'

'I didn't know,' Sophie said, cursing herself for being so sure it was the ex-soldier that she hadn't thought to look.

'I guess at least one of my groups is discreet,' Becky continued. 'The men only account for just under five per cent of the total reported cases, but it's likely to be higher. Men just don't talk.'

Sophie sat for a moment, processing what she was learning. They had looked at Geoff, acting on the assumption he was the only male attached to these women.

'Becky, these men you've worked with, do any of them know the current members of the women's group?'

'Yeah, a few.'

'Can I get their names?'

'Sure, but I don't think any of them are involved. These men are so fragile.'

'Please,' Sophie said. 'I must insist.'

Becky sighed again. 'What's your email? I'm in the office shortly. I'll get them sent.'

'Thank you.'

After giving her email, she hung up and sat back. They had been right to assume the killer was connected. Martin Goodfellow being the latest victim was confirmation. They had just been looking in the wrong direction. It wasn't the ex-soldier; it was a support group user. It made sense – who would have more opportunity, information or motivation than a man who had been a victim too? He would know everything about the other women in the group. He would empathise with their struggles. Becky said they were fragile and Sophie knew fragile people broke.

She had to rethink completely what she would do next. Now, in order to identify the serial killer calling himself The Caretaker, she would not only have to find that man but also watch the women of the support group, because one of them had to have a suspicion, a gut feeling as to who was killing on their behalf. Maybe, she speculated, they even knew. Maybe they not only knew the killer but had planned it with him. Maybe this was bigger than just one person's fight for what they deemed to be justice.

The idea scared her.

As she waited for the email from Becky, Sophie looked up Hannah Smith and discovered a police file about an alleged assault. As she read the details and looked at the photos, she realised there was nothing alleged about it. Martin had beaten her black and blue.

And he had been beaten in return.

'It's linked. It has to be,' she said to herself. She read on and discovered that despite the overwhelming evidence, Martin was never charged for the attack. She wanted to know why.

Twenty minutes after the call with Becky, a new email landed in her inbox: a list of every person the support group had worked with, ninety-three in total. Seven of them were men. Seven clients who had also survived domestic abuse, seven who understood the trauma of the three women whose ex-partners were now dead, because they shared it. She began working on learning everything she could about them and every other member of the support group.

One of them, past or present, knew the truth. One of them was the killer, and she would stop at nothing to find them, and bring them to justice before it all went to shit.

As she began to dig on the seven men on her list, a message pinged. It was Clarke, inviting her down to the mortuary.

Sophie didn't look at Clarke when she got there. Her eyes were fixed on the body lying on the slab.

'Jesus.'

'Yep,' Clarke said.

Sophie had seen many dead bodies in her career, so many that when they were on the slab, they were no longer people at all; they were relegated to a puzzle, a story. She was not concerned with their souls, or their emotional state in their final moments. She knew that to survive the job you had to leave your humanity at the door, in order to solve the crimes and give the victims the justice they deserved. However, Goodfellow, or what was left of him, made her feel a little sick. The violence required, the trauma, were hard to imagine, even for her.

She needed a break. Badly.

She could tell that Clarke felt it too. He wasn't his usual chipper self when cleaning and processing the body; he was slower, even more methodical, his brow furrowed pensively. She didn't interrupt, but waited patiently for him to look up and smile at her.

'Can you tell me anything?'

'Nothing you can't see. The Caretaker did a number on this man.'

'Yeah,' she replied. 'Seems more frantic?'

'I don't get it. The first, with the potassium chloride. It was so controlled. So meticulous. So was the bee, that was clever, considered. This kill…'

'Looks like rage.'

'The Caretaker was angry, so angry. It's like it was a different man altogether.'

'That scares me,' Sophie said.

'Why?'

'Because he is becoming unpredictable. It's hard to stop someone who doesn't know themselves, their next step. Clarke, you still understand what The Caretaker is doing here?'

'I did. Now, I'm not so sure. You?'

'Same. People are starting to like him.'

'Yep. Our killer is becoming a hero.'

'And that scares me too,' Sophie said.

Chapter Fifty-Two

Jess

After we all agreed that we needed to have a break from the support group chat on WhatsApp and that we still should carry on meeting but at a different location, I expected things to go quiet, and, just in case, I went about my day like it was any other day. I worked with Will and Eva, did the food shop, then prepared myself for a long, quiet night alone watching TV. However, as I limped on with my day, a message came from Kelly. It was a chat with me, her, Hannah and Madison. Her message was direct and revealed nothing.

KELLY

> I don't know about you, but I could do with a drink this evening?

I messaged saying I was up for it. Madison did too, and Kelly came back saying to meet at hers. She told me to bring gym wear. I didn't know why, but agreed.

Hannah replied saying she was with her mum still, taking in the shock, and we asked if she was OK. From the outside, it

Chapter Fifty-Two

looked like we were just a group of friends surviving a complex situation. There was nothing to suggest anything sinister, nothing to show we knew more than we were letting on. And I understood why Kelly created the chat and wanted to go out. People were looking for a killer and would assume he would be hiding, but by being out, ironically, we would become invisible. We were hiding in plain sight.

So instead of donning my hoodie and slippers, I dressed in gym wear and packed a pair of jeans – another pair Lewis hated me in – and a black top. I opted for pumps instead of heels like I wore on the night out with the girls, the night before I knew anything of the serial killer support group. Appraising myself in the mirror, for the first time in a very long time, I liked the woman who looked back. She was damaged – the scar on her face would always be a reminder of that – but she was healing. Perhaps not in the light, but it was there, in the distance, the darkness not quite so complete. I didn't hate my reflection anymore. I liked the woman looking back, if only a little.

Despite my flicker of self-confidence, I wasn't sure walking alone at night was a good idea, even knowing who I knew, so I rang for an Uber, which dropped me at Kelly's front door.

'Come in,' she said, giving me a hug and welcoming me in.

'Kelly, why am I in gym wear?'

'You'll see. Follow me.'

Kelly led me through her impressive house, through the room where I learned the truth of who The Caretaker was, and then out the back of the house to another building. When we stepped in, I was surprised to see several gym machines, a bench for lifting weights and a treadmill, which Madison was running on. She gave me a smile, one that didn't reach her eyes.

'Are we not going out?' I asked.

'Yeah, but we tend to work out first.'

'Why?'

'To stay strong,' she replied matter-of-factly. 'What do you wanna do first?'

'Me?' I said.

'Yep.'

'I-I don't know.'

'OK, let's get a base of where you are.'

'OK?' I replied, not really knowing what she meant.

She told me to sit down in front of a lat pulldown, and, moving the pin to 10kg, she told me to do eight reps. I did, still in a state of shock.

'How was that?'

'Fine.'

'OK, so, I want you to add a weight, keep going until eight is impossible.'

I nodded, moved the pin down one weight and repeated. And I did so until, at 40kg, I failed to get past six. I stopped, my brow sweating.

'You're strong,' Kelly said.

'Am I?'

'Ummmm, yeah.'

I stood up, my arms and shoulders aching, but with the kind of ache that made me feel good. 'What's next?' I asked.

Kelly and I worked out together for another hour. The whole time Madison ran, listening to music, unable to look at us, and I knew why. After what she had done, I'd want to run too. Afterwards, we took turns to shower and, feeling stronger, we left for the pub. It was busy for a Wednesday, and as I helped

Chapter Fifty-Two

Madison to find a table, Kelly went to the bar, returning five minutes later with three drinks.

'I got you a vodka and Coke.'

'Thanks.'

Kelly handed me my drink then put a rosé in front of Madison. Sitting at the round table, she raised her glass. I followed and Madison did too. We didn't speak when we clinked. We didn't need to; we all knew what we were toasting. We disposed of our first drink quickly and, without asking, Kelly went to the bar and returned with three more. We didn't drain the second but sat quietly sipping, three still beings amidst a swirl of noise and movement. We made small talk, mostly about how Kelly would host the next group at hers, as she had the space. We didn't talk of what had happened, didn't speak of what Madison had done. But, every now and then, I would reach over and take her hand, give her a reassuring smile. Kelly did the same, and I saw Madison relax a little. Killing someone must strip something away from a person's soul. For her, as for Kelly and Hannah before, everything had changed. I understood that, even if I didn't understand exactly how. And it was important for her to know she was still Madison, still our friend, still a good mother.

When I saw the drinks were getting low, I got up to buy the next round, and as I approached the bar, I looked along the counter. A couple sat close, whispering to one another amongst the noise of drunk, laughing, playful people enjoying a midweek blowout. Further along the bar, past two older men who clearly always sat on the same stools, no doubt talking about the same things on a loop, I saw a face I recognised. It took me a moment to place him, but when I did, I looked away. He looked so different out of his uniform, but there was no mistaking him. In the same bar as us, the same bar as three quarters of the serial killer support group, was one of the investigating officers in the case. A man who had nothing but disdain for us. A man who had stood in my flat and as good as blamed me for Lewis not leaving me alone. Drinking and laughing, without a care in the world, sat DS Jones.

Chapter Fifty-Three

Seeing DS Jones in the same bar made me feel a sharp jolt of panic. Salam in the coffee shop was one thing, but his being there made it all feel too close. He had been in my flat; he knew my story, even if he didn't give a shit about it. I didn't want him to see me. Sometimes hiding in plain sight was the right way, but sometimes it was just better to hide. I turned my back to him, so he didn't see my face, and paying for the drinks, I quickly went back to the table.

'You OK, Jess?' Kelly asked when I put the drinks down.

'That copper who was there when Geoff was arrested is at the bar. I'm sure it's him.'

Kelly looked over her glass, discreetly, then looked back to me. 'Yeah. It's him.'

Madison looked, and fear flashed across her face. Kelly reached out and took her hand. 'Hey, it's OK.'

'You think—' I started, but Kelly stopped me.

'No, no, he's just having a night off. It's just a coincidence.'

'You sure?'

'Yeah. It's fine. We're OK,' she said. 'God, I fucking hate that man.'

'Me too,' I said. 'And not just for Geoff either. He was the copper who came to my house when I called the police about Lewis breaking in. He did nothing. He was almost pissed off at me for wasting his time.'

Madison turned in her chair and looked at him, then turned back. 'He was the one I first spoke to about what Jake was doing to me. He scares me a bit,' she said, her voice barely audible.

I looked from her to Kelly, who was watching him again, the hatred in her eyes palpable.

'Kel?'

'He was the copper I spoke with when Duncan first attacked me too. And Baheela has said the same.'

'Four of us have dealt with him,' I said.

'And four of us have had no help.'

'Maybe he's just a shit copper?' I said, but Kelly shook her head.

'I'm not so sure. Look.'

I turned in my chair and we watched him across the bar. He was talking to the woman he was with, just like other couples were talking, but the way he leant in, the way he had his hand clamped on the back of her neck, the way she sat as he spoke – I knew that posture. So did Kelly. Madison too.

'Are you seeing this?' Kelly said, not blinking.

'Yeah,' I said.

'Ladies, I think I've just realised why this man failed to help us as he should.'

'No, you think?' I began.

'Look at her. Who does she remind you of?'

'Us,' I said. 'She reminds me of us, when we were with our exes.'

'Yep.'

'What do we do?'

'Let's finish this drink, then, Madison, you go home and get some sleep.'

'OK,' Madison said, slowly nodding, a tear falling from her eye.

'Jess, how do you fancy playing a little game of detective with a detective?'

I looked around at him again, watched as he laughed at his own joke, watched her flinch because of the sudden raucous outburst, and then, turning, I nodded at Kelly.

'Sounds like fun,' I said.

Chapter Fifty-Four

Madison finished her drink and, taking Kelly's advice, she hugged us goodbye without saying a word and left. She was dead on her feet, but I thought she was courageous for managing to make it out at all after the night she'd had. Being The Caretaker was a necessity, but I knew she would be irreparably damaged by it. The image of Martin flashed into my mind. How did anyone come back from doing that? Once she was gone, careful to avoid Jones, who was getting louder and more pissed, I turned to Kelly.

'Think she'll be OK?'

'Yeah, it's rough, I cannot lie. I'm having nightmares – Hannah is too – but it does get a little easier. In time I know sh —' She stopped mid-word. 'He's leaving.'

I turned and saw DS Jones, his arm tightly around his partner, head for the door. He released her to walk through, letting the door swing back into her.

'Shall we?' I said.

Putting on our coats, we drained our drinks and, with the warmth of the alcohol in my bloodstream moving me forward like steam through a locomotive, we walked through the gaggle of people and outside into the night air.

The cold slapped me hard, making me wobble more, and I could see Kelly felt the impact too.

'We need to be careful,' she said, as if reading my mind. We were drunk and following a police officer. I wasn't sure it was a good idea at the best of times. We were members of the serial killer support group – it could easily go wrong. I almost said as much to Kelly but, as I opened my mouth to speak, I thought about the way Jones's partner had sat. The way she'd flinched when he'd laughed, instinctively expecting a blow, the way she followed him out of the bar, even though he didn't give a shit. I was that woman; Kelly was too, and Madison and Hannah and everyone else in the support group. And this copper, he had failed us. He hadn't done a goddamn thing when I'd told him about Lewis being in my house. He hadn't helped Kelly, or Madison, or Baheela. How many others had he failed? How many people could have seen justice, felt safe, felt like they could get their lives back, if he'd done his job? It could be dismissed – he was just a shit police officer – but from the way he behaved with his own partner I knew that wasn't true.

As we walked, we made sure to keep him at a safe distance, so he didn't catch on to us following. If he did for some reason look back, Kelly and I had our arms linked, to look like anything but two women stalking. Thankfully, it wasn't an issue. He was drunk, loud and oblivious of us. His partner was always a few steps behind him, trying to keep up.

For ten minutes we followed, turning left and right until the main road had been replaced by modern suburbia: matching new-build houses, functional, pleasant but devoid of personality. Eventually, he and his partner turned onto a path that led to a front door, and as he fumbled with his keys, Kelly and I walked on. As we passed, his partner looked at us, her eyes heavy, tired. I knew those eyes; I had seen them a thousand times in the mirror looking back at me. I had those eyes on New Year's Eve, and I knew how that woman in the hospital, that mother with the little girl who had burned her arm, understood my secrets. You can hide almost anything, lie about almost everything, but eyes always showed the truth. Especially if you are someone who has the same burdens to carry.

We heard the front door open and then seconds later slam shut.

We stopped walking.

'Follow me,' Kelly said, and she turned back and quickly headed towards his house, then swung left and up to a garden gate. She twisted the iron ring handle, and it opened.

'Bingo,' she whispered.

We ducked into the garden, quietly closing the gate behind us, and between the wall of the house and the fence, we were perfectly hidden.

'Kel? What are we doing?'

'I wanna know for sure.'

She didn't wait, but moved along the side of the house, keeping low, placing one foot in front of the other noiselessly, until we were at the back. I kept up, anxious that we would be seen. But I trusted Kelly; she was the driving force here, and I knew I was in good hands. She first looked, then stepped into the back garden and moved towards a window. From inside, we could hear voices and, keeping low, we moved closer.

'...Pete, you're drunk, let's talk about this tomorrow.'

'No, don't deny it, I saw the way you looked at that man.'

'I didn't, I swear, Pete, please.'

'Don't lie to me, you bitch.'

We heard a thud, followed by silence, then the faintest of

cries. Looking at Kelly, I could see she had the same thought as me. I wanted to go in, help that woman, but knew I couldn't. Moments later, a door slammed somewhere upstairs, and Kelly and I began to move again, to leave. We had seen enough. I dared to look into the house. There on the floor, sobbing into her hands, was the woman, and for a moment I thought I was looking at me.

Kelly and I walked in silence until his road was so far behind us, I knew it was safe.

'He is supposed to be a good guy,' I said.

'Yeah, yeah he is.'

'How is he getting away with it?'

'Because the system is fucked.'

'Kelly, what do we do now we know?'

'I don't know,' she said. 'But we have to help her, don't you think?'

'We can't go after a copper.'

'No, we can't. But maybe we could let him know we know, somehow.'

'How?'

'I'm not sure,' Kelly said. 'But we can't just do nothing. He's a copper; he's more above the law than Martin or Duncan or Lewis.'

'I didn't realise at first, but it's obvious. You know who DS Jones reminds me of?' I said.

'Who?'

'Lewis. He's just like Lewis. We need to stop him, a copper. This is so fucked up!'

'Yeah, it is.'

'But then, he is like Lewis, and for too long he has got away with it.'

'What are you thinking?' Kelly asked.

'Fuck it, even if he is a police officer, he needs to be stopped.'

'You're finally there,' Kelly said with a smile.

'There?' I asked.

'Where I got to, and Madison, and Hannah. You're done. You aren't afraid to be afraid anymore.'

I thought about it. I was still scared of these men. Terrified of Lewis. But I was also able to follow one home. Think about challenging him. Yes, I was scared, but being scared no longer terrified me.

'Yeah, I'm there,' I said.

Chapter Fifty-Five

7th February 2025

Almost a week had passed since I'd sat in Kelly's massive hosting room and learned the truth about the serial killer support group. And still I hadn't fully absorbed it. I knew my friends were doing what they were doing – I wasn't under an illusion that it was all a mistake somehow – but in my head it still refused to feel real. It was like the whole thing was a TV series I was binge watching, one that I had absorbed into my real life. But the news wasn't lying when it spoke of three separate murders, all linked by a man calling himself The Caretaker. And the news wasn't local anymore; every outlet I could find, every tabloid paper had an image of him – or rather Madison, or Hannah, I couldn't tell – on their pages and screens. It was creating many conversations, people voicing their opinions about whether The Caretaker was a good person, bringing justice to those who needed it, or the very face of evil. And the results were in the balance. The whole country seemed divided on the subject. It was discussed on every daytime chat show, in every paper, on every online forum. It wasn't just that; ever since the second video had been posted, all of us had had hundreds of friend requests on our Facebook, and Madison's Instagram had over three thousand new followers. It seemed that what the Caretaker was doing was making us a talking point too. She had messages, some kind, offering support, some asking her what made her special. I had gained followers too, but as my name wasn't linked to a murder, I was left alone.

The video Madison had posted, raging about the lack of justice and the lengths she had had to go to, was everywhere. I had no doubt the police wanted it to vanish, as it was creating so much tension between the pro and con camps, but it simply wouldn't go away. It was like a virus, spreading, growing – who knew where it might end up? Some spoke of being afraid to leave the house, placing themselves in a self-imposed lockdown. But I knew, if they were good people, if they didn't abuse their partners, then they had nothing to worry about.

I wondered if DS Jones was afraid.

And amongst all of the talk of The Caretaker's identity and his ideology, poor Geoff was still being discussed. It had been proved that he wasn't The Caretaker, as the police had him under surveillance at the time of the third killing, but still, his life was cruelly pulled apart, even though he'd done no wrong. Geoff was one of the kindest people I would ever meet. There had to be a way to make it right. Becky had told us he had resigned from his job and had gone back to his daughter's in Scotland. I didn't blame him, and I hoped he was happier there. But I couldn't help feeling partly responsible. Even though I hadn't known anything at the time of his arrest, I did now. I asked Becky for a contact number, but she wouldn't give it. Kelly said she'd find it. We all wanted to know if he was OK.

But I had bigger things to worry about, as selfish as it was.

Knowing what I knew was weighing heavily upon me. I tried not to let it influence my actions or behaviour, but in doing so I felt exhausted; my mind was foggy, the effort snapping blinkers onto my vision, tunnelling it. Pretending to be normal, in a world that was anything but, was tough. But, as Kelly said, I was there: I was no longer afraid to be afraid.

I was so distracted thinking about how my life would never be the same, how I would never go back to being that broken woman I once was, that when I left my flat to join the others at Kelly's house for our usual Friday meeting in an unusual place, I should have checked my security cameras as I did every morning, but I hadn't. I should have looked through the spyhole in my front door before unlocking it, but again, I didn't. So distracted, I simply put on my shoes and coat and walked outside like I was just anyone. I didn't check to make sure it was safe, and as soon as I stepped out, closing my front door behind me, I knew I had made a mistake.

'Jess?' Lewis said, holding his hands up in mock defeat. 'I just want to talk.'

I was so shocked to see him standing a few feet from me, I didn't react. Then, as my fear kicked in, I scrabbled for my keys, which I had dropped into my bag. Knowing I wouldn't find them quickly enough, I instead began to move towards him. I wanted to brush past without comment, but as I got close, he blocked my way. If I pushed him, I knew he could overpower me. I stopped. My head low. I wanted to be able to look him in the eye, tell him to fuck off, but I couldn't. I was afraid, but it didn't scare me anymore, so I took a breath and lifted my head. Daring to hold his beady little eye. I heard Kelly's voice, telling me I was strong.

'What do you want, Lewis?'

'This whole thing, you know, the killings, what people are talking about, it's made me think.'

'Lewis, please,' I said.

'Just hear me out,' he demanded, and I recoiled at the small but vicious rise in his voice. It reminded me of Jones's partner when he laughed. I hated that he did this to me.

'Please,' he followed up, quieter.

'I don't want to talk to you. I need you to leave me alone.'

'Jess, just hear what I have to say.'

I felt my blood begin to pulse. How dare he say I had to hear him out? I spent years wanting to be heard, but it fell on deaf ears.

'No,' I said, and I could see he was as shocked as I was.

'What?'

'Lewis, I said no.'

'No? What do you mean, no?'

'No, I don't want to hear you out. No, I don't care what you think,' I said, quietly, calmly, but the words felt bright and strong. I didn't care; I hadn't since he'd hit me so hard I needed to have my face stitched together. But saying it, seeing the hurt in his eyes, empowered me.

'Jess—' he began, his voice small and fragile, an act I wasn't going to fall for again.

'I need you to do something for me,' I said.

'What?' he said. I could see he was wobbling, my new power knocking him off balance.

'I need you to get the fuck off my doorstep, and I need you to never, ever think it's OK to talk to me, turn up at my door, harass me in any way. If you so much as look at me, take another penny from me, so help me God I'll—'

'What? You'll what?' he said, his rage-filled eyes boring into me. I knew those eyes, but I didn't fear them anymore. Lewis stepped towards me, right into my space, so close I could smell his rancid breath. I used to back away when he got so close. Not anymore. Never. Again. 'You'll what, bitch?' he said, grabbing me by the throat. So much for him being a changed man. One little push, and his true colours flooded out. Before he could say anything else, I did something so unexpected I saw fear flash across his face. I smiled at him, even though he was choking me, his grip so tight my vision blurred. I smiled.

'You listen to me, Lewis,' I said, my words rasping as his fingers clamped hard. 'This is your final warning. Leave me alone, or I will have you fucking killed, do you hear me?'

He released his grip and stumbled back, and I fought not to cough in front of him. I sucked in big gulps of air, and I held his eye. He regained his composure, but he didn't step up to me again. He didn't try and grab me.

'Are you threatening me?' he said.

'I'm promising you, Lewis. The Caretaker is out there, hunting for men like you. I'd be careful.'

Lewis looked at me for a second longer, then he backed away.

I stood, holding my composure, until he disappeared around the corner. I didn't want him to turn and see me struggling. Once he was gone, I slumped against my wall and gulped in air. As I exhaled, it almost turned into a sob. Almost.

Just warning him that The Caretaker was out there was enough to make him panic. I wondered, could we use the same approach to help the partner of DS Jones?

Chapter Fifty-Six

Even though I had stood my ground with Lewis, even though I had won my first small victory over him, I still didn't want to board a bus alone, just in case, so I messaged Kelly and she came to mine and picked me up. Even though I wanted to talk about Lewis, about how I wanted him gone, I didn't need to. Kelly knew why I didn't travel on public transport, and she told me not to worry, things would work out for me.

We didn't discuss it further as she took me back to hers for the new support group session that wasn't really a session, and I didn't ask her to clarify what she meant. So instead we talked about the group meeting that was ahead of us. Becky had been invited to host it, as she always did, but she'd politely declined, saying it was crossing a boundary she wasn't prepared to cross. But she insisted that once it all died down, once the media got bored, the doors to the children's centre where we met would fly open, inviting us back. I respected her even more for her decision. Sometimes going against the flow, and standing firm in the face of adversity, was all anyone had.

She asked about Geoff. No news.

When Kelly and I arrived back at hers, Madison, Hannah, Vija and Rachel were on the drive waiting. Kelly apologised and let everyone in. We asked if the others were coming, but Vija said they weren't. Baheela had gone into hiding. The press was hounding her, digging up incidents from her past. Claire was uncomfortable being around us, and Steph had vanished. It didn't bode well for them. I knew that being present, in public, would be our best defence against scrutiny, if it came to that.

Despite the change of location and the absence of Becky, the session was pretty much the same as usual. We drank tea, sat in a circle, but instead of talking about our feelings, our weeks, all we spoke of was The Caretaker, and the police who were now starting to show up in our lives more and more. So far, I hadn't had that experience, but I knew I was on borrowed time. After an hour, Vija and Rachel left, the meeting came to an end, and in its wake Kelly, Hannah, Madison and I, the serial killer support group, remained.

Our topic of conversation: a certain DS Jones.

'Are you sure he is an abuser?' Madison asked, and Kelly and I nodded. She hadn't seen what we saw, hadn't heard what we heard. There was no doubt in either of our minds he was a bad man.

'We need to do something about this,' Kelly said. 'He is supposed to help people like us, but he isn't, because he is just like those we are trying to stop.'

'Kelly, are you suggesting we go after him?' Hannah asked, her usual bright and chipper attitude dulled by the death of her ex, and the media hounding her since. 'He's a copper.'

'He's no different to Duncan, or Martin, or Jake,' I said quietly.

'But he is a copper. We would have the whole police force looking for us,' Madison said.

'They are already looking for us,' Kelly said. 'Look, I get it – if you think we shouldn't consider it, then I will stop. We are a group, a team; we all have to be onboard with any decision we make.'

Madison and Hannah nodded. But I could see they were unsure.

'I think this thing,' I started, 'this group, I think it's needed, do we all agree?'

'Yes,' Madison said.

'Of course,' Hannah added.

'But now I think there is an obligation. We were failed by the justice system, all of us, as well as countless other women out there. Jones is connected to three of us sat here, and others from our small group. How many women has he damaged? How many went back home to their abusive partners, because of him? One woman every eight or nine days dies at the hands of a partner. There might be women who are now dead because of him intentionally failing to do his job. And he is getting away with it. He is worse than anyone the group have dealt with. Much worse. I think we have to do something.'

'But what can we do? He's a police officer,' Hannah said.

'I have an idea.'

I told the serial killer support group about Lewis, and the fear that had flashed across his eyes when I'd mentioned The Caretaker. 'What if The Caretaker cornered him somehow, gave him a warning?'

'It didn't work for Martin,' Kelly said quietly, and both Hannah and Madison looked down. Hannah reached for Madison's hand and gave it a gentle squeeze.

'No, but Martin didn't know who had attacked him. The

The Serial Killer Support Group

Caretaker is now famous, and feared. Lewis nearly shit his pants when I mentioned his name. If we could get Jones alone, face to face, it might be enough to help her.'

'It might work,' Kelly said.

'OK, so, if we go for it, we have to try to get him on his own, and then one of us needs to risk being there. Who is going to do it?' Madison said, and the group fell silent. I thought about how much I wanted to hurt Lewis, how I enjoyed the fear. How much Jones reminded me of him. I wanted to kill him myself, but knew I couldn't. So I volunteered.

'I'll do it, I'll be the Caretaker,' I said.

Madison asked if I was ready, and I said I was. Kelly nodded my way and then pulled out the little blue book containing notes about the men followed.

'In here is how we have done it before. You'll need a few weeks to watch, to follow. There is a step-by-step at the front of this book. Read it, learn it. I'll be there to help. But never over the phone, we only talk about this book face to face, somewhere safe. You keep this book with you at all times. If you think someone is going to find it, burn it. Understand? Even though this visit isn't about killing him, we need to do it properly and leave no trace.'

'Do you really think Jones knowing The Caretaker is watching will stop him?' Hannah said.

'I don't know,' I said. 'But it's worth a shot. We have to try to help her, don't we?'

Everyone nodded, then Kelly handed me the blue book.

'Keep it with you at all times, especially if you're still worried Lewis might get into your house.'

I nodded. I understood. I took it from Kelly and it felt heavy and hot in my hands. I didn't look inside. I simply put it in my bag, like it was just any book.

Chapter Fifty-Seven

We wrapped up the session and, needing the fresh air, I decided to find my own way home. Lewis was probably whimpering in a corner, licking his wounds, and the weight of what I had just volunteered for outweighed my fear of his retribution.

As I left Kelly's, her hug longer and tighter than usual, I headed into the cold but clean winter air, towards a bus stop. I had just said I would become The Caretaker, and even if I wasn't going to kill, I was still going to be the man everyone feared. I had work to do. I needed to research Jones's life, fill the blue book with my own findings. I would need to practise wearing the gear The Caretaker wears to kill. And as scared as I felt, I knew I wouldn't back out of being the one to stand before Jones and give him his final warning. These women were my rock, my new world order. I would do it for them, if doing it for me wasn't enough. The serial killer support group would be with me every step of the way, and knowing it made my walk that little bit easier.

As I reached the bus stop that would take me back into

town, my phone pinged. Pulling it out, I saw a text from a number I didn't know. Curious, I opened it.

> **UNKNOWN**
>
> Hey, Jess, it's Sophie Salam. I really hope you're OK with me getting your number.
>
> I'm wondering if you had time for a coffee? I could do with a person who understands how hard things are with a child with autism.
>
> If you don't want to, that's fine, I just thought I'd ask.

I should have said no, or ignored it. She was the leading investigator in a crime I was now complicit in, and for all I knew, she could know something and want to trap me. I almost said I wasn't happy for her to have my number, that I was going to put in a complaint – I had the right to – but would that be an admission of guilt? Or look like I was hiding something?

Then I wondered, would she really use her child to entrap me? Was that even legal? I saw the way she struggled, the way she was drowning as a mother. I had to believe she was being genuine. I suspected she didn't have many friends she could turn to. This wasn't a copper trying to catch me; she knew nothing about my involvement. This was a mother, a desperate mother.

Someone once said, keep your enemies closer, and although Sophie Salam wasn't an enemy – men like DS Jones were – she would see me as one if she knew what I knew. So, even though I had just confirmed I would become The Caretaker to scare a man, a police officer, I messaged her back.

> Hey Sophie, No, I don't mind, I'm free today? If you want? Anytime.

She messaged back straightaway.

> Today? That would be amazing, I'm free in an hour, same café as before?

> I'll have Lottie, is that OK?

I looked at her message, read it over and over to see if there was anything in it to suggest she knew more than she was letting on, but she didn't; she just need help. And she wasn't my enemy. But she knew my enemy, and maybe, if I helped her, she might inadvertently help me in return.

> An hour is perfect, and of course it's OK. See you then.

I wondered, was I making a terrible mistake?

Chapter Fifty-Eight

The bus slowly trundled towards town, weaving into smaller roads to pick up more passengers: happy elderly people who still had a quiet dignity in a world that moves too fast, young mothers with prams and fidgety little ones, commuters and teens and everyone in between – an eclectic mass, walking their own paths, unaware that close to them was a woman who would become the man the whole country was talking about. I was invisible to them, as was everyone to everyone else. That was how life was: we worried about what others were thinking, but mostly people were thinking about themselves. I was afraid I was projecting as someone with a secret. But really I was just a woman, slightly dishevelled, most definitely tired, also trying to just get by. I was literally just like everyone else. And it made me think, was that true of The Caretaker too? If he were real, would he be just like any other person? Weren't most people just a few steps away from being someone like The Caretaker? Weren't we all only two or three tragic moments from being someone who could kill?

How many steps away was I?

Arriving in town, I had a little time to kill before meeting Sophie Salam, so I thought I would put my sleuthing to the test. I wanted to see if I could follow someone for a while without them noticing. I hoped I could, because it would make me feel calmer. I'd not followed anyone before, not intentionally. I hoped my theory that everyone worried about their own shit was correct, and not just a thing I had created to ease my own paranoia.

I found a bench and sat and watched. Two older women walked past, deep in conversation about someone called Gary, a child or husband perhaps. They weren't my demographic. A young man passed next, head down, looking at his phone, too young. Then a woman in a suit, powerwalking, she was a potential, but then behind her I saw my target. A man, casually dressed, maybe early forties, he was very likely to be a decent bloke, going about his day, but I didn't let myself think of him as having a loving partner, being a family man – I needed him to be the enemy.

As he sauntered past me, oblivious of me watching, I got up and followed him at a short distance, close enough to hear him as he answered a call. When he stopped, taking a seat on a bench, I sat directly behind him, pretending to message on my phone. I listened as he spoke to someone, a girlfriend or wife, about dinner plans. He had a nice voice; it was light, kind. He wasn't like Lewis, deep and rough and without a hint of love. This man was a good man. But for now I had to pretend he wasn't. Before he hung up he said he loved whoever was on the other end, in a way that made me believe him, and then he was on the move once more. I followed, this time a little closer. He walked like a man without a care in the world. He turned to enter a jeweller's and I walked on. Once out of his view, I stopped. And waited. A few minutes passed, and then I heard him say 'Thank you' to the staff of the jeweller's before stepping out again. He walked straight past me without knowing I had been following him for the last ten minutes.

People only cared for their own shit. No one else's. Having it confirmed made me confident I could sit opposite a police officer and her daughter with a blue book in my bag that would incriminate everyone in the murders that were going on, and she would never know. She had her own shit too.

When I arrived at the café, I looked through the glass to see DS Salam was already inside, sat in the same space as before, with Lottie beside her, headphones on, watching something on an iPad. I pushed open the door and smiled as she saw me.

'Do you want anything?' I asked as I got closer and joined the small queue.

'No, thank you,' she said. 'I've got you one. It was a latte, right?'

I nodded. She was perceptive.

I needed to be careful.

I sat opposite her. Lottie looked up at me, and I smiled at her, giving her a wave. She didn't wave back, but there was a hint of a smile on her lips as she turned her attention back to her screen.

'Hi, Jess, thanks for meeting me,' Sophie said.

'It's OK.'

'I'm gonna say, using your number was wrong, but—'

'Honestly, it's fine,' I said. 'I should have given it to you when I last saw you, in case you needed more music to help or something. I really don't mind you reaching out.'

Keep your enemies closer, right?

I saw Sophie exhale, her shoulders releasing tension, and it said a lot. Then I realised I was holding my shoulders tight too, and I tried to subtly release them, but like me, she noticed.

'How is everything?' I asked, wanting to quickly make it all about her daughter. I figured, if I could make it about Lottie, offer some advice, she would relax and then maybe I could find out something of interest about DS Jones. At the very least, when I had completed my research, filled the pages of the little blue book and visited Jones, I would never be seen by her as a potential suspect.

'The nature sounds really help. It's why I asked you here; I wanted to thank you.'

'Good, I'm pleased,' I said, genuinely happy I had helped her.

We drank our coffees, and I talked about my career in helping children with additional needs, and shared some of the issues I faced. As I talked, I could see her relaxing more and more.

'This is so refreshing,' she said. 'I just assumed I was bad at being a mother.'

'Not at all,' I replied. 'I can see how you would feel like that, but trust me, Sophie, you're doing good, and on top of it all you have your career,' I added, testing the waters.

'Yeah, that's tough too,' she said.

'I bet, with the whole Caretaker thing. It's bloody terrifying.'

'Yep,' she said, pursing her lips a little. I could see she wanted to talk more but knew she shouldn't. I had a choice, press a little and she might clam up completely, or leave it, knowing that I might never have the opportunity again.

Life was about risk, right?

'How are you coping with it all? There's not been anything like this here, ever.'

She looked at me for a moment, and I didn't see the detective who was calm and observant; I just saw a tired woman, close to burnout.

'We thought we had our man. Now, God knows.'

We both took a sip of our drinks, and I felt the energy shift.

'Are you any closer to finding him?' I asked.

'Jess, I can't talk about the case,' she replied, but the way she said it made my skin tingle. She held my eye too. I could see she was thinking. I realised then I should have said no to meeting for a coffee.

'Yes, sorry. Of course. It's just all so scary,' I said, breaking the silence.

'Yep. Pretty scary,' she replied, again without breaking eye contact. I shifted in my seat and looked down at Lottie, who was smiling at the screen.

'Is she sleeping all right?' I asked. Salam was making me uncomfortable. I knew she was smart, too smart.

'On and off,' she replied, looking at her girl. 'Truth be told, she only really sleeps when I am there.'

'Who else cares for her?'

'My mum. But she struggles.'

'I wish I could say more to help,' I said, meaning it too.

'It's OK, you've helped a lot. Thank you, Jess.'

She looked at me again, studying me. I knew it was time to leave. I began drinking my coffee quickly, ready to make my excuses, but before I went, I wanted to shift the energy. I needed to remind her I was a victim, needing help. I could see her thinking: the men who had died were connected to the support group I was in. She was wondering how much I knew. I could almost hear her ask.

'Sophie. Can I ask about my case?'

'Your case?' she said, lowering her cup, the suspicion in her eyes fading.

'My ex breaking into my house? The video of him outside, drawing on my windows.'

'He broke into your house?' she said, confusion flashing across her face.

'Well, not really, he got a key cut.'

'Without your permission?'

'Yep.'

'Oh,' she said, and I could see she had no idea what I was talking about.

'You didn't know about this?'

'I must have missed it,' she said, but she and I both knew that wasn't the case. DS Jones didn't report it properly; he'd cut a corner. I felt like I was wasting his time that day, and it seems he felt it too.

'I can look into it, when I'm back at work,' she said.

'No, don't go out of your way. Sorry, I shouldn't have asked. I'll ring DS Jones.'

'No, it's OK. He's on leave now for a few weeks. I'll look when I'm next at work.'

'Leave? Even with what's going on?'

'Yep, even with what's going on,' she said in a way that told me she wasn't too happy about him jumping ship.

I began to think. If Jones was off, there had to be a way to find him, see where he was. If he wasn't at work, surely it would be easier for The Caretaker to pay him a visit?

'You all right?' she asked.

'Yeah, fine,' I said, abandoning the plan that was beginning to form.

She looked at me quizzically for another beat, and then, thankfully, Lottie made a frustrated sound. We both looked and saw that the iPad's screen was blank.

'Looks like the battery has died,' Sophie said to her.

'Mummy, what now?'

'Shall we go for a walk?'

'Yes.'

Sophie looked at me, and I began to excuse myself. I had heard enough, and I knew if I stayed any longer, asked any more questions, she would wonder why. As I stood to leave, she did too, and then she did something unexpected: she leant in and gave me a hug.

'Thanks for meeting up with me today.'

'No, it's my pleasure,' I replied. 'I'm glad I could help.'

'I don't have many friends, I mean, friends who understand. It's refreshing for me.'

'Anytime. I like you, and trust me, you're doing a great job with Lottie.'

'Thank you, Jess.'

I reached for my bag and knocked it onto the floor. My purse skidded out, as did the blue book. Sophie reacted quicker than me and bent to pick it up.

'Here.'

'Thanks,' I said, trying not to show my anxiety at her holding the evidence of who The Caretaker was. Inside that book was enough to have everyone in the serial killer support group locked up for life. I dropped it in my bag, along with my purse, and saying goodbye, I walked away. As I made my way out of the coffee shop, giving a wave back, I was shocked to find that even though I was a member of the serial killer support group, even though I had only met up with Sophie to learn anything that would help me attack her colleague, I meant it: I liked her, and I saw her as a friend. And thankfully, my new friend had no idea how close she had been to cracking the case.

As I made my way home, opting to walk again, I first chastised myself for being so careless. Kelly, Hannah and Madison had spent a year with this blue book, and had never had a problem. I had had it for under two hours and almost messed it up. I'd be careful from now on. After giving myself a good telling off, I focused on what I'd just discovered. I'd been worried that I wouldn't be able to get to him on his own, as he was so wrapped up in the investigation, but it seemed, thanks to Detective Sophie Salam, I had nothing to worry about.

All I had to do was find Jones and have The Caretaker pay him a little visit.

Chapter Fifty-Nine

14th February 2025

After discovering Jones was on leave, it didn't take long to find him, despite his limited social media. Through his Facebook profile picture, Kelly and I found his partner, Faye Reeves, a travel adviser whose social media were both unlocked and active. Through her, we watched their comings and goings, until, four days after we began stalking, she posted about a trip they were taking to the east coast. The Instagram tag was of them both, smiling for the camera, like they didn't have a care in the world. The post said, 'A whole week, just us, back in the beautiful town of Cromer, where we first met.'

They looked perfect, happy, and it really pissed me off. Because it was all a lie.

Things moved quickly, and after a quick message, me, Kelly, Hannah and Madison, the members of the serial killer support group met at Kelly's to discuss the plan to have Jones visited and warned by the caretaker.

For it to work, for us to stay under the radar, I needed to be both at Cromer and at home. Here and there. So, if anyone became suspicious of my activities, we had a perfect alibi.

Hannah agreed to help and shot off to pack a few things. After she was gone, I sat with Kelly and Madison by my side and rang Jenny.

'Hey, Jess, are you OK?' she asked as she picked up the phone.

'Honestly, I'm stressed with it all.'

'What do you need?'

'Jenny, I hate asking, but I need some time, a few days, just to get my head straight.'

'Take as much as you need, Jess, I won't interfere, but Samuel and I want to help, if you need it.'

'I'm OK, I just need some time. I'm sorry.'

'I understand. Take a week. Call me if you need more.'

'Thank you,' I said, hanging up, feeling immeasurable guilt for lying to my boss, my friend. But Jones needed to be warned, his partner saved. We had a duty to help. Lowering my phone, I looked at Kelly, who smiled sympathetically.

'Right then. The Caretaker is going to the seaside,' I said, my voice cracking slightly through nerves.

'Jess, you sure you're OK for this?' Madison asked, her voice so small it was barely audible. Her time as The Caretaker had taken a heavy hold.

'Yeah. I am. Jones, he's like Lewis. Just like Lewis. Fuck him. I want to do this. I want my power back, all the way back. I'm not afraid to be afraid, not anymore.'

Madison looked at me for a long time, then simply nodded, and I took that as my cue to leave, and get ready for my time being that man.

By the time I got home, Hannah had messaged to tell me she was there, outside the back of my house. She climbed into the garden and came in through my back door, and after a quick cuddle, I left the same way. Until I was home, until it was done, she was going to stay at mine, so from the outside it was like I never left. If anyone came round, I'd talk to them through my ring doorbell that was linked to a phone Kelly had given me. I would tell them I was sick, and hope it was enough. I had a different phone so I could leave mine at home, with Hannah, and still be in contact with the group. If my phone was tracked, it would look like I'd not left. If anyone needed to see me, I'd tell them through my ring doorbell I was out and returning later, then I'd leave Cromer and get home before anyone could become suspicious.

It was as good an alibi as any, if it was needed. And really, the only person who might come to my front door was Lewis.

Fuck. Lewis.

I went to the train station, boarded the train I needed and sat anonymously with the other passengers, who, like me, were minding their own business.

The train began to rumble, and I focused on the outside world, trying to keep my mind calm. The countryside flashed by so quickly that my eyes struggled to keep up. Trees streaked brown and grey, fields rolled by in a myriad dead colours, punctuated by the odd deer or hedgerow in the distance. When the train passed another coming from the other direction, the noise was like a thunderclap. I saw other passengers jump as it passed, but I didn't; I barely blinked.

I was becoming The Caretaker already.

Chapter Sixty

Kelly had booked a small B&B under the name Penny Baldwin, someone she once knew but had no contact with anymore. Arriving, I checked in with an older woman who told me about the history of the house and her role as cleaner, cook and in charge of guest relations. It was just her and her son who ran the place, and as it was off season, it was quiet. Of the thirteen habitable rooms, only three were occupied, by myself and two other guests.

Letting me into my room, a charming double with a view of the pier, she handed me the key and left me to it.

Opening my case, I pulled out a small rucksack containing the things I would need to become The Caretaker, and stashed it under the bed. I put a few pairs of shoes in front of it, so if the landlady came in, I doubted she would look inside. Then, grabbing a beanie to tuck my hair into, I left the room and went out, to see if I could find the man I would isolate and scare into being different.

The cold sea air hit me hard, making my eyes water and

cheeks sting, and I was grateful for it. I needed my cool, I needed to stay calm, and I needed Jones not to recognise me. Since it was so bitter, everyone out wore their scarfs high and their hats low, hiding their faces, and that meant I could too.

Again, hiding in plain sight.

I walked aimlessly along the narrow streets, taking in the 1920s architecture and the smell of hot chips lingering in the air. I'd never been to Cromer before; the place was pretty, charming in an old-world, slightly run-down way. I imagined in the summer it was crowded and would probably lose some of its charm.

Taking a narrow road between a clothes shop and an ice-cream parlour, I stepped out onto a platform at the top of a small hill. At the bottom was the pier itself, and not knowing where else to go, I decided I would walk along it. As I descended a wide path towards it, the burner phone pinged, and pulling it out, I saw a screenshot of Faye Reeves' Instagram. It had been posted a few minutes before from the end of the pier. In the picture, she was leaning in, one foot lifted behind her like she was a fucking Disney princess, kissing Jones on the cheek. Under it read: 'A perfect Valentines, with my perfect man.'

All of it was fake.

I felt my rage, my indignation rise. She was no doubt desperately hanging on to the man she once knew, like I did with Lewis. She wanted the good to outshine the bad, but I knew it wouldn't. It couldn't. Men like Jones, like Lewis, they didn't change. They manipulated into thinking it was you who needed to change.

She wouldn't be a fake Disney princess for much longer. I was going to make sure of that.

Fuck you, DS Jones.

Fuck you, Lewis.

And fuck you, Faye, for showing the world that lie. It didn't protect anyone; it didn't help her. It only empowered him. But then, I had done the same, for too long. I stopped myself being angry with her; this wasn't her fault. She only wanted what she posted. She was projecting her hopes, her dreams. I pitied her. I was like her once.

My heart rate increased as I approached the pier, and even though I knew how Instagram worked – people seldom posted and then uploaded – still I felt nervous.

As I walked through the entrance to the long pier, passing a gift shop, to my surprise, I saw Jones and his partner ahead of me.

'Well, I'll be fucked.'

I didn't stop, nor did I slow down, but just continued to walk. I was so close to Jones that I could smell his overpowering aftershave. Once they passed me, I slowed and looked out at the sea, then, as they left by the entrance I had just come through, I followed.

I kept a safe distance from the pair as they ascended the slope into the town. They didn't turn into the charming streets but took a route close to the sea, heading out of town. After ten minutes of walking arm in arm, posing as the perfect couple, they crossed the road to a street with small terraced houses. It made me wonder, had we got Jones wrong? I didn't follow them into the street; I didn't need to, for Jones stopped and walked up to a door, number 29. He opened it and his partner walked in first. And just for a moment, the perfect couple image slipped, before the door closed. It was so brief I nearly missed it. Jones didn't say anything, nor did Faye, but there was a tension about the seemingly relaxed and happy lovebirds.

So far, The Caretaker's little adventure to the coast had been a successful one. Within his first hour there he had found his target and learned his address. He needed to see DS Jones being the man he thought him to be, to be sure there hadn't been a mistake. Then he'd make sure Jones knew he was being watched and was on thin ice.

Chapter Sixty-One

18th February 2025

In the little blue book I had been given there were a lot of observations of how people were creatures of habit, sticking to routines, following them blindly. And even though Jones was away from his usual routine, I found that, in four days following him, his behaviour formed a pattern.

His and Faye's bedroom light, which was at the front of the terraced house, came on at just after 9am, and around 11am they stepped out of their front door and found a café, the same one in the middle of the town. She had a mint tea; he had an americano. He had a bacon sandwich with it, a large bap, covered in brown sauce. She had a granola bar.

After their late breakfast, they walked through the town, shopped, went along the pier. Then then disappeared in the afternoon for a few hours, to sleep or have sex, and then, at just after 6pm, they came out again. They went for a meal, some drinks, and then home between 10 and 11pm.

The routine was set on the evening of the day I first found them and hadn't changed.

And as I followed, listened, watched, I realised that we were right about Jones. In the day, he was controlling; she only ate a granola bar because it was what he wanted. In the afternoon, he love-bombed her with jokes and romance, and then in the evening, when drunk, he was vile. He accused her of looking at other men and seethed at her in public when he thought no one was watching; but I was watching, taking notes, planning. I had no doubt that he went on doing it when they returned home, and then he would apologise, love-bomb again, tell her he was drunk, or blame the stress of work, with the murders he wasn't helping to solve, or his mother's health – some bullshit to validate his actions.

And she was a fool, just like me and Madison and Hannah and Kelly and all of the others, because she believed him when he said those things.

I had written it all down in the book, his pattern fully established. I had prepared. I had practised putting on the Caretaker outfit; I had recorded my messages to Jones, written by me and Kelly, making sure they were short and sweet. Just a few sentences, edited to sound just like the man in the videos posted online. Only one question remained: how would I get him alone, so that The Caretaker could do what he needed to do?

I found my answer on the fourth evening of watching them.

Jones and Faye left the house at their usual time and found a quiet pub where they had a meal and a few drinks. I followed them in, sat further along the same bar, now confident that I could hide in plain sight, and ate a burger, washing it down with a cold beer whilst watching them. Jones drank a lot and, in the two hours they were there, polished off six pints. After they paid, he staggered out, taking a fresh bottle of beer with him, Faye in tow, and they headed towards the beach. I followed, sticking to the shadows, and watched as Jones tried to initiate sex on the beach. To her credit, Faye pushed him back, saying it was too cold, people would see. He didn't take it kindly, and when she refused his advances again, he slapped her across the face. I wanted to help but knew I had to bide my time. Faye didn't hang around, but said she was going back to the house. He told her to fuck off, and shouted that he could get it from anyone, anywhere.

'You're lucky to have me, Faye. You're so beneath me, it's actually embarrassing,' he shouted as she broke into a run.

Prick.

Faye passed close to where I was hiding, so close I could see the red slap mark on her face and hear her sobs. I saw me in her. I knew that pain. It wasn't just physical; it was psychological. It hurt more than any mere slap or punch or kick.

She disappeared up the ramp towards the town, and once she was gone, I turned my attention back to Jones. Not once did he look back to see if she was OK. Not once did he show any remorse. He drank his beer, looking at the sea, his body swaying with the lapping tide.

He was completely and utterly alone.

Staying hidden, I pulled off my rucksack and prepared myself for what was to come.

I didn't put on the hazmat suit, as the others had before, because it was too conspicuous for something so public, but I took time to ensure my hair was fully tucked under my hat, and then further secured with my hood and face mask, which in the darkness looked like a scarf. I did change into the wellies, four sizes too big, taped the leg cuffs, put on the gloves and then taped them too. I was pretty much airtight. What with that and the wild winter elements, I was sure I would be fine.

The Caretaker was sure he would be fine.

Chapter Sixty-Two

THE CARETAKER

Jones didn't leave the beach, but instead began to walk along it, away from the pier. The Caretaker had no idea why he did so. Perhaps he was taking a moment to re-evaluate his choices. He doubted it. It was more likely Jones was too pissed to be thinking at all.

In the blue book, the word 'serendipitous' had been written, The Caretaker guessed it was simply that. The world wanted him to do what he had been doing; that was all there was to it.

Jones continued to wobble along the shoreline, his feet soaking in the swell of the sea, and The Caretaker followed, walking as far as possible in the surf so any footprints would be swept away. Even though The Caretaker wasn't going to kill, he knew, because he had been taught by the others, to leave no trace.

Jones stopped abruptly, and The Caretaker paused as his prey stood facing the sea and took a piss. The Caretaker slowly began to walk again, hoping Jones was too drunk to turn and see him, and as he walked, he scanned the beach. They were alone. Completely alone.

The Caretaker took off his rucksack, unzipped it and pulled out a telescopic baton that Kelly had bought online a long time ago, just in case it was needed for when The Caretaker came to life. Extending it, he continued to advance, his breathing deep, as Jones sang to himself and voided his bladder in the surf. Then, as Jones shook and tucked away his penis, The Caretaker charged, hitting Jones on the back of the head and sending him crashing to the ground.

Stunned and moaning, soaking wet as the tide washed over him, Jones rolled onto his back and spat sand out of his mouth. When his eyes adjusted, he saw The Caretaker standing a few feet from him, the baton pointing at him.

'What the fuck?' Jones said, his eyes still struggling to focus from the blow.

The Caretaker pressed play on his phone, and the pre-recorded message, edited to sound like the others, began.

'Jones, I know the type of man you are, I know how you treat Faye.'

'What?' Jones said, trying to get up, but The Caretaker was too fast, and he struck the police officer once more, in the ribs, winding him. He then pressed play on the second pre-recorded message.

'Consider this a warning. Your first and last. Change, Jones, or leave her, but if you hurt her again, I will come back, and I will kill you, just like I killed the others.'

Before Jones could argue or speak, The Caretaker swung the baton one more time, catching him on the side of the head, knocking him out cold.

Chapter Sixty-Three

JESS

21st February 2025

When I woke the morning after attacking Jones, I dressed and packed to leave. I had another few days on the booking, but I told the kind B&B owner something had come up at home and I needed to get back. She wished me safe travels. Then, as I walked through the town towards the beach, I listened to the buzz of news spreading about what had happened. I wanted to hear more, curiosity getting the better of me.

As I left the narrow streets to emerge onto the large platform that overlooked the pier, I saw, to my left, in the distance, several police officers milling around, some press among them. Beside me, an older couple stood nursing a hot cup of something, and I turned to them.

'What happened?' I asked.

'They say The Caretaker was here, last night,' the woman replied.

'What?' I said, feigning shock. 'Has someone—'

'No, the man was hurt, but he wasn't killed. Poor man.' she added, and her husband, who until that point hadn't engaged with even a smile, looked at her.

'Poor man? If it was The Caretaker, he had it coming. Poor man? Really, June?'

'If he's not been tried, then he is innocent,' she replied, and the husband, shaking his head, turned to leave. She followed, and I listened as they bickered all the way along the road about whether The Caretaker was good or bad.

I looked along the beach for a minute longer, picturing Jones coming to, raising the alarm because he had been attacked. I wondered if he would say it was The Caretaker. If he did, he would get the whole force involved, but it would be damning. Either way, people knew; word had got out somehow and Jones would now been known as an abuser. I had done enough. Smiling, I turned and headed for the train station.

By the time I had arrived back home, said goodbye to Hannah, who snuck away through the garden, unpacked my bags and slept that day away, news had broken of the near miss on the North Sea. A police officer had been linked, but Jones hadn't been named yet. The next day there was more speculation, but the second day after leaving Cromer, the day I was sure Jones would be named, the story was all but dead. Without a death, the incident had been dubbed a copycat. At first I was pissed, but then I thought about it: we hadn't set out to have Jones named; we'd set out to scare him. As long as he paid heed to my threat, that was enough. But even so, I wanted more. I wanted him to pay.

As I readied myself to leave to meet at Kelly's house for our usual Friday session, again opting to hide in plain sight, my phone pinged and I saw it was from Lewis. His message was short.

LEWIS
> We need to talk.

He was probably freaking out about the new attack, but still, his message angered me. Even now, even after all he had done, he was still demanding things of me. *We need to talk*, no *please*, no *thank you*, no *how are you and could we maybe …* just four words. Demanding more of my time. I replied. My message just as direct.

> No.

His reply came quickly, and any doubt I had about The Caretaker visiting him vanished.

> Bitch.

He wanted my time. Once he could have had it all, but no more. For him, time was finite.

My anger at Lewis replaced my anxiety about leaving the house. Since I'd come home from Cromer, I hadn't been out, and part of me wondered if, when I did, people would know I had posed as The Caretaker. However, as I put on my coat and took a final look in the mirror, I saw I didn't appear different at all. It was like it never happened. I might well have believed it was just a weird dream, or another moment from a TV programme.

The journey from mine to Kelly's was uneventful. I had half expected to hear more from Lewis. I knew he was planning something; his rage at my rejection would burn deep, and he would no doubt be working on a way to make me pay. But I didn't care anymore. I wasn't afraid to be afraid. Though I waited for him to call, message or turn up, he didn't, and I arrived at Kelly's front door slightly wired. She opened it before I could ring the bell and, without saying anything, took me in her arms and hugged me tightly. Then, when she released me, she led me to her hosting room, where Hannah and Madison sat waiting for me. We exchanged a smile, they gave me a nod – well done – and then we sat.

Kelly handed me a cup of tea, and the four of us began the meeting.

'Have you seen it's all eased off? They believe it was a copycat,' Hannah said, and we all nodded.

'Yep, it's time to release the video,' Madison said.

'Video?' I asked.

'It's ready to go,' Kelly said, pulling out her MacBook.

'What video?' I asked again.

'We assumed because he wasn't killed, people would dismiss the attack. So we made another video. Jones won't be able to hide from this,' Hannah said.

I smiled. 'Good.'

Kelly opened her MacBook and loaded a video she had made when I was in Cromer. She told us it was being sent via a fake email and bounced around so as not to reveal its IP address. I didn't know what any of it meant, but I trusted her. Before she shared it, we sat and watched it together. It was weird seeing The Caretaker talking about how Jones was a bad man, worse than any other The Caretaker had come across, that he had warned Jones not to abuse his power. We sat in silence as The Caretaker spoke of justice being a thing no man should be able to avoid. A police officer had received his final warning, and if he ignored it, he would die too. No abuser would be safe, regardless of their station in life.

When the video finished, Kelly looked at us all, we nodded, and without ceremony, she hit send, uploading it onto YouTube, where we knew it would spread on to all the social media platforms. Once the upload was competed, she deleted the video, closed her laptop and picked up her tea.

'What now?' I said quietly.

'Now, we plan for your trip away.'

'Trip away?'

'You want Lewis dealt with?'

I nodded, all doubt gone.

'For us to do it, you need to be far away. When you were by the coast, Hannah found you a break.'

'Where am I going?'

'Canaries.'

'What? I can't afford tha—' I began, but Kelly cut me off.

'It's done. It's fine. We didn't book without showing you first. Wanna see?'

I nodded.

Kelly opened her phone and scooted closer, and as she began to show me what was on her screen, a lovely quiet hotel on Gran Canaria, her front doorbell rang. We all snapped upright, tension flooding the room.

'It's probably just a delivery,' Kelly said, anxiety lacing her words. She got up and walked towards the front door, and I followed.

The doorbell rang again and Kelly looked more anxious. She tried to hide it with a sing-song 'Coming' but I could tell she was thinking the same as me: the police knew something.

When she opened the front door, we were both shocked to see a woman standing there. Maybe the same age as me, tall and slim and clearly distressed. She tried to speak, but the words didn't come. Tears replaced them, and as she wiped her eyes, I could see deep purple bruising on her wrist.

'Can I help?' Kelly said, and the woman let out a little sob. 'Is anyone with you?' she continued, and the woman shook her head.

'No, I'm alone,' she said, her voice no louder than a faint breeze.

'Do you need to come in?' I added, hoping Kelly wouldn't mind, and the woman nodded.

Kelly stepped towards her, put an arm around her shoulders and gently guided her inside. I moved on ahead to the others, who were perched on the edge of their seats, and told them we had company. Kelly then entered and stood beside the woman. We watched, unsure what to say or do.

'Are you OK?' Hannah asked, eventually, her voice calm and light.

'I need help,' she replied.

'Help?' I said, looking at Kelly, who was just as alarmed as I was.

'Jay, my husband, I can't stop him, and The Caretaker ... he has been helping women like me, they say on the news that you know him?'

'We don't,' Madison said. 'We don't know him.'

'How did you find us?' I asked.

'You are all over the news. They have been here. I— I grew up in the area and I knew the house when I saw it. I'm sorry for coming, I really don't know where else to go.'

'It's OK,' Kelly said, but I could hear the tension in her voice, the tension we all felt. Our secret group wasn't as secret as we hoped.

'They say that he is helping you, that he has stopped your men.'

'We have lost people, yes,' I said.

'I need The Caretaker to help me. Please, I don't know where else to turn. Please.'

The woman burst into tears, and not knowing what else to do, I gave her a hug. She held me tight and sobbed harder than I thought possible. As she cried, not letting me go, I looked at the others, wondering what the hell we should do. We should have helped her, we all knew it, but could we? Our eyes found Kelly, and she simply shook her head. The risk was too high.

We did what we could to console the woman, and then we put her in touch with Becky, who came round, picked her up and took her away. The time from her knock on Kelly's door to Becky's coming to help was less than an hour. In the woman's wake, we were more shaken up than we had been in all the time before.

'Fuck,' Kelly said, once the woman and Becky had left, and no one commented.

The woman had come to us, to find The Caretaker, and we knew that if she could, anyone could.

Then, as we were reeling from our visit from a stranger, who was so close to The Caretaker it was frightening, things got worse. My phone pinged and I saw an incoming call. I stepped away and answered.

'Miss Pendle?'

'Yes?'

'It's Detective Salam.'

'Oh, hi, Sophie.'

'Detective Salam, please. We need you to come down to the station. Can we arrange a suitable time?'

I forced myself to breathe, worried that if I didn't, I would pass out. Leaning against a wall, I agreed a time to come down to talk under caution. After I hung up, my hands feeling numb, I staggered back to the others.

'Jess?' Kelly said.

'That was the police. They have asked me to come into the station.'

'Fuck,' Kelly said again, and straightaway her phone began to ring.

Chapter Sixty-Four

SOPHIE SALAM

When the video from The Caretaker was released, claiming that the warning to DS Jones was his work and not that of a copycat, the force needed to act. Thankfully he hadn't been killed, but having a police officer attacked, warned, proved no one was safe. So far, the identity of The Caretaker had eluded them. Since their prime suspect had been proved to be in Scotland, they had no real leads. It was time for drastic action.

Geoff had become a ghost, and Sophie couldn't help but feel for him. His life had been flipped upside down. She hated to admit it, but he was their instant prime suspect because he had done military service and looked the way he did. It was enough for the nation's media to condemn before any charges were made. It was enough for her to think she was right. He was just the wrong-looking man in the wrong place at the wrong time. They were no closer to finding their killer.

What she did know was that, whoever the Caretaker was, he was connected to a small group of women who met for therapy once a week. And although Faye wasn't a member of the group,

Jones was connected to it; in an interview in the Mail Online Faye had confessed that Jones was an abuser. How The Caretaker had discovered this, Sophie didn't know. Whatever type of man Jones was, they had to act fast. All the current members of the group, as well as some past members Sophie had highlighted after receiving a detailed list from the therapist who ran the group, were called in to be individually interviewed, and with the department in meltdown, having seventeen people arriving at once to be questioned put it under a lot of strain. But one of theirs had been targeted by The Caretaker, and making an arrest was time-sensitive.

Interviewing so many people in such a short time was mentally and physically exhausting, and even though the department split to manage the load, Sophie had to interview six of them alone: a man named Tim, a current victim of domestic violence, Becky, the therapist, Kelly, Vija, Rachel and lastly her new friend Jess.

As Jess came into the room, she looked at Sophie, held her gaze and gave her a small smile. It told Sophie that Jess understood that their friendship, if you could call it that, would be frowned upon. Sophie nodded back, and then offered a seat.

'Good afternoon, Miss Pendle. May I call you Jess?'

'Sure.'

'Thank you. And thank you for coming in at such short notice. For the record, this conversation will be recorded, and anything you say can be used in court. You do not have to answer any of my questions, and if you would like legal representation, I can arrange that for you now.'

'No, it's not necessary.'

Sophie nodded again. Jess didn't. 'Jess, do you know why you have been asked to come in today?'

'The Caretaker.'

'What can you tell me about him?'

'Only what I have read and seen. He is a man targeting abusers.'

'Anything else?'

Jess shook her head. 'I'm trying to not read too much about it.'

'Why not?'

'It makes me feel uncomfortable.'

'Uncomfortable?'

'That a killer is out there, that somehow he is linked to the support group.'

'Jess, tell me about the support group.'

'What do you want to know?'

'How did you find them?'

Jess told Sophie all about the New Year's Eve incident, and how when Lewis was arrested, she had the flyer pushed into her hand. As much as Sophie wanted to be objective and neutral, she felt for her new friend. Jess then spoke of how they met every Friday, until the media began to hound them. Now the group had been disbanded.

'I'm sorry to hear about your situation,' Sophie said, meaning it.

'It's OK.'

'Jess, to your knowledge, could anyone connected to the support group be doing this?'

'No. If I did, I would have called you.'

'OK,' Sophie said, holding Jess's gaze until she had to look away.

Thanking Jess for her time, Sophie concluded the interview, and once the recording stopped, she spoke a little about how Lottie was doing. She knew she shouldn't, as someone could be watching, but she needed to see how Jess responded. Jess talked lightly, not unlike how she spoke in the café, only this time, Sophie noticed, Jess was finding it hard to hold her gaze.

'Jess, we might have more questions, so if you are planning on going away—'

'I am, actually.'

'Where?'

'Just to get some winter sun. This year has been rough. But I will have my phone with me.'

'We are going to need to know where and when and for how long.'

'Sure, OK. I'll get the details across to you. Say hi to Lottie for me.'

Sophie nodded, and Jess left the interview room. Once the door was closed, Sophie sat on the edge of the table and folded her arms. Jess was hiding something; she didn't know what. She hoped it wasn't anything that would get her into trouble, but she felt sure Jess knew something about what was going on. She knew she should report it, but then, if she was wrong, she had no doubt Jess would report her for using her number without permission. For now, she had to keep her gut feeling to herself.

'Shit,' she said quietly.

Chapter Sixty-Five

JESS

As I walked towards the exit of the police station, I tried my best to look calm, despite the wave of panic that wanted to flood out of every pore in my body. Sophie hadn't said anything, but I could tell from the way she looked at me that she knew I knew more than I was letting on. She didn't suspect me of murder – if she did, she would have arrested me on the spot – but she knew I knew something.

I had to be careful. No slip-ups, no mistakes. If I did, I had no doubt my new friend would pounce.

As I moved towards the exit, I saw Madison sat on a blue plastic chair, waiting for her turn to speak to the detectives. She looked at me, a flash of relief on her face. I nodded her way, my message small but clear. I was telling her it would all be OK. I wished I could give her a hug – she looked like she needed one – but I didn't want to have any eyes look my way, so I continued walking out of the station, and then made my way home.

DS Salam, Sophie, was bright, determined. She didn't need to tell me she was the kind of woman who didn't give up;

everything about her exuded that. Which was why I liked her so much, and why I was now afraid of her. The pressure from high up, maybe as high as central government, to stop The Caretaker would be intense. Pressure forced people to act. Some coped and thrived; some crumbled. Sophie Salam wasn't a woman to crumble.

I knew that what we had planned for Lewis when I went away would have to be paused. Sophie was too close, and I could feel my resolve slip.

Midway through my walk home, my phone pinged a notification and I saw my ring doorbell had picked up something. I assumed it was post, but when I opened it, I was surprised, even now, even after everything, to see Lewis there on my doorstep. I assumed he would leave when he realised I wasn't in, but he didn't. He stood there, waiting for me.

'Jess. If you're in, open the door. I want to talk.'

I spoke back through the app.

'Go away.'

'You need to hear me out, OK? I know I've not been great and made mistakes.'

'Not been great? That's what you'd say if you weren't pulling you weight at home or had neglected me. You hit me, Lewis.'

'Jess, please.'

'You hit me many times. I don't want to hear it, Lewis. You had your chance to fix those mistakes.'

'Jess.'

'And didn't you call me a bitch only a few hours ago?'

'I know, I'm so—'

'I don't want to hear it.'

'Fuck you, Jess. Please. I thought you were better than this, just hear me out, OK?'

I didn't reply, instead I closed the app, and, knowing it would piss him off more, I walked faster.

Fuck me?

Fuck me?

No, Lewis, fuck you.

By the time I got to my front door, I was sweating from the exertion, and Lewis, who had been sitting on my doorstep, stood up. He began to speak, to validate himself, his apology only driven by fear because of what The Caretaker was doing to men like him. I didn't give him the chance. Bounding up my path towards him, I grabbed his face with my right hand. Caught off-guard, he stumbled back into the door.

'Jess. Stop,' he mumbled as my hand forced his mouth open, but it only fuelled me. I squeezed harder, my fingers digging into his face, so hard I could feel his teeth through his thin cheeks. I pushed again, banging his head against the door. I realised I should have fought back a long time ago. Lewis wasn't strong or domineering; he was a coward, a fucking coward. My aggression wasn't being matched. He was afraid of me.

'Lewis, you listen to me now. You need to leave, and you need to never come back. If you do, you won't have to worry about The Caretaker, I will fucking kill you. Am I clear?'

He nodded, the whites of his eyes showing.

'Good,' I said, letting him go, and he stumbled forward, grabbing his face. He looked at me, a mixture of shock and terror, and as he massaged his cheeks, I could see blood in his mouth from where I had crushed the inside of his cheek against his teeth.

'You, you fucking psycho,' he said, backing away. I didn't reply. I simply smiled and waited for him to leave, knowing that this would be the final time I would see him. The image of him, cowering, afraid, couldn't be any sweeter.

Lewis turned and began to half walk, half run down the street away from me. My doubt in the plan had faded. Sophie Salam wasn't a woman who would crumble under pressure. But I wasn't one either.

Just before he turned the corner, Lewis looked back at me, the shock still written on his face.

'Who's the bitch now,' I said.

Chapter Sixty-Six

SUPPORT GROUP CHAT

23rd February 2025

VIJA 7.34PM

I'm freaking out after the police interviews. Did we all get called in? What do we do?

Rachel has left the group.

CLAIRE 7.35PM

Rachel has left the group.

😮 2

VIJA 7.35PM

Baheela left it last week too.

KELLY 7.35PM

Following the recent conversations with the police, I fear we are going to be watched.

The Serial Killer Support Group

CLAIRE 7.35PM

> We haven't done anything wrong!

KELLY 7.36PM

> No, but I don't want the police hounding me, or the press. I think it might be best to close this group chat, the police can have a copy if they want, but I worry if we talk about it at all they will continue to want to interview us. Don't talk about the day at the station, it will all blow over. We just need to be like Geoff, keep our heads down until an arrest has been made.

CLAIRE 7.36PM

> This sucks. What about Friday meets?

KELLY 7.39PM

> I think its best we don't attract any more attention. Lay low ladies.

VIJA 7.40PM

> Speak soon.

> 🙂

Vija has left the group.

CLAIRE 7.41PM

> 🖤

Claire has left the group.
Steph has left the group.

MADISON 7.43PM

> See you soon.

HANNAH 7.44PM

See you soon.

KELLY 7.47PM

Jess, are you sorted for your trip?

JESS 7.47PM

Yep bags packed, passport ready. I've told the police where I am, and I'll have my phone, if they need me.

MADISON 7.47PM

I bet you can't wait?

JESS 7.47PM

It feels weird going with all this happening, but I need this break. This year has felt rough.

KELLY 7.48PM

Have a good trip away, you deserve it. Let's catch up when you're back.

JESS 7.48PM

I'll message when home.

> Jess has left the group.
> Madison has left the group.
> Hannah has left the group.
> Kelly has left the group.

Chapter Sixty-Seven

THE CARETAKER

25th February 2025

Even though Jess was the newest member of both the therapy group and the serial killer support group, she had become integral to them and was loved. What she had had to endure, what she was still living through, fuelled Kelly. With her first kill, Kelly had had more time to prepare and to research, but although she had only dedicated half the time to being ready for Lewis that she had to being ready for Madison's ex-partner, Jake, she knew she would succeed. The Caretaker's legend would be enough to get her halfway there.

Vengeance, even by proxy, was a powerful accelerant, and with Jess safely out of the country, lying on a sun lounger in a small hotel, hopefully drinking nice cocktails and sleeping like a small child at night, Kelly readied to kill.

Jess had told Kelly about the latest incident on her doorstep, and just before she flew, the two women sat down together, and Jess told Kelly everything she could about Lewis: where he worked, where he drank, his address and phone number. Kelly didn't say, because she didn't want to freak out Jess even more, but a lot of the information she already knew. Since that day sat in her kitchen when Jess had said she wanted The Caretaker to get Lewis, Kelly had been working, and even though Jess had the little blue book still – it seemed unsafe to be passing it around, in case the police were watching them – she had made her own notes.

Lewis worked for an insurance company, settling claims for domestic damages, and at times investigating them, and to his credit, he was fair. On Mondays he worked until late; Wednesdays he played badminton with some friends; Fridays he went to the same pub, the Lion's Head, where Kelly and Hannah had sat at a table next to his as he drank his usual Peroni. She had learned, in that one night of listening, that he liked a dirty kebab, wasn't a fan of Marvel films and had strong opinions about modern marriages being weak, as people didn't fight hard enough.

If you didn't know he'd done what he'd done to Jess, you'd never guess. Lewis looked and sounded and acted like he was a decent guy.

But that was the point, wasn't it? Didn't most?

In her short time following, learning, listening, Kelly knew that on a Tuesday Lewis usually had a quiet one at home. He lived in an apartment in the city centre, opposite a Premier Inn. Kelly booked a room online using a different name, this time one of Hannah's childhood friends, Olivia Patterson. She had requested a street-view room, and when she checked in, high up on the fourth floor, she looked out of the window. To her right, five windows away and two floors lower, was the window that looked into Lewis's living room. It was a risk, booking a hotel room based on so little research, but, thankfully, Lewis was like everyone else, a creature of habit. As Kelly sat there, eating a

Pot Noodle so she didn't have to go out, she looked down into the street and wasn't disappointed. Lewis was coming home. She looked at her watch; it was just after six. As she finished her Pot Noodle, she watched his window, and a light flicked on. Within half an hour, he was sat in jogging bottoms and a jumper, TV on, eating. Kelly watched as his face glowed blue from the screen. After he ate, he sat flicking through his phone. He masturbated at just before 10pm, and at 10.17pm the lights went out.

Kelly then stood, closed the curtains, grabbed the rucksack from the bed and got changed. She couldn't become The Caretaker fully, but with the wellies on, the trousers taped up and the hat secure, she only needed to don the hazmat suit, gloves and face mask.

She took a final look at herself.

Then The Caretaker set to work.

The Caretaker left the hotel and, approaching the apartment block's entrance, stopped and gave the impression he was fumbling for his keys in his bag. He carried on, acting the part of a person growing more and more frustrated with not being able to find them, even going so far as faking a phone call to a partner who wasn't picking up. Finally a man approached to go inside.

'Mind if I follow you in? I can't find my keys, and my other half isn't picking up his bloody phone.'

The man smiled. 'Sure, no problem.'

'Thanks, you're a lifesaver,' The Caretaker said, enjoying the irony.

The man held the door open and The Caretaker stepped

inside. Then, as the man walked to the lift, The Caretaker took the stairs, holding back when he got to the second floor in case the man who let him in got out of the lift there. He didn't, as The Caretaker saw the lift go all the way up to the seventh. Staying in the stairwell, The Caretaker quickly pulled the hazmat suit on, as well as the gloves and face mask, and then, taking out the item he would need to use on Lewis, he approached his front door.

He had learned that although he presented as a well-adjusted man, Lewis had a mean temper: he didn't like being proved wrong, he didn't like being embarrassed and he didn't like being woken up.

Banging on his front door, The Caretaker hoped Lewis had fallen asleep. When he didn't answer the first time, The Caretaker banged again. He heard a moan from the other side, followed by Lewis saying, 'What the fuck?' Then the front door opened, and Lewis registered shock at seeing in front of him the serial killer who had been all over the news. The Caretaker held a taser in his right hand, one he had found and purchased through the dark web at the very beginning, when the serial killer support group was just an idea. He pressed it into Lewis's chest. He didn't have time to react or scream, as every muscle in his body went rigid and his jaws clamped shut. Lewis fell back into his apartment, and The Caretaker continued to hold the taser to him, until he shook so violently he passed out and urinated in his light grey trousers. The Caretaker stepped over him, dragging him further into the apartment, and closed the door.

When Lewis woke, it took him a full minute to work out where he was and what had happened, and then, as he remembered the man standing on his doorstep, the man the country knew as The Caretaker electrocuting him, fear shot into his body and he tried to move and cry for help. He quickly learned he couldn't. His hands had been cable-tied behind his back, his legs bound together with almost a whole roll of gaffer tape. In his mouth was some of his dirty laundry, stuffed in and then secured with more gaffer tape, which had been looped around his head, as with Jake. Even though he knew he couldn't move, he tried to, until The Caretaker slapped him across the face, snapping his panic into focus.

'There is no point trying to call for help. Inside your mouth is your underwear from the wash basket. I felt it was a nice touch, given what you wanted her to say on New Year's Eve after you hit her.'

'You're a woman?' Lewis said, confusion etched into his features.

'No, Lewis, I am a man, just like you.'

Lewis couldn't immediately place what The Caretaker meant by the dirty underwear, but, like a lightning bolt, he remembered, and understood what The Caretaker was talking about. When he hit Jess, he'd demanded that she say she'd tripped over laundry and banged her face. When he made the connection that The Caretaker was there because of what he had done to Jess, and knowing, because of what was all over the news, what was coming next, he pissed himself again. The Caretaker saw, and even though his face was covered, Lewis knew he was smiling.

The Caretaker wanted to take his time with Lewis, enjoy it, make him suffer as he'd made Jess suffer, but this kill was rushed and time wasn't on his side, so The Caretaker began.

'You have suffocated a beautiful woman with your violence towards her, Lewis. You need to pay for your crimes.'

Lewis tried to move again, to crawl away, to hide, but The Caretaker was strong, the year-long training was for exactly these moments, and before Lewis could get anywhere, The Caretaker stamped him back to the floor. He then dropped onto his target, pressing his full weight into his chest, and reached towards his face. Lewis tried to move again, so The Caretaker struck him hard across the nose. It had been effective before, and it was again; blood began to pour down the side of his face. The Caretaker grabbed his face and pointed it towards the ceiling, so the blood poured down the back of his throat, then, still pressing down, he pinched his nose tight. With his mouth bound shut, stuffed with his own underwear, Lewis began to buck, desperate to draw in a breath, but The Caretaker held firm. Lewis thrashed, fought, his trapped voice desperate to escape, to cry out, to breathe. The Caretaker didn't relent. The thrashing became wilder, and then it stopped. The Caretaker continued to squeeze for another minute, until even the spasms had been reduced to involuntary electrical twitches.

Standing up from the body of Lewis, Kelly fought to catch her breath, and then prepared to record a video and leave the flat. She enjoyed the fact that when they found him and discovered his own underwear in his oesophagus, even though he was dead, he would be humiliated.

A final 'fuck you' to a fucking awful man.

With all traces of her presence cleaned up, besides a bloody bootprint which she knew wouldn't be an issue, she once more became The Caretaker, positioned the camera to show Lewis's lifeless eyes staring up and recorded her message for the world.

'Tonight, I have struck again, another man who didn't pay for the crime he had committed. For the way he suffocated the life from an innocent woman.

'There has been a lot of speculation as to who I am, and who knows of me. I am alone, I act alone and I move alone. And to men like this one behind me, you may think you are clever, getting away with it, but you aren't hard to find. I know how you think; I can spot you in a crowd; I can see you for what you are, even when you think you present as the perfect partner.

'I will come for you, if I have to.

'And finally, to the police, to DS Salam and others in your team, you are no closer to knowing who I am, but I don't want you to try to find me. That's not my point in this. I want you to find them, these men who are getting away with crimes equal to mine, and I want you to stop them. Stop them, and the killings stop. It is as simple as that.'

Chapter Sixty-Eight

SOPHIE SALAM

Several days of interviewing almost two dozen people and re-watching footage made exhausting work, and the more Sophie watched, the more it appeared that anyone could be a suspect – or no one. Going around in circles wasn't helping, and even though, when she finished work, she knew she needed to go home and relieve her mum, she also needed a moment to compose herself, to unwind. She needed a drink. Lottie was asleep anyway – Mum said she had had a good day – so, after checking in to make sure it was OK to be an hour late, Sophie messaged Clarke, inviting him to the pub.

When they arrived, Sophie bought the drinks and found a quiet table. She swallowed a mouthful of red wine, and Clarke matched her by drinking almost half his pint in one go.

'Needed that,' he said.

'Me too.'

They chatted about the investigation, the interviews, and Sophie told him she was hitting a dead end. She didn't say that she had a gut feeling about Jess Pendle being involved, and she didn't know why. She reasoned that, until she had proof, a gut feeling was all it was, but deep down she wondered if maybe she liked Jess a little too much. A long time ago, Sophie had blurred the boundaries between job and life, with life-altering consequences, and resulting in a daughter. She vowed to never make a mistake like that again.

But still, she didn't tell Clarke about her suspicion.

'Can you believe Jones? Do you think he's like that?' Clarke asked, rousing Sophie from her moral dilemma. She shrugged. 'His partner says so.'

'He seems like a decent chap.'

'You would think that,' Sophie said. 'You're a man.'

'You mean you are not surprised?'

'Honestly, no. I've never really felt OK in his presence.'

'Shit, I had no idea. Male privilege,' Clarke said. 'You just don't know what happens behind closed doors,' he added to himself. Sophie could see he was struggling to work out why a man would be like Jones and the others that dominated their lives at the moment.

'What I can't work out,' Sophie continued,' is how The Caretaker knew Jones was an abuser.'

'What do you mean?'

'We work with the man and had no idea. How did The Caretaker discover this? And why didn't he kill him?'

'He's a copper – maybe The Caretaker knew it was a step too far?'

'Yeah. Maybe,' Sophie said, raising her glass. If The Caretaker didn't kill Jones because he was a copper, what did that tell her? He was one himself? Or he respected the law? Or maybe The Caretaker was afraid to kill a police officer, maybe he wasn't as ruthless as they thought?

'Soph?' Clarke said. 'You OK?'

'Yeah, just thinking. I gotta know how he found out Jones was—'

Before she could finish, her phone rang. She saw it was the DI and answered quickly, her stomach dropping, fearing the worst.

'Boss?'

'There's been another. Where are you?'

'Shit, OK, I'm with Clarke.'

'Good, bring him. I need you both on this, now.'

Hanging up, Sophie looked at Clarke, and he knew without needing to be told. 'I'll drive,' he said.

Leaving the pub, Sophie and Clarke ran to his car. As they got in, an address came through to Sophie, which they put into his satnav, and they set off. According to the satnav it would take fifteen minutes to get there, and the pair drove in silence. Arriving at a scene of a murder wasn't easy, particularly for both Clarke and Sophie, since this was their first serial killer. While they were mentally preparing for the scene, the questions, the swarming media, Sophie's phone pinged again with a news update, the title short and terrifying.

Serial killer vigilante strikes again.

'Shit,' she said.

'What?'

'The Caretaker has posted another video. I'm finding it now.'

Clarke nodded, but didn't take his eyes off the road as Sophie went online. It only took seconds to find The Caretaker's video on TikTok. She turned up the volume so Clarke could hear, and sat in silence watching, seeing the lifeless eyes of the latest victim staring into nothing, only reacting when she heard The Caretaker call her by name.

'Did he just say—' Clarke began.

'Yeah, yeah, he did.'

'Sophie, I don't like this. I don't like this at all.'

'You and me both.'

By the time they arrived at the scene, Sophie had watched the video five times, looking for any clue to who The Caretaker was. She had no doubt it was connected to the support group, but she just didn't know how. The men in the group were coming up cold. None of them had it in them. She had done the work, profiled everyone they had spoken to, watched the interviews; these men were broken, none of them strong enough. The only ones she had spoken to who were brave, strong, were…

'Oh, shit,' she said.

'What?'

'We might be looking at the wrong people with this.'

'What do you mean?'

Sophie was about to explain her idea, that her gut feeling about Jess knowing could be more than that, and therefore something she had to act on, but then Clarke rounded the corner to the address in the satnav, and the chaos stopped her in her tracks.

Outside the apartment building, the media were everywhere, snapping pictures and questioning anyone in uniform who happened to be nearby. Not just the media – people were out in their dozens, wanting to see the latest victim's body removed on a gurney. As Sophie climbed out of the car, she heard both civilians and press shouting to her, a cacophony of aggression and demand. She was even booed – by a gathering of people who had crude handmade signs calling The Caretaker a hero.

'Have you seen that?' she said to Clarke, who read the signs and looked back at her.

'It's all gone to shit.'

Pushing their way through the crowds, helped by uniformed officers, Sophie and Clarke went into the building and, going up two flights of stairs, they came to the scene of the crime. Sophie could see the body in the living room, his feet sticking out into the hallway. Clarke went ahead to suit up and begin to look at the body, and she approached Edwards, the PC who had been at the first murder scene. That day, she recalled, he had looked green around the gills, but not now. Already The Caretaker had hardened his resolve.

'How are you doing, Edwards?'

'Tired, Ma'am. You?'

'Same. What can you tell me?'

'Victim was bound and suffocated, using what we think is his own underwear. Still working out how he was overpowered to begin with.'

'Who is he?'

'His name is Lewis Nixon.'

'Lewis Nixon?' Sophie said. 'I know that name.'

'You do?'

'Hang on,' Sophie said, taking a step away to try and remember where she had heard it before. It took her a minute, but when it came, she gasped. 'Shit, Jess.'

'Who?'

'Jess Pendle. She is a member of the support group. The man is her ex.'

She stepped away and, pulling out her phone, looked up Jess's number and rang it. The ring tone was Continental, and she recalled Jess informing them she was going away. She hung up. Jess was out of the country on the same day her ex was murdered, proving straightaway that she didn't do it. It was convenient. But was it too convenient? It made Sophie wonder: where were the other women when their exes were killed?

She had no proof, but she was confident that these women weren't just protecting The Caretaker; they were more involved. More hands-on.

Stepping back into the room, she walked past a slightly bemused Edwards and headed for Clarke.

'You OK here? I think I've got something. I need to get back to the station.'

'Yeah, fine, we'll be hours.'

'OK, ring me if you find something more than what we already know.'

'Will do.'

Making her way out of the apartment, Sophie fought through the gathered press, and once away from the building she flagged down a taxi. Sitting in the back, she logged into her secure work profile and looked at the investigation. Jess was in Spain. She had complied with the police request to be available if needed. But Sophie didn't want to talk to her yet. Instead she looked back to the first crime, the murder of Jake Murray, the body-builder killed with a calculated amount of potassium chloride. But she didn't dwell on the cause of death, even though the taping and binding were similar to the scene she had just left; she looked at his ex.

At the time of the killing, Madison was away on holiday with her sister.

Duncan Miller was next, killed by anaphylactic shock.

His ex, Kelly, was away with work.

Martin Goodfellow, beaten to death.

Hannah, away at her mother's.

None of them were at home the night their ex died.

Not one.

Coincidences happened, but not like this.

As Sophie began to try and piece together how it all made sense, her phone began vibrating. It was her mother calling.

'Hey, Ma, everything OK? Is Lottie all right?'

'She's fine; she's sound asleep.'

'That's good.'

'Sophie, a man just called. He said he needed to get hold of you. Said it was important.'

'Who was it?' Sophie said, wondering why someone would ring her home phone and not her mobile.

'He didn't leave his name, but said you and he knew each other back when you were in the Cambridgeshire force, before Lottie. He said you and he were friends.'

Sophie sat upright in the back of the cab. She didn't keep in touch with anyone from the cadets, very specifically, because of one man.

'Mum, what did he sound like?'

'He had an accent. I think it was Newcastle maybe?'

Sophie felt sick. 'Mum, did you tell him about Lottie?'

'What? No, of course not. Sophie, are you OK?'

'Did you tell him anything?'

'No, I just said you were at work, and he said he'd call back another time.'

'If he calls again, hang up.'

'What's going on?

'Mum, please.'

'OK, OK, I will.'

Sophie made her mum swear, and then, hanging up, she

went onto Google and typed his name, sighing with relief to read that nothing had changed.

But something had; somehow, he had found her. Managed to get her home phone number. Used his prison privileges to call. He knew about her. She tried to push down the sick feeling that rose from somewhere deep inside, and to focus on the job at hand, but the picture she was trying to build of the connections between the killings, and how The Caretaker was doing them, was gone. Instead, her mind was filled with the image of Karl Kendrick: a man who had done many bad things, a man who was the father of her little girl and didn't know it.

To try to do something to lift a dread that felt closer than it had since the day he was arrested, she again rang Jess, this time to break the news and gauge her reaction. The phone rang and rang and went to voicemail.

Chapter Sixty-Nine

JESS

26th February 2025

When the news came, I was sitting in the hotel bar, talking with an elderly couple, Veronica and Peter, who, I understood, pretty much lived abroad during the winter months. I was sipping my third cocktail of the night and enjoying the cool evening breeze, which was still a damn sight warmer than it would have been at home. It teased me with the smell of the ocean, and with it a kind of hope. I hadn't been messaged – I didn't have my phone – but I saw the news on the TV mounted near the bar's ceiling. Although I couldn't hear what was said, I saw The Caretaker and behind him Lewis. I was expecting to feel something, anger, grief, shock, but I didn't. He was there, and he was clearly dead, and I didn't care that much about it.

I guess I knew it was coming.

The news bulletin was over within a minute, and the bartender put on Eurosport, which showed highlights of a skiing tournament. As far as I could tell, no one else saw that

The Caretaker had struck again. People continued to drink, talk, play cards, and I allowed myself to be swept up in one of Peter's stories of how, a long time ago, he and Veronica would visit what was then Yugoslavia. I found their stories uplifting, romantic, and exactly what I needed to hear after seeing my ex-partner dead.

But knowing he was gone, I didn't feel anything at all.

By the time I staggered back to my room, I was five cocktails deep, and unsteady on my feet. I wandered over to the wardrobe and pulled my phone out of the safe. I had dozens of missed calls, hundreds of new messages on Facebook and Instagram, as well as scores of new followers and requests. I ignored the social media and looked at the call list. I saw that Sophie had called and I knew I needed to at least try and call back. Struggling to focus, I looked at the time on my phone: just after three. She might be awake, but likely not. Though I hoped for the latter, I rang to show I was being compliant, and prepared a voice message in my head, saying I was out, and I hadn't had my phone with me. I knew I needed to sound like I didn't know, like I wasn't affected. That would be easy.

As I hit call to Sophie Salam's number I sat on the edge of the bed and waited, blinking blearily. It rang three times and then she answered.

'Hello?'

Shit.

'Sophie, it's Jess. I missed your calls.'

'How are you?' she replied, her voice clipped and tight and impossible to read.

'Yeah, I'm good, this holiday is exactly what I needed. I'm not in trouble, am I?'

'Trouble?'

'For not answering my phone.'

'Jess, listen, something has happened to Lewis.'

'What? Is he OK?'

'I think you can guess what.'

'Oh, shit.' I said, trying to sound shocked, too shocked to respond properly.

'It's on social media. Avoid it.'

'Oh God, are you sure?'

'Yes, I've been there. I'm sorry.'

I didn't reply but listened, unsure what to say next.

'Jess?'

'Sorry, I just— It's a lot to take in.'

'Is it?'

Those two words jolted me into sobriety, and I stood up.

'I-I don't know what you mean.'

'Is it a shock? That The Caretaker got to him?'

'Yes, yes, of course. I-I mean, I have wondered if he was safe.'

'Why?'

'Because The Caretaker seems to know everyone who's connected to us.'

'And why is that, Jess?' she asked. The lightness and kindness in her voice that I had come to like when we were talking about Lottie had disappeared.

'I don't know.'

'Jess, why did you go to Gran Canaria?'

'I needed a break. What with the assault and the separation and what's happening, I felt so stressed.'

'I understand,' she replied. 'See you when you get home.'

'Do you want to meet for coffee?'

'We'll need to talk to you at the station.'

'Yes, sorry, of course.'

'You do know he is dead, right? That The Caretaker has killed him?'

'Yes.'

'It's just – forgive me, but you don't seem that bothered.'

'It's a lot to take in,' I replied, knowing I needed to get off the phone as quickly as possible.

The line went quiet.

'Sophie?'

'Goodbye, Miss Pendle.' She hung up.

I realised that DS Sophie Salam knew, without a shadow of doubt, that I was involved in what was going on.

Chapter Seventy

28th February 2025

I was wired, unable to sleep, and sobering, I paced and waited for a WhatsApp call between me, Hannah, Madison and Kelly. The three of them had stayed at Kelly's house, so that, if it came to it, there would be two witnesses to the fact that Kelly hadn't left it. The call came at 7:10 and, with my head pounding and my muscles aching from hangover, I saw my three friends appear on screen.

'Hi, Jess how are you?' Madison said.

'I'm OK.'

'Are you sure?' Hannah asked.

'Just hungover.'

The girls smiled, but the smiles faded and their faces became serious.

'Is it OK to talk?' I asked.

'Yes, unless they have a tap on my phone, we should be OK,' Kelly said.

'We might have a problem,' I continued, and I told them

about my history with Sophie Salam. I went all the way back to the beginning, the random bumping into each other, her daughter, and how I helped. I said I should have told them all then, but I didn't want them to kick me out of the group, or think I was in with the police. She was just a mother, needing to help her kid, and I helped. They seemed to be OK with it. Then I told them about the interview with her, and the call I'd made in the night.

'She knows I know something. I suspect she knows about all of us,' I said.

'What do we do?' Hannah asked Kelly, who went very quiet for a moment, weighing up the options.

'Do we kill her?' Madison asked, her voice so small, almost expressionless.

'What?' I said.

'If she knows, she might come for us, and then we are all fucked,' Madison continued.

'No, no, we can't kill her.'

'But you are saying she knows.'

'She knows something, but she can't prove it,' Kelly said, calming us down. 'If she could, we would all be arrested. Jess too – she would have the Spanish police bring you in.'

'Mads, I can't believe you just suggested that,' I said.

'We have killed these men, Jess. I don't want to go to prison. I have suffered enough; we have all suffered enough. This is about us becoming free, not ending up behind bars.'

'She isn't them though. She's a woman, a mother, just doing her job.'

'Hey, calm down, both of you,' said Kelly. 'Jess, we aren't going to kill her. But we are going to keep an eye on her. I'm going to do some digging, find out what I can. The Caretaker is going to vanish now. He has done what he needed to do. We are free, and, more, the whole country is talking about domestic violence and its victims, all the way up to the prime minister. Things will change. They have to now. We have shone a bright light on it, which is what we set out to do. The Caretaker will become infamous – and a ghost. We are done. As long as we keep our shit together, DS Salam can think what she wants; it will never come back to us. Jess, you have the blue book, right?'

'Yes, it's in my suitcase.'

'You know what to do?'

'As soon as we have said goodbye, I'll get it done.'

'Good, now enjoy the rest of your trip. We'll collect you from the airport when you get home.'

As the call finished, I felt shaken up. Killing Sophie wasn't part of the plan, and I hoped to God that whatever Kelly dug up, using her work contacts, it wouldn't mean I had just signed her death warrant.

Throwing on some clean clothes, I quickly brushed my teeth and then, grabbing the blue book, with all its notes on the four men we had killed, dropped it into my day bag and headed out of the hotel.

The location of my break was remote, the transfer from the airport almost two hours' journey, and so far only three hotels had been built along this secluded part of the Atlantic shore. There were skeletons of others in various stages of construction, but I'd yet to see anyone working on them.

As I headed out of the hotel lobby, I stopped at a little shop that sold everything from beach inflatables to painkillers. The latter were something I very much needed, so I bought a packet of paracetamol and a bottle of water – and along with them a box of matches and some lighter fluid.

After washing down two tablets, I placed the purchases in my bag and set off for a long walk.

As I strolled along the coastline, the Atlantic lapping at my feet, I was struck by the contrast: the beach was beautiful, peaceful, but it also reminded me of violence and murder. The ocean knew my crimes, and with each murmur of the tide I could hear it telling me so.

I repressed the thought. Kelly was right: The Caretaker was done, finished. It was over. All I had to do was return home, ride the media storm until the press got bored, and then I could get on with my life, with my friends, our secret safe.

I just had one thing left to do.

Once I was sure I had walked far enough to be out of sight, I stopped and with a piece of driftwood dug a small hole in the sand. Then I pulled the blue book out of my bag and dropped it in, doused it in lighter fluid and lit it. The book burst into flames, and each time they died down I squirted in a little more accelerant until nothing but ash was left. The plans, the secrets and evidence were gone.

I stayed on the beach until the tide swept up and over the hole, removing all evidence of the blue book ever having been there. Confident that not a trace would ever be found, I walked back towards the hotel to rest before my flight home in a few days' time.

Lewis was gone; so were Martin and Duncan and Jake. Four men who'd ruined the lives of women, killed by a group of women who had, with any luck, saved the lives of many, many more.

The Caretaker would be a hero forever, and a secret for just as long.

Chapter Seventy-One

2nd March 2025

As the plane began to descend, making my ears pop with the change in air pressure, I looked over what was my home. Even in early March, the colours were astounding. A week on an island that was effectively arid desert made me appreciate the textures of our Blighty. Under where I sat, thousands, tens of thousands, were getting on with their lives, loving, living, dying, having children, losing, winning. They were living in hope, fear and everything in between, and for a moment I was present in it all.

By the time the plane touched down, though, my thoughts were more mundane. I was just Jess, returning from her holiday. But I was returning home to questions around my ex-partner's death. The world wasn't pretty and green; it was on fire. Everyone was picking a side.

As I made my way through passport control, I expected to be stopped, since the police no doubt wanted to talk to me. I assumed a flag would have been put on my entry, and I would be quietly whisked into an interview room. But I got through without incident, and then, grabbing my case, I made my way towards the exit, walking through 'Nothing to Declare'.

Then the shitstorm began. Somehow the press knew I was coming home, and on the other side of a metal railing, dozens were gathered. Airport security and some police kept them from climbing over when they saw my face. The cameras began to flash, and questions were fired at me. I kept my head down, kept moving.

'Jess, what can you tell us about the death of your violent ex?'

'Jess, Jess, what would you say to The Caretaker if he was here right now?'

'Miss Pendle, do you know who The Caretaker is?'

The last question made me stop, just for a beat, but then I continued walking, ignoring them.

As I fought through to the exit, where Kelly was waiting for me in the short stay car park, I tried not to react. No glances, no pauses, no beats. I was just a woman coming home, grief-stricken. Once outside, I looked for Kelly. She beeped her horn and I ran towards her. She helped me put my case in the car and, as I got in, I looked back. Sophie was there, standing slightly apart from the crowd, her arms crossed. She didn't wave, didn't nod. She just watched me. And I just looked back. We both knew we both knew. And although that made me anxious, I had to remind myself that she couldn't prove it. If she could, I would have been arrested at passport control. Sophie didn't blink, and I didn't flinch, until I closed the car door.

Kelly got in the driver's seat and fired up the engine.

'Sophie Salam is here,' I said, making sure my face was turned towards Kelly so no reporter could read my lips.

'Where?' she asked.

'Behind us, further along Arrivals, near the second door.'

She looked into her rear-view, adjusted it and squinted a little. 'So she is.'

'What does that mean?'

'Nothing. Don't worry, our friend Sophie Salam has some secrets of her own. She isn't going to do anything.'

'What do you mean?'

'I've done a little digging on her, spoken to some old friends for help. She isn't exactly what she appears to be. None of it can be proved, but Sophie Salam has a black mark on her record, and I think she is a little more like us than we realise. I'll explain all when we are back at mine.'

Kelly didn't add any more and pulled away. We had to turn around at the end of the car park and drive back past the press, who tried to get more pictures. Sophie was still there, in the same spot, watching us leave.

Chapter Seventy-Two

SOPHIE SALAM

She wanted to doubt her gut instinct. She wanted to dismiss her new friend as a suspect, but the way Jess had looked at her as she climbed into the car, the unflinching eye contact, even from a distance, told her that despite her wanting Jess to not be involved, she was.

And the way Kelly looked at her as she drove past told her she was too.

And Madison.

And Hannah.

And probably the rest of them.

She'd thought for a while they knew who The Caretaker was. Now she was almost sure she had got it wrong: these women weren't protecting anyone; they weren't sheltering a man; they were looking out for each other.

After the car left, Sophie began walking towards her own. Her phone rang, an unknown caller.

'Hello?'

The line was quiet, but she could hear someone was there.

'Hello?'

'Hello, Soph. Long time no speak.'

The voice stopped her in her tracks. She'd not heard it in many years, but she knew who it was instantly. 'Karl? How did you get this number?'

'Oh, I have my ways.'

'I have nothing to say to you.'

'You do. You just don't know it yet.'

'You know I'm a police officer. You know that what you are doing right now isn't legal?'

'I also know you're not going to tell anyone, are you, Soph? It wouldn't end well for you now, would it?'

Sophie didn't reply.

'Your silence says it all. Speak soon, yeah?' Karl said, and then the line went dead.

Sophie managed to get to her car. Climbing in, she closed the door and fought to regulate her breathing.

Sophie wasn't a religious woman, but in that moment she prayed to God Karl didn't know about Lottie. If he did, she didn't know what he would try to do. Firing up the engine, Sophie began to leave the airport, all thoughts of The Caretaker and Jess and the murder victims gone. She just wanted, needed, to get home to her baby and hold her tight.

Chapter Seventy-Three
JESS

As we pulled up at Kelly's house, I was shocked to see that on the street, just on the edge of her property, more press were waiting, and as her Range Rover approached, they sprang into action. More questions, more pictures and film.

'What the fuck?' I said.

'It's been like this for most of the week. Not just here, but at Madison's and Hannah's too.'

'You think they all know?'

'I think they are latching on to us, because they have no idea who The Caretaker is.'

'But we are—'

'They don't know it, Jess, none of them, and now The Caretaker is gone.'

'Yes, sorry, you're right.'

As we made our way slowly up Kelly's drive, the front door opened, and as soon as the car stopped we both shot out into her house, leaving my suitcase in the boot. Kelly closed the door behind her and managed a shaky smile.

'It will ease down. I promise,' she said, and I nodded, then turned to see Madison and Hannah. I hugged each of them tightly and then we all moved into the kitchen. As I sat down, Madison opened a bottle of wine and, in silence, poured out four glasses. We raised them and toasted without speaking. What we set out to do was done. The Caretaker had come into the world, done what was needed to make us safe, and was gone again. We took a large drink in unison, and collectively sighing, we settled.

'How has it been here?' I asked.

'Have you followed it at all whilst away?' Hannah said.

'No, I didn't want to, in case my picture was anywhere. I didn't want people seeing it and then me.'

'It's been crazy,' Hannah said. 'There are stories coming from all over the country, men handing themselves to the police, confessing to being abusers.'

'What?'

'There's more. There have been protests outside parliament for the laws to change to protect women. The Caretaker has a fan club on all of the social media platforms. Last night, I read that two women beat partner of one of them. He had been abusing her for years.'

'Shit,' I said.

'The Caretaker has ignited something here. We wanted justice for us, but it seems we are going to help a lot of people,' Kelly said.

'And all we have to do now is get on with our lives,' Hannah said, taking another sip of her wine.

'And not get caught,' I said, damping the excited energy.

'We won't,' Kelly said.

'But Sophie Salam—'

'What about Sophie Salam?' Hannah asked, sitting up.

'She was at the airport. She didn't say anything; she just watched me. She knows.'

'That we know who The Caretaker is?' Hannah asked.

'No, I think she knows it's us.'

'But, as I said, she can't prove it,' Kelly swept in. 'If she could, we would all be arrested.'

'They did call us in for an interview,' Madison said.

'Because they had to be seen to be doing something. A police officer was threatened. Ladies, we have planned for this. We have all got alibis. The police can't touch us, especially Sophie Salam. She isn't any better than us really.'

'What do you mean?'

'She has a past.'

'What?'

'I've found out, calling on favours from defence solicitors who owed me, that she was undercover, years ago, and she crossed a few lines. Ending up no better than us.'

'If she broke the law, how is she still a copper?'

'If anyone can make things vanish, it's a police officer. I can't prove anything, of course, but Sophie Salam has many secrets.'

'What was she undercover for?'

'A money-laundering outfit. She went in and worked her way to be a bit on the side for the boss. She overstepped the mark. If she leans on us, we'll let her know we know things too.'

'When was this?' I said.

'Seven years ago.'

I thought of Lottie, how she was around six, how there was no father figure. I didn't say anything to the group, because despite it all I liked Sophie Salam, and the idea of her daughter being dragged into something didn't sit right with me.

Kelly continued to reassure us that the police had nothing,

and would get nothing, because of how careful we had all been, and it was now over. We all settled into the feeling, enjoying our wine, and as the alcohol took hold we began to relax further, talking just like a bunch of women, and not like the killers we all were. We laughed, shared and did so knowing we were completely safe with one another.

Later in the evening, with a third bottle open, we began to talk of our dreams, of what the future held for us, and we realised that none of us had got that far in our heads. I was new to the now disbanded serial killer support group, but these women had been working on this for a year, focusing solely on the present, on making it work and not getting caught. They had had no thoughts about the future. But the future was now, and as we quietly began to wonder what our individual futures might be, Kelly's phone pinged on the table between us. She scooped it up, and her face morphed into confusion.

'Kel?' I said quietly, gaining the attention of the other two, who also looked at her.

'We've been invited to an event.'

'What?'

'Some woman named Kimberley has invited us to an event in Norwich.'

'What kind of event?' I asked.

'She says it's a conference for survivors of domestic violence. She wants us to come and talk about our experiences.'

'No way. Someone has made this up, just to get us all together and talking about The Caretaker. I'm not interested,' Hannah said.

'Jess, Google Women Against Abuse. It's the name of the organisation she claims to be from,' Kelly said, as she continued to read.

I picked up my phone and did as she asked. 'It's a registered charity. They hold events up and down the country for women who have suffered domestic violence. The woman who founded it is called Kimberley Murphy.'

'Yeah, that's who messaged me.'

'What else does her message say?' Hannah asked.

'Only that they hold retreats for women who have recently come forward, and that they want us to come and talk with them about surviving. She says she can pay for our travel and accommodation. She also says that no one will know before the event that we'll be attending it. So there will be no press. She says we have become a symbol of hope. Our being there will make such a difference to those who are at the start of their journeys.'

'I still don't like it,' Madison said.

'I'm not sure either. It could be a trap of some kind,' Hannah added.

'Jess? What do you think?' Kelly asked, and I shrugged.

'All I know is that before meeting you and knowing I wasn't alone and that I could survive, I was a mess and didn't see a way out of it. Becky's group helped me; you all helped me. If we can be sure, it's not a scam, I would be up for it. And this Kimberley, she has an OBE. I think she's for real.'

The women fell silent.

'Besides, hiding in plain sight, right?' I added, and Kelly nodded.

'Yeah, hiding in plain sight. We need to be reacting to the world, not controlling what happens in it. Hannah?'

'I'd want assurances.'

'Of course. Madison?'

She looked at us all, then nodded.

'All right,' Kelly said. 'Let me speak to her. If I'm convinced it's legit, I'll book us to go. Jess is right; we need to get on with our lives, and hiding in plain sight has always been how we were going to do it. Talking to a charity is only going to strengthen our innocence in all this.'

Chapter Seventy-Four

JESS

11th March 2025

It had been nine days since I returned home from Gran Canaria to a crowd of press, three weeks since I walked along the beach at Cromer. For the most part, the media furore had died down. The Caretaker wasn't killing anymore; there were no more videos, so the world moved on. There were other things happening, other stories. The Caretaker had been reduced to a footnote. Fortunately his legacy raged on, with more protests and more conversations in government about changes to the laws to protect victims of abuse. But without The Caretaker committing crimes, keeping fear tangible for those who should fear, I worried that within a few months nothing would have changed.

We had, though. For good or bad, the members of the serial killer support group would never be the same again.

Even though the attention was dying down, the pressure wasn't: we were all being watched, being followed, if not by the press then by the police, and I wanted nothing more than to hide away until it was all over. So I went to work; I did the food shop; I even went to meet Lewis's mum to help her with the funeral arrangements. It was tough, knowing I was the reason he was dead, but I think Lewis would have eventually killed me, and I would rather help with his funeral than attend my own.

After our drink at Kelly's on the day I returned home, Kelly did what she did best and investigated Kimberley Murphy's life and her charity. What came back was clean, the offer to attend the talk was a legitimate request, so we agreed to go. I wanted to appear like I wasn't sneaking off, so on the afternoon we were leaving for Norwich, Kelly opting to drive us all there, I went for a coffee. If anyone saw me, they would see I was relaxed, quiet, grieving, but still a woman with nothing to hide. So I ordered my latte, found a seat by the café window and watched the world go by. I had a small bag beside me, with some things for an overnight stay, and I enjoyed the quiet before we women got together and the anxiety of our having to talk in public took over.

I watched people outside being buffeted by the high winds as the fourth or fifth storm of the winter began to move in. They said that Storm Frieda would be the worst yet, with winds expected to hit over one hundred miles an hour on the east coast. It would be fiercest in the night, but it was making its presence known early, turning umbrellas inside out and driving the rain sideways, and those outside were so caught up in their own lives and running away from the storm, they barely looked up. Then I saw someone crossing the road, someone I hadn't seen since I'd left the airport. She didn't see me at first, as she was talking to her daughter. I wondered if I could slip out of the café before she entered, but I knew all I would do was bump into her, and she would know I was trying to leave. So I looked away, picked up my coffee and pretended I hadn't seen Sophie Salam approaching.

As she entered, I dared to look, and still distracted by Lottie, she didn't see me. She joined the queue, still oblivious of my presence, and even though I knew I should look away, I didn't. She ordered a drink, and while they made it, she turned and looked around the café, no doubt trying to find somewhere to sit.

Then our eyes met.

In the nine days since I'd seen her at the airport, Sophie and I hadn't spoken at all. I knew this would be the case: it was too close to home, and she couldn't talk to me anymore. I suspected she wouldn't talk to me now, so, after we locked eyes, I nodded and then turned my attention to the world outside once more. But I was still aware of her presence in the room. The rain intensified, creating a static-like noise as it pounded the café roof. Most of the people inside looked up at the din, myself included. Sophie did too, and we looked at each other once more. She walked past me and put her drinks down on the table a few away from mine. Lottie scooted into a seat and, seeing me, smiled and waved. I waved back, and before Sophie could stop her, and to my surprise, she came over.

'Hi,' she said.

'Hello,' I said back. 'How are you, Lottie?'

'Good.'

Sophie, having no choice but to talk to me, came over.

'Lottie darling, come and drink your hot chocolate.'

'Bye bye,' Lottie said to me, and wandered off back to her seat. Sophie lingered.

'I'm surprised she approached you. She doesn't usually approach people. Sorry.'

'It's OK. She looks happy.'

Sophie smiled. 'She is doing well at the moment. We seem to have found a new rhythm.'

'I'm glad to hear it.'

'Thanks again for helping with that.'

'Pleasure.'

Sophie, unable to hold my gaze, looked down at the bag at my feet. 'Are you going off somewhere nice?' she asked, trying to sound light and non-detective like, and I nodded. This woman didn't miss a trick.

'A few of us have been asked to talk at a dinner for survivors of what we have experienced. It's just an overnight thing.'

'I see, that's good.'

'I'm nervous if I'm honest, but I remember when I first said out loud what I was living through, if I hadn't had people around me, I might not have been OK.'

'People as in the rest of your support group?'

'Yes, without them I'd be lost. I just want to try and help others.'

'I see,' she said, able to look me in the eyes once more. Only this time, the mother in her was gone; it was all police in her stare.

'Sophie, you look tired,' I said.

'So do you.'

'How's the investigation going?' I added, feeling I was close to overstepping the line.

'Not sure you should ask that, Miss Pendle,' she said.

'No, no, perhaps not, Detective Salam,' I replied.

Then Lottie called out, and we both looked towards her. 'Mummy, look, birdsong,' she said, pulling her headphones on. She smiled. I did too, and when I looked back at Sophie, she was still watching her daughter.

'You know, this whole nature sounds thing has helped us so

much,' she said. Then she did look at me. 'Jess, I can't talk about work, not with you. Not now.'

'No, I understand, it's too close. But, and I'm saying this as a friend, you have to look after yourself.'

'I should say the same to you.'

'I'm OK.'

'Jess, I know you know something, and I know you know this. I'm going to find out what. That's my job.'

'I'm sorry, Sophie, but you won't find anything.'

'We'll see.'

Outside, a horn beeped and, turning to look, I saw Kelly's car. She waved towards me, smiling, and I couldn't tell if she had seen Sophie and was convincingly cool, or if she didn't know I was talking to the detective investigating our crimes.

'This is my lift,' I said, finishing my coffee and standing up. 'Bye, Detective Salam.'

'Bye, Miss Pendle,' she said, stepping back just enough for me to pass. As I left, I waved to Lottie, who beamed back, her chin covered in hot chocolate, and then I ran quickly to Kelly's car. As I climbed in, rainwater dripping down my face, I gave my friend a hug.

'Is that Salam?' she said.

'Yeah.'

'What did she want?'

'Nothing, she was just with her daughter.'

Kelly reversed out of the parking space, and as we began to drive away, I looked into the café. Sophie was sitting opposite her daughter, but her attention was solely on me in the car. Once again, Sophie Salam watched us drive away.

Chapter Seventy-Five

The drive to Norwich took just over two hours, and even though I was quick to dismiss Sophie's comment about knowing I was involved, I couldn't entirely ignore it. But I didn't tell the others what she had said, because I didn't want to stress them out too, so I appeared relaxed as we rattled through the country to the postcode punched into Kelly's satnav. Even though we all talked about The Caretaker and about how we were feeling, about the weird dreams we'd had since, and what the press were doing now, we didn't linger on the subject. Instead we listened to music and chatted about the usual things friends talk about. It was odd; I was in a car with a group of killers: the women I was talking to had murdered for one another, for me, and even though I hadn't killed, I knew that if we were discovered, I would be tried as a murderer – but it didn't feel that way. We were bonded by our trauma, immortalised by our crimes. I loved these women, more than I had ever loved any man, and I knew that this love would not be betrayed.

As we drove, the storm making it difficult, the day began to turn to night, ink-black, and the roads reduced from dual carriageways to single lanes as we weaved around the Norfolk countryside. We all stopped talking so Kelly could concentrate. The towns were becoming further apart and shrinking in size and facilities, until we were driving through tiny hamlets. The roads narrowed further, until it was barely wide enough for Kelly's car, and buffeted by the wind, the trees' lifeless branches looked like gnarled skeletal hands reaching to grab us.

'Where the bloody hell are we going?' Madison asked, her voice tense with anxiety.

'It says we are arriving in ten minutes,' Kelly replied.

'To where, a field?' Hannah said, trying to sound light, and failing.

'Kel, are you sure this is legit?' I asked beside her.

'I think so,' she replied, not taking her eyes off the road ahead.

For several more minutes, we bounced along the narrow lane, and then, just when I thought we would go on forever seeing nothing, a large house came into view. I looked at the satnav. We had reached our destination.

'Looks like this is the place,' Kelly said, turning into the manor's large drive, where six cars were parked.

'It's like Bates Motel,' Hannah said, and although she said it as a joke, none of us laughed. The house was exactly that. It was old, a little spooky, but grand. Once it would have been the talk of the area. Now it was tired; impressive, but still tired.

Getting out of the car, we made our way quickly to the front door and no sooner had we passed between the large pillars that flanked the entrance to the beautiful house, it opened, and Kimberley Murphy stood there smiling. She was more striking and more beautiful than the pictures on Google suggested. She had the kind of look that reminded me of the black and white movies I'd watched on a Sunday afternoon when I was young. Tall and long-distance-runner slim, with a wide, inviting smile and high cheekbones, she exuded confidence. But, as she looked at us, there was intelligence in her cool eyes too. She wasn't to be mistaken for someone who relied on her looks alone. Kimberley Murphy absorbed who we were, and for a moment I thought she saw things others didn't.

'You made it,' she said.

'Yes, weather has been a little tricky,' Kelly said, offering her hand, and she took it.

'Come in. Come in.'

We entered the house, and were taken aback by the beauty of its interior. A large entrance hall, with a spiral staircase in the middle, a chandelier, and even a baby grand in the corner.

'Woah, this place is beautiful,' Hannah said.

'Stunning, isn't it? We rent places like this, up and down the country, to provide retreats for, well, women like us. We then invite women to come for a few days, to unwind, be pampered, but more importantly to talk about what has happened, and how to heal. And again, thank you for coming to us, it means a lot to have such strong women visit.'

'We are hardly strong. Just survivors,' I said, noting how she said 'us', not 'them'. Kimberley was a survivor too.

'That's all these women need. They just need to look in the eye of someone who is out the other side.'

I nodded, remembering how I felt after my first session at the Friday morning group.

'Right, if you'd like to follow me, I'll show you all to your rooms for the evening, then, if it's OK with you, I'll gather the women at seven, and we can meet before dinner?'

'Yes, of course.'

Kimberley led us up the stairs and then, one by one, showed

The Serial Killer Support Group

us our rooms. The anxiety we'd all felt had melted. This woman was one of us; she was someone who had come out the other end, maybe not in such extreme circumstances, but she wanted what we wanted. And I could tell we wanted to help all the more. Kimberley excused herself to go and prepare for our talk, and after she left, the four of us, the disbanded serial killer support group, all ducked into my room to help each other get ready.

Chapter Seventy-Six

An hour later, changed and freshened up, the four of us were waiting in our rooms, and then Kimberley collected us. I was nervous to meet these women, not because of the secrets we four shared, but because they were looking to us to say something or act in a certain way to give them hope, and I was so worried I would fail them.

Kimberley led us into a large dining area, and sat at the table were six women who stood and greeted us. When she'd invited us, she had said that no one would be aware of it, and yet the women didn't seem surprised we were there. They knew our names, welcomed us, thanked us for coming, and then, introductions over, we took our seats. Kimberley had spread us out, which made sense; she wanted us to be in amongst the other women on the retreat, but I felt uncomfortable not being next to Kelly. I could see Madison was uncomfortable too, so I offered a reassuring smile, which helped us both.

The meal was exquisite, five courses served by staff Kimberley had brought in to ensure a five-star event, each dish beautifully presented and divine to taste. I didn't really know what I was eating, but I devoured it feverishly. As we ate, we drank wine and talked. I was sat next to Michaela, an older woman from Leeds, who had left her husband of twenty-three years, deciding two decades of abuse were more than enough. He wasn't letting go easily, though, and was persistently harassing her to come home. Across the table sat Geeta, from near the Welsh border, who had had an arranged marriage and stepped into a violent life on her wedding night. These poor women had had it rough, rougher than I ever did, and I wondered for a moment, was it right to make The Caretaker disappear? Was there still a need for him? I dismissed the thought. There was no way he could come back. The police were close, and although I was confident they would never directly come for us, if The Caretaker came back, the chances of us making a mistake would be increased. The Caretaker was created for a specific reason and had served his purpose. I had to accept that to help these women, we had to do what we were now doing: talking, sharing, helping – with words, not actions.

Once the meal was over, Kimberley invited us into what looked like a study, with huge wingback leather chairs and a bookcase that ran from floor to ceiling along one of the walls. It looked like a room where men would go for a cigar and brandy after a meal in bygone years. I found it fitting that it was now full of women. The staff served us more wine, and we settled and began to talk. It was an informal question-and-answer session, some of it about the impact the recent weeks had had on our lives, but mostly it was about who we were going to be now. We told them we still hadn't quite worked it out.

Hours passed, with us talking, sharing and drinking, and at just after ten thirty, Kimberley publicly thanked the staff for serving us, and we all joined in. The staff then tidied away, said farewell and left. We continued to talk casually, and I learned that the women in the room came from all over the UK, which made what Kimberley was doing even more impressive. We, via The Caretaker, had helped victims across the country very publicly; she was doing the same without attracting any attention.

Once the final member of staff had left and the front door closed, I watched as Kimberley looked through the window of the study, until they had all driven away. She then turned, picked up a letter knife from the grand old desk she stood behind and tapped her wine glass. We all stopped chatting, and turned our attention to her.

'Thank you, everyone. I just wanted to say a few words, if I may. But before I do, I want to say a massive thank you to Kelly, Hannah, Jess and Madison for coming to join us this evening and sharing their stories.'

The women all clapped, and we smiled back.

'When I started Violence Against Women, I had a mission, to help women who were like me, alone, beaten down by the ones they loved, not knowing how to escape. I was staggered by the sheer number of women – some men, but mostly women – who were like me. It took my ex almost killing me for me to get away. I didn't die at his hands, not because I was strong, or I spoke out; I was simply lucky that night. But, as we know, many more aren't, and I wanted to create change, not just for me, but for as many women as I could. Here this evening, we have women from all over the UK. From all social classes, with different beliefs and nationalities and faith systems, but we are all connected by one thing.'

She paused, and I expected her to say that we were connected by our abusers, but she didn't. What she did say pull the rug from under my feet. As it did Kelly and Madison and Hannah too.

'Ladies, we need to know how you did it.'

'Did what?' Kelly asked.

'We need to know how you created The Caretaker.'

Chapter Seventy-Seven

We sat stunned for what must have only been a beat, a second at most, but for that short time the silence was all-consuming. Kelly was the first to compose herself.

'We don't know what you are talking about. Ladies, I think we should leave.'

She stood and began to move, and her action forced us to do the same.

'We are with you. We are on your side,' Kimberley said, but we didn't stop walking. 'Please.'

I stopped, turned and looked at her.

'This is why we have come here: we want to learn how you did it.'

'We don't know what you're talking about,' I said, echoing Kelly. I caught up with the others as they marched out of the room. When we reached the front door, Madison tried to open it, but it wouldn't budge.

'Let us out,' Kelly said, turning back and coming face to face with Kimberley.

'I will. I'm not going to keep you, if you want to go.'

'We want to go,' Hannah said,

'Just, please, stay a few minutes more. Let me explain.'

'Open the door!' Kelly said again.

Another voice came from behind Kimberley, a small voice, weak with unshed tears.

'I cannot go home. He'll kill me,' Geeta said. 'I'm not allowed to leave. I had to lie to come here, to meet you. If I go back, I know he will kill me. I need help.'

'We can't help you,' Kelly said, her voice wavering.

'Can't or won't?' Kimberley said. 'Please, just hear us, you don't have to speak. Just listen, please, and if in a few minutes you want to go, I'll unlock the door.'

'This feels like entrapment,' Kelly said.

'How can it be? You've done nothing wrong,' Kimberley replied, and I wasn't sure if she meant we had done nothing wrong because she didn't believe we were The Caretaker, or we had done nothing wrong because she validated our actions. Either way, a few minutes wouldn't hurt.

'Kelly, let's hear her out,' I said quietly, and as she turned to look at us, both Hannah and Madison agreed with me. Kelly nodded.

'You have five minutes.'

'That's all we ask for,' Kimberley said, taking a teary Geeta by the arm and walking back into the study. We followed, and whereas before the energy felt light and relaxed, now it was tight, attentive.

'Please, sit down.'

We did as asked, and Kimberley sat down as well, Geeta beside her, mopping her tears.

'You don't have to say anything, but we believe that you four, somehow, are The Caretaker.'

'Your five minutes are shrinking,' Kelly said.

'We don't want you to be The Caretaker for us. That's not why we asked you here.'

We didn't reply. We had vowed to keep The Caretaker buried, and we were women of our word.

'You have done enough, and we cannot even begin to understand how you are coping with the pressure of it all. We'd not ask you to do it again. What we want is something else.'

None of us spoke.

'Since The Caretaker went public,' Kimberley continued, 'there has been more change for women like us than ever before. More are talking, sharing, opening up. Abusive partners are seeking help, handing themselves in because of their fear. Calls to our hotline number have increased by over three thousand per cent. Women are no longer afraid to reach out. What The Caretaker has done has achieved more for victims in a few weeks than I have managed in fifteen years. We think The Caretaker is a hero.'

'Many don't agree,' Kelly said flatly.

'People are divided, yes, but we here, and thousands of others like us, can't afford for The Caretaker to vanish as he has.'

I waited for Kelly to say something, but she didn't. She simply waited for Kimberley to say more.

'We don't want you to be The Caretaker. We don't want you to do anything.'

'What do you want?' I asked.

'Teach us.'

'What?' Hannah asked.

'Teach us how you did it. Show us how you planned it, how The Caretaker came to exist.'

'If we knew what you were talking about, and I mean if,

The Serial Killer Support Group

why do you want to know?' Kelly asked, still tense, still sizing up the situation.

'So we can take The Caretaker home,' Geeta said.

'I'm sorry?' I said.

'We want to learn so we can go home to our networks, our own support groups, and share our knowledge. We need The Caretaker too,' she said, gazing at me. 'From what you have told us tonight,' Kimberley continued, 'we can all see that thanks to The Caretaker your fear is gone, you have taken charge of your lives once more. We want the same, not just for us, for thousands more like us, like you, who are out there still, hiding their pain.'

'If we knew what you were talking about, how would we know we could trust you?' Kelly asked.

'I guess you don't,' Kimberley said.

Kelly nodded, then, for the first time since we'd sat down, she turned to look at us. We made sure we were all in agreement, and then Kelly looked at me. I don't know why she was handing me the reins, but I took them.

Turning my attention back to Kimberley, I offered a small smile, opened my mouth and began to speak.

'Well, then, I guess I'll start with: welcome to the Serial Killer Support Group.'